GATE

— OF THE —

GODS

TYLER GILREATH

Author of *Gospel over Gods*

GATE

OF THE

GODS

REVELATION, THE MESSIAH, AND THE
SECOND COMING OF BABYLON

DEFENDER

CRANE, MO

Gate of the Gods: Revelation, the Messiah, and the Second Coming of Babylon
Tyler Gilreath

Defender Publishing
Crane, MO 65633

© 2024 Defender Publishing
All Rights Reserved. Published 2024

ISBN: 978-1-948014-67-0
Printed in the United States of America.
A CIP catalog record of this book is available from the Library of Congress.

Cover design by Jeffrey Mardis
Interior design by Pamela McGrew

DEFINITION

Babylon: The Babylonians call their city bab-ili, bāb-ilu, or bab-ilani, meaning "gate of the gods."

CONTENTS

PREFACE

This book builds upon my original work, *Gospel Over Gods*, which tells the story of the three divine rebellions recorded in the Bible:

- The serpent in Eden (Genesis 3);
- The angels (i.e., the sons of God) who sinned with women and fathered the Nephilim giants (Genesis 6:1–4); and
- The angels (i.e., the sons of God) who rebelled following the Tower of Babel event and became the gods over the nations (Deuteronomy 32:8–9).

While I strongly recommend that readers become familiar with the content of my earlier work, I revisit the basics in this book to lay the groundwork for the new material I cover. This book tracks the supernatural war in the book of Revelation by investigating the mysterious identity of Babylon the Great. I argue that it's not all about Rome.

It is entirely understandable why Rome gets so much attention in Revelation; the seven churches of Asia Minor lived under Roman rule. Although John doesn't name "Rome" anywhere in the book, it's universally believed that he uses "Babylon" (Revelation 14:6; 16:19; 17:4; 18:2, 10, and 21) as a cryptic cipher or substitute for Rome. This conflation makes a lot of sense. Babylon and King Nebuchadnezzar leveled Jerusalem, destroyed the Temple, and carried its people into exile just five hundred years before Rome did it to Israel in AD 70. So Babylon's past actions against the Jewish community became *archetypal* to Rome's cruelty against God's people in the first century. This is well documented in many contemporary and later Jewish texts (see 2 Baruch 1:1; 33:2; 67:7; 79:1; Sybilline Oracles 5:140–143, 158–61, 434; 1 Peter 5:13).[4] That John and the early Church saw Rome as a *latter-day* Babylon is indisputable.

However, what if I told you that when John discusses Babylon in the book of Revelation, *Old Testament* (OT) *Babylon* was fundamentally on his mind? What if I told you John saw Rome as the latest national *string puppet* in a long line of marionettes manipulated by the puppeteering angels from the Tower of Babel? The shocking content in this book will prove precisely that, and it will shatter your paradigm concerning Babylon's identity in the book of Revelation.

In our study of Revelation, we will discover many unique connections to OT Babylon and recover *John's hidden Babylonian framework* that lies within. These subtle and sometimes drastic pen strokes will lead us far beyond the time of Rome—back to Babylon, Babel, and the ancient gods of the primeval world.

Revelation promises that the Messiah *will* finish off the devil and his angels. Reading this book will show you how.

Fight the good fight,

Tyler Gilreath

THE OLD TESTAMENT
IN REVELATION

Before we investigate Revelation's cosmic war, we need to discuss the book's blueprints—the Old Testament.

While many commentators often leverage the context of the Greco-Roman world to guide their readers through Revelation's murky waters, they are unaware the Old Testament is embedded in the book's DNA. This resource will uncover many hidden links that tie Revelation—sometimes called the Apocalypse—to the writings of the Hebrew prophets. For example, consider the following chart by professor and author of numerous books, Steve Moyise, which tallies how often Revelation utilizes the OT:

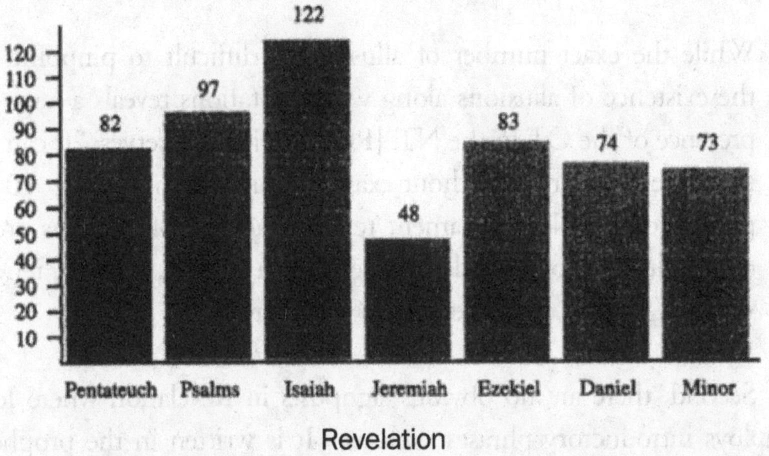

This is an exorbitant use of the Old Testament by John; it is truly remarkable. To put things in perspective, notice a similar chart by Moyise on the book of Hebrews, a New Testament book known for its many Old Testament echoes.

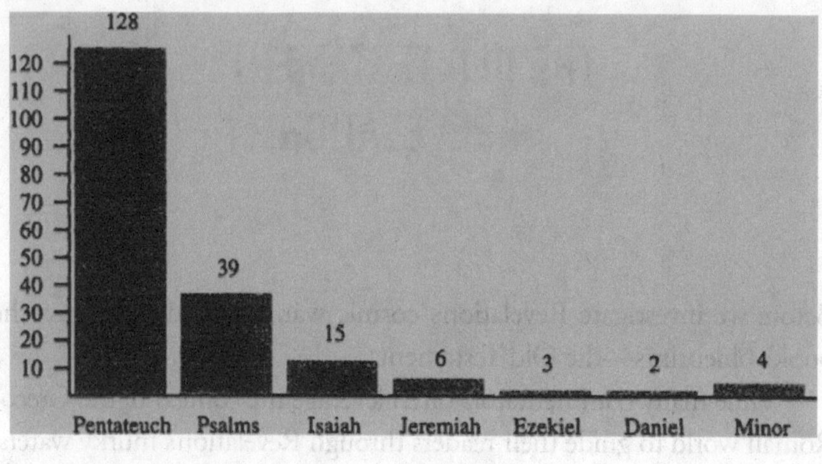

There are three primary reasons Revelation's readers rarely detect the Old Testament's presence in the Apocalypse. First, many Christians are unaware of the New Testament's dependence on the Old Testament as a whole. Michael J. Vlach writes:

> While the exact number of allusions is difficult to pinpoint, the existence of allusions along with quotations reveals a large presence of the OT in the NT. [Roger] Nicole observes, "It can therefore be asserted, without exaggeration, that more than 10 percent of the New Testament text is made up of citations or direct allusions to the Old Testament." On average, for every ten verses in the NT, one is reliant on OT wording.[5]

Second, there are no obvious signposts in Revelation where John employs introductory phrases such as, "It is written in the prophets"

(John 6:45), or, "The word that is written in their Law" (John 15:25). Moyise writes:

> The book of Revelation, however, never uses introductory formulae to introduce its Old Testament references, but weaves its words and phrases into its own composition. The index of allusions and quotations in the back of the United Bible Societies Greek New Testament reveals that Revelation contains more Old Testament allusions than any other New Testament book, but it does not record a single quotation.[6]

Third, not only are readers unaware of the signposts that point back to the writings of the prophets, but on average, today's Christians aren't very familiar with the Old Testament. This reality, coupled with John's seemingly invisible allusions, has created utter chaos for readers who approach the pages of Revelation with palpable anticipation of learning how the biblical story ends. *Sadly, most readers are doomed to fail before they ever open the book.*

Indeed, John's Apocalypse makes very little sense without readers wielding the element of awareness and familiarity. Revelation is nearly a continuous allusion to the OT and was written to be read in a constant intertextual relationship with the Hebrew Scriptures.[7] Only in recent years have a few scholars thoroughly explained how Revelation is rooted in the writings of the Hebrew prophets. In fact, prior to 1984, only one work (published in 1912) discussed John's use of the Old Testament in the book of Revelation. Moyise writes:

> [Adolf] Schlatter's work (1912) remained the only scholarly book on John's use of Scripture until 1984. [L. Paul] Trudinger (1963) and [Charles] Ozanne (1964) both produced dissertations on the language of John's allusions, but these were never published. Articles appeared in Italian, French and German, but

very little was published in English. As Beale says in his Fest-schrift article, "In comparison with the rest of the New Testament, the use of the Old Testament in the Apocalypse of John has not been given a proportionate amount of attention."[8]

In Brian Tabb's book, *All Things New: Revelation as Canonical Capstone*, he carefully summarizes the various ways John's Apocalypse utilizes the Old Testament. What he says is enlightening and paramount to seeing the signposts John left behind. He first discusses how Revelation develops important *scriptural themes* such as creation/new creation, plagues of judgment, and a new-exodus redemption of Yahweh's people. Second, he notes how the content of John's visions frequently suggests an *analogy* or *comparative relationship* with OT people, places, and events. Balaam and Jezebel in Revelation 2:14, 20 are a good example of this when John conflates Old Testament characters who were infamous for idolatry (Numbers 31:16; 2 Kings 9:22) with troublemakers in the Church. Third, Tabb notes how Revelation frequently uses *typology*, which demonstrates a redemptive-historical continuity. Examples of this include designating the Church as "kingdom" and "priests" (Revelation 1:6; cf. Exodus 19:6) or the trumpet and bowl judgments that correspond to the plagues on Egypt (Revelation 8:7–9:21; 11:15–19; 16:1–21; cf. Exodus 7:14–11:10). Fourth, Tabb discusses how Revelation announces the direct fulfillment of OT prophecies (Revelation 10:7). An example of this is when John sees "one like a son of man" (1:12), signaling that Daniel 7:13 has been fulfilled. Fifth, Tabb notes how John uses prophetic segments of OT prophecy as *blueprints* or *literary prototypes* for his own prophetic compositions (e.g., Daniel 7 in Revelation 13; Ezekiel 26–27 in Revelation 18). Sixth, Tabb points out how the book of Revelation reflects *stylistic usage* of Old Testament language.[9] Some of these OT links are more obvious than others. For example, a case where John dips in to the OT to make a subtle point is in Revelation 1:9–11:

I, John, your brother and co-sharer in the affliction and kingdom and steadfastness in Jesus, was on the island called Patmos because of the word of God and the testimony about Jesus. I was in the Spirit on the Lord's day, and I heard behind me a great sound like a trumpet saying, "What you see, write in a book and send it to the seven churches: to Ephesus and to Smyrna and to Pergamum and to Thyatira and to Sardis and to Philadelphia and to Laodicea." (Revelation 1:9–11, LEB; emphasis added)

In verse 9, the text begins, "I, John." Most readers wouldn't think this is significant. However, "I, John" is a clear stylistic marker of introduction unique to the prophet Daniel. Daniel uses "I, Daniel" seven times in the apocalyptic sections of his book (7:15; 8:15, 27; 9:2; 10:2, 7; 12:5).[10] Note the following passages from Daniel:

7:15 (LEB)	As for *me, Daniel,* my spirit was troubled within me, and the visions of my head terrified me.
8:15 (LEB)	And then when *I, Daniel,* saw the vision, and I was seeking understanding there was one standing before me with the appearance of a man.
8:27 (LEB)	And *I, Daniel,* was overcome, and I became ill for some days, and I performed the business of the king, and I was dismayed over the vision.
9:2 (LEB)	In the first year of his kingship *I, Daniel,* observed in the scrolls the number of the years that it was that were to be fulfilled according to the word of Yahweh to Jeremiah the prophet.
10:2, 7 (LEB)	In those days, *I, Daniel,* I myself was in mourning for three whole weeks....And I saw, *I, Daniel* alone, the vision; and the people who were with me did not see the vision.
12:5 (LEB)	Then I looked, *I myself, Daniel,* and look, there were two others standing: one on this bank of the stream and one on the other.

Why is this important? In the era of the Kingdom, it's no longer just the Old Testament prophets through whom the Spirit speaks; it's Jesus' apostles. Their writings are just as valid as those of Daniel or Moses. By introducing himself as "I, John," the apostle establishes himself as a true prophet like Daniel. He's also setting the reader up for a much more prominent link to the Son of Man in Daniel 7, which we will discuss later in the book.

Lastly, Tabb notes how Revelation frequently *conflates* multiple Old Testament texts and expands upon specific Old Testament texts by employing universal terminology. He cites Revelation 1:7, where John combines Daniel 7:13 and Zechariah 12:10 and also applies Zechariah's prophecy concerning "the inhabitants of Jerusalem" to "every eye" and "all tribes of the earth."[11] Indeed, Revelation's dependence on the writings of the Hebrew prophets is quite extensive. Ultimately, John weaves hundreds of OT threads into the book of Revelation, many of which we will be unable to cover in this book.

It should also be clarified that, just because the book of Revelation is highly *intertextual* with the Old Testament, it doesn't mean John did not actually *see* the things described in the Apocalypse. He certainly did.[12]

Throughout this study of Revelation, you will discover many OT clues John left behind. These clues will prove to be the blueprints for the Apocalypse and clarify why it's considered the pinnacle of biblical prophecy. Understanding John's use of the OT allows us to zoom in to the cosmic conflict in Revelation and see the vivid tapestry of the Messiah at war with Babylon the Great more clearly.

With our foundation firmly established in the Old Testament, let's begin.

ANGELS IN THE CHURCHES

The mystery of the seven stars which thou sawest in my right hand, and the seven golden candlesticks. The seven stars are the angels of the seven churches: and the seven candlesticks which thou sawest are the seven churches.

~Revelation 1:20, KJV

IN A NUTSHELL

In this chapter, we will discuss the angels of the seven churches of Asia and how it is consistent with Old Testament thought to interpret the angels as real spiritual beings, not mere mortals. We will also look closely at the letters themselves and discuss subtleties in the text that point to the sin of *idolatry* as the primary component of Jesus' rebuke to the churches.

DIGGING DEEPER

The Seven Angels of the Seven Churches

The seven angels of the seven churches are well-known entities in the Apocalypse. They are not, however, well understood. Commentators often make the angels of the churches mere men, members of the congregation. They suggest that, of the seventy-seven times the term ἄγγελος, "angel, messenger," appears in Revelation, all refer to supernatural beings *except* those assigned to the seven churches.[13]

This is a red flag.

Dismissing the presence of God's heavenly host among groups of believers is a mistake. Indeed, angels *are* among us.

Churches having assigned angels or "sky guardians" reflects a familiar Old Testament principle in which angels are appointed to watch over the nations of the world. Note Deuteronomy 32:8:

> When the Most High distributed nations as he scattered the descendants of Adam, he set up boundaries for the nations according to the number of the angels of God. (LES)

The book of Daniel also reflects a Deuteronomy 32 worldview in which the angelic princes/commanders/beings of Persia and Greece fight against Israel's angelic guardian, Michael (Daniel 10:20–21).

The Church is now spiritual Israel, God's elect covenant people. As such, angelic members of God's household are assigned to watch over each local church, as Jesus mentions in Revelation 1:20. Angels' presence among the churches confirms that God is not ashamed of His people and that His angels stand guard to protect His Beloved Bride. John reaffirms these truths by saying the One who holds these stars/angels in His hand walks in the midst of the churches (lampstands). The language of God walking in the midst of His congregation is rooted in the Old Testament (Leviticus 26:12), where we read that God promised to "walk among" His people Israel. It is now the Messiah who walks among the seven churches with His angelic host.

That the angels attend to the interest of the seven churches is evidenced by their actions in Revelation 15:5–16:1. Here, seven angels are described as "heavenly priests" because their action of pouring out God's wrath purifies the earth (Revelation 15:5–8). These messengers are described as dressing in "pure, bright linen, with golden sashes around their chests." This wardrobe is obviously rooted in Levitical garments (Ezekiel 9:2, 3, 11; 10:2, 6, 7; Daniel 10:5; 12:6, 7).[14] The high priest also wore these garments on the Day of Atonement (Leviticus 16:4, 10, 23). This is also why Christ is depicted as wearing the golden sash in John's introductory vision (Revelation 1:13b), for He is our High Priest.[15] The "bowls" the angels pour out are not to be thought of as ordinary bowls; they are *libation* bowls used in ceremonies of purification at the Temple/tabernacle (Exodus 25:29; 27:3; 38:3; Numbers 4:14–15; 7:13–89; 1 Chronicles 28:17; 2 Chronicles 4:8, 21).[16] At times, these bowls were used to carry out the ashes and fat of sacrifices. So, the bowls of Revelation 15 will be used primarily for *purification*. Revelation 15–16 depicts that the earth will be purified at Babylon's expense by these angels. The nuances behind this concept derive from Isaiah 51:17 and 22, where we read that the bowl of the cup of God's wrath would leave Jerusalem and be poured out on their pagan tormentors.[17] So, each subsequent bowl of wrath brings humanity closer to an eschatological Edenic utopia, where sin, death, and all chaotic supernatural forces are no more. As the trumpet judgments of Revelation 8 signaled holy war against Babylon, the poured-out bowls of wrath prophesy the same devastation for Babylon.[18]

It should also be noted that John's readers may have associated these seven angels with the seven archangels in Second Temple literature. First Enoch 20:1–8 reveals their names to be Uriel, Raphael, Raguel, Michael, Saraqâêl, Gabriel, and Remiel.[19] We will discuss their cosmic significance later in the book.

The Battle for the Churches

The powers of darkness are not uninterested in tarnishing Christ's Bride; they're relentless and obsessed with recapturing the heart of what the Messiah values most—His people. Hell's insatiable appetite for Jesus' followers is evidenced by the speeches to the churches. Evil made inroads and set up camp in many pods of believers in Asia Minor. This conflict must be parsed through a supernatural lens, because when there is war in the seen world, there is war in the unseen world. One can only imagine the conflict between the angels of the churches (who were tasked with guardianship) and the fallen angels who were trying to tarnish the holiness of believers and shipwreck their faith.

In the Old Testament, Israel was selected to be Yahweh's holy nation and royal priesthood. The Levitical priesthood was ceremonially cleansed *by blood* at the foot of Mount Sinai (Leviticus 8:4–35). John, the inspired penman, is counting on his readers to remember this when he writes: "To the one who loves us and released us from our sins by his blood and made us a kingdom of priests." This is not just a loose connection of ideas, however. In Revelation 1:5–6, John grammatically links his writing with Exodus 19:1–6.

Notice the parallel language between Exodus 19:1–6 and Revelation 1:5–6:

Exodus 19:3–6 (LEB)	Revelation 1:5–6 (LEB)
And Moses went up to God, and Yahweh called to him from the mountain, saying, "Thus you will say to the house of Jacob and you will tell the Israelites… you, *you will belong to me as a kingdom of priests* and a holy nation." These are the words that you will speak to the Israelites.	To the one who loves us and released us from our sins by his blood *and made us a kingdom, priests* to his God and Father—to him be the glory and the power forever and ever. Amen.

To understand why John links these verses, we must first understand the context of Exodus 19:3–6. God had great plans for His beloved people Israel. His priests of the royal house were to shine brightly as priests of Yahweh into the dark, pagan world. The prophet Isaiah noted this in Isaiah 61:6:

> But you shall be called *the priests of Yahweh*, you will be called servers of our God. You shall eat the wealth of the nations, and you shall boast in their riches. (LEB, emphasis added)

Sadly, the biblical record reveals that Israel failed God, their mission, and their lost Gentile neighbors. By using the verbiage of Exodus 19:6, John communicates that Israel's duties of being a *kingdom of priests* have now been stripped away from the apostate nation and given to the Church.[20] The New Testament writers understood that citizens of the Kingdom must now take up the mantle of the priesthood by preaching the Gospel of Jesus Christ to a lost and dying world as the new exodus community.[21] Where Israel fell prey to the allure of dark spiritual forces, the Church mustn't fail.

The following New Testament passages are parallels to Revelation 1:6 and have the Church functioning as the new priests of Yahweh:

Revelation 5:10 (LEB)	...and made them *a kingdom and priests to our God*, and they will reign on the earth.
Revelation 20:6 (LEB)	Blessed and holy is the one who has a part in the first resurrection. Over this person the second death has no authority, *but they will be priests of God and of Christ,* and they will reign with him a thousand years.
1 Peter 2:9 (LEB)	But you are a chosen race, a royal priesthood, a holy nation, a people for God's possession, so that you may proclaim the virtues of the one who called you out of darkness into his marvelous light.
Revelation 1:5–6 (LEB)	...with the result that I am a servant of Christ Jesus to the Gentiles, *serving the gospel of God as a priest,* in order that the offering of the Gentiles may become acceptable, sanctified by the Holy Spirit.

To be blunt, *priestly service, not mere salvation,* is the aim of the Kingdom of God. That is not to say redemption by blood isn't essential, for we could not be cleansed priests without it. However, it's not just what God has saved us *from*; it's what he has saved us *for*.[22] Our purpose is to serve and praise Yahweh (1 Peter 2:9), just as that was Israel's purpose (Exodus 19:6).[23] At the *releasing* of our sins (Revelation 1:5), He gracefully places us into our WHY—our purpose. By His mercy, we serve in the ministry of the heavenly priesthood alongside Jesus, our Great High Priest. So, we are a kingdom of priests not simply because Christ has cleansed us in His blood, but because that is God's desire for us. He wants us to function in this divine role as *cleansed sons and daughters* of His royal house.

In Revelation, the powers of darkness want nothing more than to tarnish the priesthood as they did with the entire nation of Israel in the OT. Revelation's letters, therefore, reveal just how effective sinister forces were in luring God's priests into pagan practices.

Idolatry in the Churches

Before we discuss the idolatry problem in many of Revelation's churches, I want to briefly discuss the topic in general. They are many false assumptions regarding idolatry. In *Gospel Over Gods*, I covered them at length. I will briefly summarize that content here.

Some verses depict the nations' gods as being simply lifeless idols—nothing more, nothing less (Psalm 135:15–18). However, we must take into account the sum of Scripture. Earlier in the book of Psalms, in Psalm 106:36–39, we read that the idol worshipers were sacrificing to *demonic entities*. Their idolatry was merely symbolic for who they really worshiped—angels and demons, the panoply of the powers of darkness (1 Corinthians 10:18–21; Revelation 9:20; Isaiah 65:11; and Colossians 2:18). Early Christians, even after the first century, understood these truths.

At times, even God's allotted portion, Israel, venerated these same spirit gods. Not coincidentally, this is revealed in—drum roll, please—Deuteronomy 32:16–21. The Gentile nations knew without the shadow of a doubt that they were worshiping real, supernatural, higher entities. They payed homage to their gods through their idols. These graven images, or statues, were often sculpted to mirror their gods' likenesses or perceived attributes (Daniel 3:25). Idols functioned as divine abodes for spiritual beings. Consequently, idol worshippers thought of graven images as *access points* to their gods.[24]

The book of Revelation ends with a warning to the seven churches of Asia: They were not to add or take away from the book (Revelation 22:18–19). Typically, we see this as a *general* warning, but this actually speaks to idolatry. John is alluding to a series of passages in Deuteronomy that warn against a teaching that suggests idolatry could *coexist* with the God of Israel (see Deuteronomy 4:3 [which alludes to the Baal-Peor episode of Numbers 25:1–9, 14–18] and Deuteronomy 29:19–20).[25] Note the following:

Deuteronomy 4:1–2; 29:19–20	Revelation 22:18–19
Hear the statutes.... You shall not add to the word...nor take away from it" (4:1–2 [likewise 12:32]). And it will be when he hears the words...every curse which is written in this book will rest on him, and the Lord will blot out his name from under heaven.	I testify to everyone who hears the words: ...If anyone adds to them, God will add to him the plagues which have been written in this book, and if anyone takes away from the words of the book...God will take away his part of the tree of life and of the holy city.

With John concluding Revelation by applying the Deuteronomy problem *analogically* to idolatry in the churches, it shows how prevalent idolatry had become among believers. The rest of this chapter will flesh this out.

Pergamum (Revelation 2:12–17)

Jesus recognized the residency of Satan in the city of Pergamum; Satan's throne was there, and his strong presence *permeated* the Pergamene church. The city was not coastal like Ephesus and Smyrna. It sat inland about sixteen miles and was located sixty-five miles north of Smyrna. It belonged to Rome. However, it was not conquered by Rome like most Roman-controlled cities.[26]

Christ tells John to address "the angel of the church of Pergamum and write, 'This is what the one who has the sharp double-edged sword says'" (Revelation 2:12). He wants the church at Pergamum to know His *words* are, in fact, words of judgment. God's spoken words are often combined with a sword or rod throughout the Bible (Isaiah 11:4, 49:2; Hebrews 4:12; Ephesians 6:17). Here, He stands over Pergamum as an authoritative Warrior-Judge who is about to reveal their collective sin by the sharp words of His mouth.

The Lord then says to the Christians in Pergamum that they live where Satan's throne is. Christ reveals Pergamum to be not just a city under the influence of Satan, but the very *seat* of his dark reign, his locus of evil and ruling authority.[27] New Testament scholar David E. Aune identifies several possibilities in Pergamum for the "throne of Satan: 1) The temple of Augustus and Roma, also known as the "Sebastion"; 2) the Great Altar of Zeus Soter; 3) the judge's bench or tribunal where the proconsul sat to judge; 4) the temple of Asklepios; 5) Generally, Pergamon as a center of Christian persecution; 6) Pergamon as a major center of the imperial cult; and 7) Pergamon as an important center for Greco-Roman religion.[28] Whatever Jesus is alluding to in the passage, Satan holds a seat of power where the church of Pergamum resides.

Indeed, being neighbors with Satan comes with a high cost to those who aren't fully dressed in the armor of God.

The people of the Pergamene church let their guard down and

Satan walked in the back door. They have some who hold fast to the teaching of Balaam, who taught Balak to put a stumbling block before the sons of Israel, to eat food sacrificed to idols, and to commit sexual immorality. These imposters were called the Nicolaitans. The Nicolaitans were said to hold fast to the teaching of Balaam. This is puzzling, since Balaam is an Old Testament figure. To grasp Jesus' condemnation of these false teachers, we must understand who Balaam was and what he did. Balak, the king of Moab, hired Balaam (a pagan prophet) to pronounce a curse on Israel. God made him bless Israel instead (Numbers 22:5–24:25). However, Balaam devised a plan for some of the Moabite women to entice the Israelite men to "defect from the Lord" (31:16) by fornicating with them and joining with them in the worship of their pagan gods (25:1–3). Sadly, the plan was successful.[29]

The notorious figure Balaam became the poster boy for heretical teaching. His name became a biblical catchphrase for those who influence God's people to engage in ungodly practices.[30] Evidently, the Nicolaitans led some in the church into idolatry.

Linking the Nicolaitans to Balaam is Jesus' way of appropriately labeling this camp of sinners who seek to drive the church into apostasy through sexual immorality with pagan women (in a religious setting) and/or spiritual adultery with feasts to foreign gods (see Isaiah 57:3, 8; Hosea 2:2–13). It's easy to see why Jesus does this when examining the parallel accounts of Balaam and Pergamum.

Additionally, we know the Nicolaitans and Balaam are linked by their etymology. "Nicolaitan" means "overcomer of the people," and, according to Jewish rabbis, "Balaam" means "consume the people." This suggests conflation.[31]

Interestingly, there seems to be a pattern of sexual immorality, food sacrificed to idols, and falsehood in the communities of Ephesus, Pergamum, and Thyatira. These sins get linked with Baalam (the Nicolaitans) and even with Jezebel of the Old Testament.

Comunity	Designation of the Problem Group	Specific Characterization
Ephesus	evildoers Nicolaitans	claim to be "apostles"—falsely
Pergamum	Satan's throne, teaching of Balaam, Nicolaitans	"sexual immorality" "food sacrificed to idols"
Thyatira	woman Jezebel, deep things of Satan	claim to be "prophetess"—falsely "sexual immorality" "food sacrificed to idols" [32]

Because of this church's tolerance of these issues, Christ calls *everyone* in the Pergamum congregation to repentance.

As Balaam and those he led astray in Israel discovered, compromise is costly. It means going to war with God. War is a frequent scene in Revelation to those *outside* the church (Revelation 12:7; 13:4; 17:14). But here, it's against those *inside* the church.

This threat of bringing a sword to the Nicolaitans echoes back to the drawn sword of the angel who stood offensively before Balaam, ready to strike him, and later, to Balaam's being killed with a sword for his continued disobedience. Note the links among the following passages:

Numbers 31:16 (LEB)	Revelation 2:14 (LEB)
Behold, *these women caused* the Israelites, *by the word of Balaam*, to be in *apostasy* against Yahweh in the matter of Peor, so that the plague was among the community of Yahweh.	But I have a few things against you: that you have there those who hold fast *to the teaching of Balaam*, who taught Balak to put a *stumbling block before the sons of Israel*, to eat food sacrificed to idols and to commit sexual immorality.

Just like Balaam was put to death by the sword for advising the Midianites to lure the people of Israel into sexual sin at Peor (Numbers 31:8, 16), so the Balaamites (the Nicolaitans) will die by the sword if they continue down this treacherous path.[33] The decision by the Pergamene church to *harbor* spiritual compromisers now threatens the whole church. But there is hope if they repent. Those who refuse to participate in pagan feasts will be given hidden manna, the heavenly food God provided Israel in the wilderness. They will also be given a white stone. On the white stone is written a "new name." In the ancient world, being given a new name was a signal that one had a new status, and this was the promise to Israel in Isaiah 56:5; 62:2; and 65:15. This promise to the church at Pergamum confirms they are considered *Israel* and will receive all things prophetically promised, including a new name. The new name is also mentioned in Revelation 3:12. Just as Christ was given a new name in His victory over the grave, Christians who conquer will receive new names as well.

Thyatira (Revelation 2:18–29)

The Lord now turns His attention to the angel stationed forty-five miles southeast of Pergamum, to the city of Thyatira. As the evil one's looming presence influenced the Nicolaitans to urge the church to fellowship with demons through idolatrous meals, Revelation 2:18–29 discusses a powerful Jezebel woman who is poisoning the church at Thyatira through pagan seduction. Those who remain faithful to Yahweh and resist the woman's sexual immorality will be given the morning star and authority over the nations.

Let's drill down deeper.

Jesus begins His commendation of the Thyatiran church by saying the Thyatirans' faith, love, work, and endurance have grown, not shrunk. This is the *opposite* of what was said about the church at Ephesus.[34]

Despite their growth, Christ has something against them. They have tolerated the woman Jezebel, who is said to deceive Christians into committing sexual immorality and eating food sacrificed to idols. Jezebel is a seductive Old Testament figure (1 Kings 18–21; 2 Kings 9).[35] Like her Old Testament counterpart, the Thyatiran Jezebel influences the people of God to forsake their loyalty to Yahweh by promoting *tolerance* toward and *involvement* in various pagan practices.[36] Like the Nicolaitans (the Balaamites) at Pergamum, this Jezebel in Thyatira has influenced her brothers and sisters in Christ to *compromise* and *flirt with* God's supernatural rivals by eating food offered to idols. Paul addressed this in 1 Corinthians 10:19–21, where he emphasized that pagan meals are inseparable from demons.

This deception is a tactic Satan has used for centuries. Christians can't give a place to the devil, even if it seems as innocent as eating a piece of meat once sacrificed to a god.

Jezebel's stubborn disposition will now reap fatal consequences from the Hebrew King of promise; He's throwing her and her lovers into a sickbed and killing her children with deadly disease. The punishment fits the crime, since a bed is often the place of intercourse (Hebrews 13:4). Her harlotry with other gods is her fatal undoing, and it also spells death for her "children." Jesus' verbiage about the death of her children echoes back to the punishment of Ahab and Jezebel's seventy sons in the Old Testament (see 1 Kings 21:17–29; 2 Kings 9:30–37; 10:1–11).[37]

Jesus quotes parts of Jeremiah 17:10 when He says this fatal blow will show all the churches He is the One who searches minds and hearts and who will give to each according to their deeds. Like Yahweh found idolatry within the congregation of Israel, the Son of God finds idolatry within the church at Thyatira.

God's Son then addresses the remnant the Thyatiran Jezebel hasn't seduced, the ones who haven't known the deep things of Satan. They are to be given authority over the nations. This makes little sense without understanding cosmic geography and the Deuteronomy 32 worldview. Believers will replace the fallen angels and be added among God's council.

At Babel, the nations were handed over to select angelic members of God's council (sons of God) to rule over them well (Deuteronomy 32:8–9). They rebelled against Yahweh, their Creator, abused their authority, and led the nations astray (Psalms 58; 82). Jesus' description of our shared authority demonstrates that believers displace and replace the fallen sons of God who presently rule over the nations.[38] This is a direct fulfillment of Daniel 7:18 and 22, where we read that saints were promised shared authority.[39]

Not only will the Thyatiran church share in Jesus' authority over the nations, but they are also to be given the "morning star." This language conjures up divine-being talk (Job 38:7) and, most importantly, Messiah language (Revelations 22:16; Numbers 24:17). The message is that we are allotted shared authority to rule with Him in His council.[40]

Sardis (Revelation 3:1–6)

The church at Sardis is dying like its city, fading out to nearly nothing.[41] While Jesus is specific about their spiritual condition, He is ambiguous about why they are spiritually dead. Is it due to false teaching or false apostles? Are they being infiltrated by a synagogue of Satan, a sect of Nicolaitans, or Jews who are not of God?[42] We aren't explicitly told. However, the precipitous decline of their spirituality is undoubtedly evident *to them*. They know precisely the poison that has stolen their vitality.

Like He told Lazarus who came forth from the grave, Jesus tells the congregation at Sardis, "Wake up, and strengthen what remains and is about to die, for I have not found your works complete in the sight of my God" (Revelation 3:2, ESV). If Jesus is playing on the historical rise and fall of the city itself, His command to "wake up" is especially meaningful because the city has fallen *twice* due to a lack of watchfulness by lookouts at the city walls.[43]

Though the church at Sardis has the appearance of life and has perhaps paraded many past accomplishments and accolades, the church's glory is quickly fading—like that of the city in which they live. As Jesus reveals, Sardis is on the brink of devastation and ruin. Similar to Christ's remedy for the Ephesian church, they are to strengthen what remains and remember what they have received and heard: Keep it and repent.

The Son of God then gives the Christians at Sardis a gulp-worthy warning: "If you do not wake up, I will come like a thief, and you will not know at what hour I will come against you" (Revelation 3:3, ESV). Jesus says something similar in Revelation 16:15. His coming "as a thief" to Sardis and His statement about not knowing the hour of His judgment connects to something He said in his earthly ministry regarding the destruction of Jerusalem and His eschatological return to earth (Matthew 24:42–46). The message to the Sardians is that if they don't repent and become *watchful,* Christ's coming will catch them by surprise as it did to those who did not heed the warnings during the destruction of Jerusalem in AD 70.

However, despite the harsh warning, there are some "who have not yet soiled their garments" (Revelation 3:4, ESV). The soiling of "their garments" likely involves pagan and idolatrous practices.[44] Consequently, others in the congregation are likely suppressing their witness by keeping a low profile in their idolatrous community or paying homage to the gods of the guilds to hedge against financial hardship.[45]

The remnant of unsoiled believers, Jesus says, "will walk with me in white." The language about "walking" echoes back to the Old Testament, where we read that Enoch, Noah, and Abraham "walked" with God (Genesis 5:22; 6:9; 17:1). The fact that the "unsoiled" will walk with Jesus in "white" is steeped in both cultural connotations and Old Testament theology. The standard apparel for deity worship in antiquity was white or linen. Those who resist pagan worship will be therefore awarded *their* white garments in the next life.[46]

Jewish records[47] reveal that unworthy priests who soiled themselves with sin were dismissed and wore *black,* while the faithful wore *white.*[48] Ultimately, Jesus' words intentionally point back to Daniel 11–12, where the white robes signify the end-time Tribulation of the eschaton, where the saints are made white through the fire of persecution (Daniel 11:35; 12:10).[49] The white garments can be viewed as a reward for martyrdom, loyalty, and faithfulness amid persecution and temptation. This is how those who die in the Lord are depicted throughout the Apocalypse (Revelation 4:4; 6:9–11; 7:9–14). Jesus said in our passage, "Those who will walk with me in white are worthy.… I will confess his name before my Father and before his angels" (Revelation 3:4–5, ESV). Both the "worthiness" language and the promise to be "confessed" before God and the angels link to Jesus' statement in Matthew 10:32–38 (also to its parallel account in Luke 12:8).[50]

Matthew 10:32–38 (KJV 1900)	Whosoever therefore shall confess me before men, him *will I confess also before my Father which is in heaven.* …He that loveth father or mother more than me *is not worthy* of me: and he that loveth son or daughter more than me *is not worthy* of me. And he that taketh not his cross, and followeth after me, *is not worthy* of me.
Luke 12:8 (KJV 1900)	Whosoever shall confess me before men, him shall the Son of man also confess before the angels of God. He that overcometh…*I will confess his name before my Father,* and before his angels.
Revelation 3:5– 4 (KJV 1900)	Thou hast a few names even in Sardis which have not defiled their garments; and they shall walk with me in white: *for they are worthy.*

In both the Gospel accounts (Matthew 10 and Luke 12) and Revelation 3:4–5, disciples face persecution. Those who fall under the weight of family persecution in Matthew 10:32–38 *are not* worthy, and those who stand in the face of persecution in Revelation 3:4 *are* worthy. Those who "confess" Christ (i.e., "witness") in the Gospel accounts (Matthew 10; Luke 12) and Revelation 3:5 are, in return, both "confessed" before the Father and the angels in Heaven. So, in Revelation 3:4–5, Jesus uses parallels to and contrasts with His statement in the Gospels.

Then, Christ says of those who conquer in Revelation 3:5: "I will never blot his name out of the book of life" (ESV). The Old Testament background for this is the *census book of Jerusalem*, the land God caused Israel to inherit. For example, when Moses prays that if God does not forgive the sin of his people, he asks God to blot out his name from Israel's registry book (Exodus 32:32–33).[51] Other OT passages pick up this language about a divine ledger. Isaiah 4:3 mentions all those recorded for life in Jerusalem. Psalm 69:28 begins by saying, "Let them be blotted out of the book of the living" (LEB). Daniel 12:1 says everyone who is found inscribed in the book (of the living) will be lifted up. So, Jerusalem's book of life *prefigures* the New Jerusalem's book of life.[52]

Those whose names are written in Revelation's book of life are considered citizens of the New Jerusalem, the land the Lord has promised *we* will inherit. This profound truth would have motivated those who have not soiled their garments with idolatry to continue in their faithfulness. Likewise, the Christians at Sardis who were spiritually dead would have found the blotting out of names very troubling.

Laodicea (Revelation 3:14–22)

In Revelation 3:14–22, Jesus addresses the saints in the lavish city of Laodicea. So far, in the Messiah's address to the churches, His message has been meant to reinforce that *He is Lord*. The way Jesus is described by the Laodicean angel contributes to the book's pattern of high Christology. The Messiah is called the "Amen, the faithful and true witness." Jesus titling Himself as the "Amen" is a clear reference to Isaiah 65:16, where Yahweh calls Himself the "Amen." Transferring the divine title to Jesus demonstrates, as we have continually seen in Revelation, that

Jesus is God in *every* way. The Hebrew word ʾāmēn is primarily a verbal seal of acknowledgment and confirmation that something is valid and binding.[53] There is not a higher name to make an oath or pledge to than the God of Heaven. He, as opposed to other gods, is always faithful, trustworthy, and true.[54]

Jesus wants the Laodicean church to know that He and His message should be trusted. This tells us that Jesus' message is without error, deception, or exaggeration; He gives us "the truth, the whole truth, and nothing but the truth."[55]

When we look closely at the Isaiah 65:16–17 passage, we notice that the "Amen" language is in the vicinity of the "new creation" language. This is vital because of what Jesus says next: "And to the angel of the church in Laodicea write: 'This is what the Amen, the faithful and true witness, *the beginning of God's creation, says.*'" Jesus' words link to Isaiah 65, not only to assign God's "Amen" title to Himself, but also to connect to the prophesied new creation in the passage.

Many commentators wrongly point to the Genesis Creation and Jesus' role as Creator in the beginning (John 1:1–3; Colossians 1:15, etc.) because they are unaware Jesus has Isaiah 65 in mind. However, by Jesus referencing Isaiah 65:16–17, His meaning is unmistakable. "The beginning of God's creation" here in Revelation links to the eschatological *new* creation (the New Jerusalem, the New Heavens, and the New Earth). But, how is Christ the beginning of God's *new* creation?

The Resurrected Christ is called "the beginning, the firstborn of the dead" in Colossians 1:18. While the new creation will be finalized upon the return of Christ, Jesus' bodily Resurrection marked the *beginning* of the new creation. Even now, those who are in Christ have *begun* their eternal transformation, as Paul discussed in 2 Corinthians 5:15–17.[56]

Next, Jesus tells the Laodicean church: "I know your works, that you are neither cold nor hot. Would that you were cold or hot! Thus, because you are lukewarm and neither hot nor cold, I am about to vomit you out of my mouth!" (Revelation 3:15–16, ESV). Jesus is tapping into the state of their local water supply to reveal their repulsive spiritual state. While the cold water of Colossae is refreshing and drinkable and the hot water of Hierapolis is medicinal, the lukewarm water of Laodicea is nauseating. Their conduct as believers sickens Jesus.[57] The language of God "vomiting" people out of His mouth *may* echo back to two Old Testament passages. There, God would vomit the idolatrous Canaanites out of the land of promise upon Israel's entry into Palestine and potentially expel Israel from His mouth should they disobey by worshiping idols and other gods.[58]

Leviticus 18:25–28 (LEB)	Leviticus 20:22 (LEB)
So the land became unclean, and I have brought the punishment of its guilt upon it, and *the land has vomited out its inhabitants*. But you (neither the native nor the alien who is dwelling in your midst) shall keep my statutes and my regulations, and you shall not practice any of these detestable things (because the people of the land, who were before you, did all these detestable things, so the land became unclean), *so that the land will not vomit you out when you make it unclean just as it vomited out the nation that was before you*.	And you shall keep all my statutes and all my regulations, and you shall do them, so that the land, to which I am bringing you to inhabit it, *shall not vomit you out*.

This context makes sense, since idolatry has been the downfall of the churches thus far. Jesus' warning that He will "vomit them out" of His "mouth" may reveal that idolatry is what plagues this church, too.[59]

Naturally, their witness for Christ would have been nonexistent as they pandered to pagan deities.

When Jesus says, "Because you are saying, 'I am rich, and have become rich, and I have need of nothing,' and you do not know that you are wretched and pitiable and poor and blind and naked" (Revelation 3:17, LEB), He is not exaggerating. These are wealthy people. Laodicea is where millionaires live. The city refuses to receive financial aid from the government, even after natural disasters.[60]

Jesus' assessment exposes their self-perception of being rich, prosperous, and in need of nothing. They are wretched, pitiful, poor, blind, and naked.[61] Jesus' cutting words demonstrate that they have fallen into the same self-congratulatory trap as did Israel, like we see in Hosea 12:8.

Hosea 12:8 (LEB)	Revelation 3:17 (LEB)
And Ephraim said, "Surely, *I am rich, I gained wealth for myself*; in all my toil they have not found guilt in me that is sin."	Because you are saying, "*I am rich, and have become rich, and I have need of nothing*," and you do not know that you are wretched and pitiable and poor and blind and naked.

Jesus intentionally linking Laodicea's spiritual bankruptcy to Israel's in Hosea, yet again, points to this church's struggle with idolatry. The book of Hosea sets forth that Israel had prospered through dishonest gain (Hosea 12:7) and idolatrous practices (Hosea 1–2). As biblical commentator G. K. Beale points out, Israel assumed it was *idolatrous gods* that made them prosper (Hosea 2:5–8). The prophet Hosea states that God found them worthless, not rich (Hosea 12:11).[62]

The people of the church at Laodicea need to *refine* themselves and become spiritually rich by buying spiritual resources from God. Jesus gives them the remedy by saying:

I advise you to buy from me gold refined by fire, in order that you
may become rich, and white clothing, so that you may be clothed
and the shame of your nakedness may not be revealed, and eye
salve to smear on your eyes, so that you may see. (Revelation 3:18)

The idea of spiritually bankrupt people buying what they need from
God (rich, healthy food) comes from Isaiah 55:1–3, in which we read
that the people of Israel needed to buy "eye-salve" for spiritual discern-
ment so they would see the danger idol worship posed to their faith in
Jesus.[63] This antidote would have been significant to them because of the
local medical school in Laodicea, where the famous ophthalmologist,
Demosthenes Philalethes, practiced.[64]

Next, Jesus tells the saints at Laodicea in Revelation 3:19: "As many
as I love, I reprove and discipline" (LEB), referring to Proverbs 3:12. The
Lord then says:

Be zealous, therefore, and repent! Behold, I stand at the door
and knock! If anyone hears my voice and opens the door, indeed
I will come in to him and dine with him, and he with me.
(Revelation 3:20)

As Robert Mounce points out, contextually, this is not a direct invi-
tation to the person outside the community of faith to be converted,
but one directed to those within that community to be renewed.[65] If
the church at Laodicea will respond to Jesus' message and renew their
relationship, the one who conquers (overcomes), Christ says, will sit
down with Him on His throne, as He also has conquered and is seated
with His Father on His throne. However, while the New Testament
discusses saints sitting on the throne in the New Jerusalem, the righteous sitting on God's throne is originally an Old Testament concept.
Note Job 36:7:

He does not withdraw his eyes from the righteous, but he sets them forever with kings on the throne, and they are exalted. (LEB)

The books of Chronicles make it clear that the throne of Israel was, in actuality, God's throne, and that God's chosen kings sat on His throne.[66]

1 Chronicles 28:5 (LEB)	And from all my sons—for Yahweh has given many sons to me—he has chosen Solomon my son over Israel. Whosoever shall confess me before men, him shall the Son of man also confess before the angels of God. He that overcometh…*I will confess his name before my Father*, and before his angels.
1 Chronicles 29:23 (LEB)	Then Solomon as king in place of David his father. And he prospered, and all Israel obeyed him.
2 Chronicles 9:8 (LEB)	Blessed be Yahweh your God who took delight in you, to as king for Yahweh your God.

As the Old Testament kings of Israel sat on God's throne in the holy city, we will sit on His throne with Christ in the New Jerusalem. Furthermore, as Jesus' victory over His supernatural enemies was the basis for Him sitting on the throne, the Laodicean saints' *overcoming* is the basis for their seating on the throne, too.[67]

Ephesus (Revelation 2:1–7)

What Jesus relays to this church is a pattern for the other churches to follow as they attempt to flee idolatry. They must be courageous and let their lights shine into darkness, no matter the cost.

Let's dig deeper.

Jesus says to the Ephesian church that they are not able to tolerate evil. They put evil to the test by testing individuals who call themselves apostles but are not. They are said to have endured many things because of the name of Christ, and have not become weary. Jesus knows this church by not just abiding in their presence, but by observing their inner workings and activities. His articulation of their ability to discern between falsehood and truth proves this. But, the church at Ephesus has become *unbalanced* in its mission as they busy themselves with heresy hunting.

This needs some explanation.

Jesus says He is against them because they have "left their first love." On the surface, it seems like He is saying they've stopped loving God. Most commentators suggest this, and others indicate they've lost their love for *one another*. These interpretations are problematic and seem to be at odds with what Jesus has already confirmed. He has already told them they "have patient endurance, and have endured many things *because of* [*His*] *name*, and have not become weary" (Revelation 2:3, LEB). Their willingness to endure many things for the name of Christ doesn't *sound* like they have lost their love for God. People don't die and suffer for someone they do *not* love.

So, if these brethren have not stopped loving God or each other, what can Jesus mean? Beale suggests this means they have *lost their passion for the message of the Gospel.*

Their focus has been on maintaining the inward purity of the church, for which they are commended, so the rebuke must deal with their focus toward the outside world. The Ephesians are to remember how far they have fallen in the loss of their first love, and to return to what they had done at first (verse 5)—a reference to the days in which the entire province of Asia heard the Word of the Lord through Paul and the Ephesian church (Acts 19:10). Otherwise, their lampstand will be removed.[68]

This explanation makes the most sense contextually and later on in the book of Revelation, where the lampstands are God's prophetic *witnesses* (Revelation 11:3–7, 10).

Jesus' use of the Old Testament here must not be overlooked. Israel was once a lampstand (Zechariah 4:2, 11). The prophet Isaiah recorded that Israel was to be "a light to the nations" (Isaiah 42:6–7; 49:6). Israel's failure to evangelize the nations caused this responsibility to be passed to another—the Church.[69]

However, the Ephesian brethren (God's lampstand in Ephesus) are following in Israel's foul footsteps. This is why Jesus then says to the church at Ephesus: "Remember therefore from where you have fallen, and repent and do the works you did at first. But if you do not, I am coming to you, and I will remove your lampstand from its place, unless you repent" (Revelation 2:5, LEB). "Do the *works* you did at first"? If Jesus means the church at Ephesus no longer has love in their hearts for God, "work" is a strange remedy and choice of words. However, if He means they're no longer active in *bearing light* to those in darkness, then recommitting themselves to the "work" of evangelism makes total sense.

Just as one can love *somebody* or *something* (such as a university, a hobby, a favorite movie, a restaurant, etc.) Christ reveals that the church in Ephesus has lost their love for the *work* they did at first. The church of Ephesus *at first* loved saving lost souls with the Gospel. Jesus is saying, "Bear light like you once did. Rescue those in darkness like you used to do. Be a lamp of witness in the pagan city of Ephesus again. *Use your light, or I will remove your lampstand* as I did with Israel."

The church at Ephesus needs to stop being so inward-focused and start being outward-focused. They need to stop being *unbalanced* and distracted with orthodoxy and actively reach the lost. The two hundred thousand citizens of Ephesus will remain in their sins if they aren't told the Gospel of Jesus Christ. They will die loyal to their patron goddess Artemis (also called "Diana" in Acts 19:24–35 and "Ashtoreth" in

1 Kings 11:5). This is what's at stake, and this is why the church there needs to get to work.

Jesus concludes His message to the Ephesian Christians by saying, "Those who have ears, let them hear" (Revelation 2:7). Though Jesus said this often during His ministry (Matthew 13:9–17; Mark 4:9, 23; Luke 8:8), the phrase originated with the Hebrew prophets (Ezekiel 3:27; Jeremiah 5:21; Isaiah 6:9–10).

This expression is intended to *enlighten* genuine believers and *blind* unbelievers.[70] Those who receive Jesus' message will *conquer*.

Smyrna (Revelation 2:8–11)

After calling the church of Ephesus to repentance, Jesus turns His attention forty miles north to Smyrna, a stronghold for the imperial cult. The city of Smyrna vies with Ephesus for regional prominence, glory, and grandeur. Smyrna was even often called "the first of Asia in size and beauty" on ancient coins.[71] It boasted large architectural structures such as the temples of Tiberias, Livia, and the Senate.[72] It also had scores of pagan temples dedicated to various gods and goddesses.[73]

The passage reads:

> To the angel of the assembly in Smyrna write: "The first and the last, who was dead, and has come to life says these things: I know your works, oppression, and your poverty (but you are rich), and the blasphemy of those who say they are Jews, and they are not, but are a synagogue of Satan. Don't be afraid of the things which you are about to suffer. Behold, the devil is about to throw some of you into prison, that you may be tested; and you will have oppression for ten days. Be faithful to death, and I will give you the crown of life. He who has an ear, let him hear what the Spirit says to the assemblies. He who overcomes won't be harmed by the second death." (Revelation 2:8–11, WEB)

Jesus tells John to write that this letter is from "the words of the first and the last, who died and came to life," something He stated in 1:17. As we previously learned, this is a clear allusion to Isaiah 41:4; 44:6; and 48:12, where God is called "the first and last." This reminder encourages the church in Smyrna because it signals that Christ is Lord and God.

Next, Jesus says He knows their tribulation and poverty. Christ's statement is incredibly telling of the living environment of this church. They don't have nice things or big houses. They are poor. But why? It isn't because they aren't intelligent or hardworking; it's because of whom they serve (Jesus). While they are *rich* in faith (Matthew 5:3; Matthew 6:19–21; Luke 12:21; 2 Corinthians 6:10; James 2:5), these uncompromising brethren find it very difficult to make a living, primarily because of a sect of local Jews. Jesus says they are being "slandered by Jews who were of the synagogue of Satan." Scholars have confirmed that at least some Jewish community members collaborated with the local officials to repress Christians.[74] This is not surprising when we consider the biblical evidence in the book of Acts (Acts 13:50; 14:2; 14:19; 17:5; 18:12; 24:5).

The Jews' chumminess with Roman authorities, mixed with their growing hatred of "false believers" (Christians), has put a target on the back of every member of the church in Smyrna. However, as Jesus clearly states, it is not Christians who are the pretenders; it is the unbelieving Jews who have forfeited their heritage and aligned themselves under the "synagogue of Satan." Interestingly, this is the same description the Essenic Jews at Qumran gave their Jewish *apostate* brothers in the Dead Sea Scrolls (DSS).[75]

Jesus then tells the church at Smyrna not to fear what they are supposed to suffer; the devil is about to throw some of them into prison. False accusations against Smyrnean Christians, ultimately, are Satan's work. His blasphemy is driving the Jews' unbelief and deceit. Blasphemy/slander (Greek: *blasphēmia*) is a characteristic trait of the beast throughout the book of Revelation.[76] It means "to do another harm by words."

Revelation 13:1, 5–6 (LEB)	Revelation 17:3–5 (LEB)
And I saw coming up out of the sea a beast that had ten horns and seven heads, and on its horns ten royal headbands, and on its heads a *blasphemous* name.... And a mouth was given to him speaking *great things* and *blasphemies*, and authority to act was given to him for forty-two months. And he opened his mouth for *blasphemies* toward God, to *blaspheme* his name and his dwelling, those who live in heaven.	And he carried me away into the wilderness in the Spirit, and I saw a woman seated on a scarlet beast that was full of *blasphemous* names, having seven heads and ten horns. And the woman was dressed in purple and scarlet and adorned with gold and precious stones and pearls, holding a golden cup in her hand full of detestable things and the unclean things of her sexual immorality. And on her forehead a name was written, a mystery: "Babylon the great, the mother of prostitutes and of the detestable things of the earth."

Satan's puppeteering of the Jews and Rome is uncanny, but not uncommon. He has worked in the shadows for millennia, whispering and influencing the nations. Now, the faithful of Smyrna are feeling the full effect of evil and suffering. Antipas of Pergamum has already been killed (Revelation 1:13), and Jesus warns Smyrna they may be next—or at the very least, they must brace themselves to be *thrown into prison*.

Christ then tells the church of Smyrna that they will have tribulation for ten days. Jesus links their tribulation with that of the prophet Daniel and his three friends who refused to participate in idolatrous practices. Note:

"Please test your servants *for ten days*, and let them give us some of the vegetables, and let us eat and let us drink water. Then let our appearances and the appearance of the young men who are eating the fine food of the king be compared before you, and then deal with your servants according to what you see." So he agreed to this proposal with them, and he tested them *for ten days*. And at the end of *ten days* their appearances appeared better and they were healthier of body than all the young men who were eating the fine food of the king. (Daniel 1:12–15, LEB; emphasis added)

Daniel's test and food that were undoubtedly linked to idolatry are the perfect analogy of what the Christians in Smyrna are facing. They are continually tempted to compromise in this area, since the pagan meals in Asia Minor are so frequent.[77] Smyrna must channel the strength and endurance of Daniel and his three friends. They must not *bow* to the Beast. Jesus then tells them to "be faithful unto death" so they can "receive the crown of life." He doesn't promise a way of escape; quite the opposite—and He all but prophetically forecasts their martyrdom.

History confirms that many Christians died in Smyrna. Polycarp's death is legendary. He was a disciple of the Apostle John and a leader in the church at Smyrna. He died on February 23, AD 155, at the hands of Rome and traitorous Jews. Upon his gruesome death, the church at Smyrna wrote a letter, commonly referred to as "The Martyrdom of St. Polycarp," to the church of Philomelium entailing Polycarp's departure from this life and his great faith in the shadow of death. It's chilling.[78] The faith Polycarp and the other Christian martyrs demonstrated in Smyrna meant that Jesus' words in Revelation 2:10, "I will give you the crown of life," would now be their eternal reward. It would not be the crown of Smyrna's goddess Cybele, which was pictured on their coinage, but one that doesn't fade away, eternal in the heavens (2 Timothy 4:8; 1 Peter 5:4).[79]

The Lord/Spirit ends the exhortation to the Smyrnean Christians by saying, "The one who conquers will not be hurt by the second death." The magnitude of the *second death* quickly overshadows that of their mortal death. While they will be thrown into prison (and many killed), they will *not* be thrown into the Lake of Fire (Revelation 20:14–15). This is Jesus' eschatological promise to all victors and martyrs who die with their allegiance to the Gospel well intact.

Philadelphia (Revelation 3:7–13)

As we have studied, the churches of Asia at this time are under attack by Satan (the deceiver). Some Christians are overcome by participating in *idolatrous* practices, a gripping temptation reinforced by local temples and guilds dedicated to pagan gods. When studying Jesus' words to the church at Philadelphia, believers receive no such rebuke. They are a model of faithfulness. Jesus' words to this church serve as an antidote for fleeing idolatry; they must busy themselves with spreading the light.

The issue Jesus addresses to the Philadelphian church is how the apostate Jews in the city of Philadelphia are attempting to stonewall their entrance into the Kingdom of God. Since Jesus holds the key of David (a concept we will discuss in greater detail later in the book), local Jews *cannot* forbid them entrance into the true Kingdom. Ethnic Israel is not the divine agent of salvation; the Messiah is.[80] This opportunity of Kingdom *acceptance* for these predominantly Gentile Christians sheds light on Jesus' next statement about an "open door" in Revelation 3:8–9. He says He knows their works and has set an open door before them that no one can shut. He says that though they have little strength, they have kept His word, and have not denied His name. Though the church is small and has little power, their Lord is the Almighty, and He has *opened* the door of the New Jerusalem for these faithful Christians.

Next, Jesus tells the Philadelphian church that He will make those of the synagogue of Satan (the ones who call themselves Jews and are not), kneel down before them in acknowledgment that God's love has extended beyond national Israel to the whole world. These ethnic Jews who trust in their circumcision and reject the true Messiah are apostates (Romans 2:28–29). Jesus says to the Philadelphian brethren, "I will make them [apostate Jews] bow before the feet" (Revelation 3:9). This phrase is a collective allusion to the writings of Isaiah stating that the Gentiles would one day bow down to believing Jews in a postexilic utopia. Note the following passages (italics added):

Isaiah 45:14 (LEB)	Thus says Yahweh: "The acquisition of Egypt and the merchandise of Cush and the Sabeans, tall men, shall pass over to you; they shall be yours, and they shall walk behind you. They shall pass over in chains, and *they shall bow down to you*; they will pray to you.
Isaiah 49:23 (LEB)	And kings shall be your guardians, and their queens your nurses. *They shall bow down, faces to the* ground, to you, and they will lick up the dust of your feet. Then you will know that I am Yahweh; those who await me shall not be ashamed.
Isaiah 60:14 (LEB)	And the children of those who oppressed you shall come to you bending low, and all those who treated you disrespectfully *shall bow down at the soles of your feet*. And they shall call you the city of Yahweh, Zion of the holy one of Israel.

However, in Revelation 3, the roles are reversed. Gentile Christians are in good standing with Yahweh; apostate Jews must grovel before *their* feet. Scholar James Moffatt, as cited in Mounce's commentary on Revelation, calls this the "grim irony of providence."[81]

The Messiah then commends this church for having patient endurance and urges them to stay the course so no one can take their after-life crown. He also says those who conquer (in their battle against evil) will be made a pillar in the Temple of God and will never go outside again. The Temple to which Jesus is referring is not an earthly one made with hands; it is the heavenly Temple of God's presence.[82] The Philadelphian

Christians will be *pillars* in the New Jerusalem. Paul noted that the apostles functioned similarly as pillars of foundational truth for the early Church (Galatians 2:9; 1 Timothy 3:15). The idea there and here is *stability* and *permanence*.[83] This is why Jesus says "they will never go out" of the city, a statement that may also have a *protective* flair, which connects to the conflict-ending battle of John's Apocalypse.[84]

Christ continues in Revelation 3 by saying He "will write on his faithful the name of God and the name of the city of God" (Revelation 3:12). Aune calls this a metaphor of divine ownership and dedication of the one so inscribed to God.[85] John's phrase also recalls Numbers 6:27, where we read that the name of God was put on the people of Israel, and Ezekiel 48:35, where the city wore the name of God.

Numbers 6:27 (LEB)	Ezekiel 48:35 (LEB)
And they will put *my name on the Israelites*, and I will bless them.	All around the city is eighteen thousand cubits, *and the name of the city* from that day is "*Yahweh Is There*"!

While followers of the beast will bear the mark of its evil name (Revelation 13:17), Christ's faithful will be *graffitied* with His name and with the name of the holy city of Jerusalem that comes down from Heaven from God.[86] *Bearing the name* of God is at the heart of spiritual warfare, and those who stand for Christ and flee idolatry will wear His name in the New Jerusalem (Revelation 3:12; 21:2, 10).[87]

LOOKING AHEAD

The writhing conflict of spiritual warfare has been on full display in this chapter. It's apparent that the churches are under fire by hostile supernatural forces whose desire is to keep the churches in a holding pattern of idolatry. In the next chapter, we will begin our study of how Revelation frames Jesus as the divine messenger of promise and why that matters for believers under enemy fire.

2

JESUS IN THE OLD TESTAMENT

Now I want to remind you, although you know everything once and for all, that Jesus, having saved the people out of the land of Egypt, the second time destroyed those who did not believe.
—JUDE 5, LEB

IN A NUTSHELL

Jesus is described as a mighty angel in Revelation 10. While this seems strange to our modern ears, interpreting Jesus as the angel does not undermine Him as being God; it *reinforces* His divinity. This chapter dips into what scholars call "angelomorphic Christology," the "identification of Christ with angelic form and functions, either before or after the incarnation."[88] To understand all of this, we will revisit several passages involving the Angel of Yahweh in the Old Testament, which ultimately links this figure to Yahweh Himself. We will also discuss how New Testament writers place Jesus in the historical narrative of the OT and why that's not inaccurate. Understanding that Jesus was literally present on earth for much of OT history frames John's discussion of why Jesus' struggle with historical Babylon is not out of place.

DIGGING DEEPER

Revelation 10 opens with John saying:

> I saw a mighty angel coming down out of the sky, clothed with a cloud. A rainbow was on his head. His face was like the sun, and his feet like pillars of fire. (Revelation 10:1, WEB)

This is no ordinary angel; this familiar OT description tells us that. Him being "wrapped in a cloud" hearkens back to Daniel 7:9–13 and the "son of man." Having a "rainbow over his head" links to Ezekiel 1:28, where the referent is God. In the New Testament, having a face "like the sun" is a clear connection to Matthew 17:2. These references and their amalgamation lead us into what scholars call the earlier-mentioned term, "angelomorphic Christology."[89]

What John is doing here is "blender theology." He takes terms from the Old and New Testaments that describe Yahweh and the Divine Christ and throws them into a blender. What comes out is a portrait of a *divine figure* who is *angelic*. So, in Revelation 10, Christ is an angel *functionally*, not ontologically (in other words, He's still the Creator, not a created being), as Charles Gieschen, author of *Angelomorphic Christology*, writes:

> Therefore, angelomorphic depictions of Christ, and even texts which explicitly identify him as an angel, do not signify that the author understood him to be from the ranks of created angels.[90]

It's clear from John's description that Jesus plays the role of a mighty angel in the chapter. Admittedly, even saying this feels a bit strange. However, interpreting Jesus as the angel does not undermine His being God; it reinforces His divinity and is completely harmonious with OT theology. To understand how, we need to revisit the Angel of Yahweh in the OT.

The *Lexham Glossary of Theology* defines the "Angel of Yahweh" as "a divine being often depicted as a direct representative of Yahweh or the embodiment of Yahweh in human or angelic form."[91]

In some OT passages, there is *distinguishability* between this angel and Yahweh; in others, there is *zero distinction* between the two. In Exodus 23:20–23, the angel is clearly distinct from Him, but not entirely separate from Him:

> Look, I am about to send an angel before you to guard you on the way and to bring you to the place that I have prepared. Be attentive to him and listen to his voice; do not rebel against him, because he will not forgive your transgression, for my name is in him. But if you listen attentively to his voice and do all that I say, I will be an enemy to your enemies and a foe to your foes. When my angel goes before you and brings you to the Amorites and the Hittites and the Perizzites and the Canaanites and the Hivites and the Jebusites, I will wipe them out. (LEB)

Though this text doesn't specifically call this figure the "Angel of Yahweh," it's pretty much universally accepted that He is, because, as God said, "my name is in him." Though *distinguishable* from Yahweh, Israel understood the Exodus 23 being to be a visible representation of God Himself, a visible stand-in for God's abiding presence. Other texts present the Angel of Yahweh as *the same being as Yahweh*, meaning they are *indistinguishable* from one another (i.e., Judges 6:11–24). So, the OT presents the Angel of Yahweh as both Yahweh Himself and as a distinguishable, visible stand-in.

This angel's role in the OT narrative is extensive. The *Baker Encyclopedia of the Bible* summarizes this figure's *tenured* presence with OT Israel:

The angelic figure served Israel positively as guide and protector (Ex 14:19) and companion in the wilderness wanderings (Ex 23:20; 33:2; Nm 20:16) or negatively as assassin or destroyer (2 Sm 24:16), yet always acted to preserve the sanctity of Israel's covenant with God. Certain individuals such as Hagar (Gn 16:7; 21:17), Balaam (Nm 22:21, 22), and Abraham's servant (Gn 24:7, 40) were also confronted by the divinely commissioned messenger (cf. further references 1 Sm 29:9; 2 Sm 14:20; 19:27; 1 Kgs 19:7; 2 Kgs 19:35; 1 Chr 21:15; 2 Chr 32:21).[92]

Passages like Exodus 23:20–23 and Judges 6:11–24 spurred Jews to believe in *two* Yahweh figures—one visible and one invisible. The two powers in Heaven were considered *co-powers* prior to the first century.[93]

Certain NT passages seem to link Jesus to the Angel of Yahweh. For example, note the language of Jude 5:

Now I want to remind you, although you know everything once and for all, that Jesus, having saved the people out of the land of Egypt, the second time destroyed those who did not believe. (LEB)

Jude's citation clearly places Jesus in the OT. According to Jude, Jesus saved Israel from Egypt. Phase 1 of His deliverance of Israel is recorded in the burning bush scene of Exodus 3 where the Angel of Yahweh called Moses to be a leader among God's people. The Aramaic Targum of this passage calls the "Angel of the Lord" the *Memra*, meaning the "Word." Note the following:

And Moses was pasturing the flock of his father-in-law Jethro, the *lord* of Midian, and he led the flock behind the wilderness, and he reached Mount Horeb, *above which the Glory of the Shekinah of the Lord was revealed.* And the angel of the Lord was *revealed* to him in flames of fire from the midst of the thorn bush; and he saw, and, behold, the thorn bush was aflame in the fire, but the thorn bush was not *burned*. And Moses said: "I will turn aside now and I will see this great vision: why the thorn bush is not burned." And *it was manifest before* the Lord that *Moses* had turned aside to see, and *the Memra of the Lord* called to him from the midst of the thorn bush.[94]

That the *memra* or the "Word" was in the bush is astounding and should sound very familiar to NT readers. John famously calls Jesus the "Word" in John 1:1–14.

The angel's presence in the bush and wilderness wanderings were helpful antecedents for the NT authors and their audience to *embrace* Jesus as "the Word who became flesh and dwelt among us." It also left the unbelieving Jews without an excuse. When Christians began linking Jesus to the *visible* Yahweh figure described in the Hebrew Bible the two powers in heaven stance was soon rejected in Jewish circles.[95]

So, casting Jesus as the "mighty angel" of Revelation 10 doesn't diminish His divinity or sovereignty; it reinforces that Jesus has always been both God *and* God's visual representative (Hebrews 1:2–3).

As stated, the over-the-top descriptions of this angel prove He's divine and to be thought of as Jesus, the same Jesus who appeared in angelic form in the OT. Notice again how John describes the "mighty angel" in chapter 10:

I saw a mighty angel coming down out of the sky, clothed with a cloud. A rainbow was on his head. His face was like the sun, and his feet like pillars of fire. (Revelation 10:1, WEB)

If there were any doubts about whether Jesus is the "mighty angel" in Revelation 10, John's next line puts all doubts to bed:

He [the mighty angel] cried with a loud voice, as a *lion roars*. When he cried, the seven thunders uttered their voices. (Revelation 10:3, WEB)

Assigning the angel the vocalization of a lion connects to several OT passages about the voice of God. Note below:

Amos 3:8 (LEB)	Hosea 11:10 (LEB)
A lion has roared! Who is not afraid? My Lord Yahweh has spoken, who will not prophesy?	They will go after Yahweh; he roars like a lion. When he roars, his children will come trembling from *the* sea.

The picture John wants his audience to see in Revelation 10:1–3 is *the lion of the tribe of Judah* (Revelation 5) roaring over the land and sea *with* the mighty voice of God.

What has not yet been stated is that this entire scene (in Revelation 10) *was arranged to mirror Daniel 12:5–9 and the divine man* (the angelic figure) who stood above the waters with His hand raised to swear by Heaven:

Then I looked, I myself, Daniel, and look, there were two others standing: one on this bank of the stream and one on the other. Then he said to the man who was clothed in linen who was above the water of the stream, "How long until the end of the wonders?" And I heard the man who was clothed in linen who was above the water of the stream, and he raised his right hand and his left hand to heaven and he swore by the one who lives forever that an appointed time, appointed times, and half an appointed time would pass when the shattering of the power of the holy people would be completed; then all these things will be accomplished. Now I myself heard, but I did not understand, and I said, "My lord, what will be the outcome of these things?" And he said, "Go, Daniel, for the words are secret and are sealed up until the time of the end." (LEB)

Biblical scholar James M. Hamilton Jr. explains in his book, *With the Clouds of Heaven: The Book of Daniel in Biblical Theology*, the shared likeness of these two scenes:

A similar instalment in a pattern in Revelation that bears a resemblance to Daniel...is found in the similarity of angelic action in Daniel 12:7 and Revelation 10:5–6. In Daniel 12:7, "the man clothed in linen, who was above the waters of the stream; he raised his right hand and his left hand towards heaven and swore by him who lives for ever...." The analogue for this in Revelation describes an angel "standing on the sea and on the land [who] raised his right hand to heaven and swore by him who lives for ever and ever." (Revelation 10:5–6)[96]

That the actions of the mighty angel in Revelation 10 mirror that of the divine man/angel of Daniel 12:7 just further proves this is no *ordinary* angel; this is Jesus Christ. Seeing Jesus as the mighty angel of Revelation 10 is an important thread woven into the tapestry of John's cosmic war.

LOOKING AHEAD

In the next chapter, we will fast-forward to the end of Jesus' ministry and see that Revelation frames Christ's victory over death with a set of *cosmic keys*. The region these keys control illuminates the Messiah's authority in the netherworld.

JESUS IN THE UNDERWORLD

I was dead, and behold, I am living forever and ever, and I hold
the keys of death and of Hades.

~REVELATION 1:18, LEB

IN A NUTSHELL

This chapter explores how the Resurrected Christ holds the keys of
Death and Hades in His hands (Revelation 1:18). One of the many
implications of Jesus taking these keys away from Death and Hades is
that cosmic evil is now *legally* defeated in Yahweh's court.

DIGGING DEEPER

Having not seen Jesus in nearly sixty years, John once again suddenly
finds himself standing in Christ's presence, as we read in the book of
Revelation. But things have changed. Jesus is now deified in His God
state; He's not in corruptible flesh and blood. He's now:

...dressed in a robe reaching to the feet and girded around His
chest with a golden belt, and his head and hair were white like
wool, white as snow, and his eyes were like a fiery flame, and his

feet were like fine bronze when it has been fired in a furnace, and his voice was like the sound of many waters, and he had in his right hand seven stars, and a sharp double-edged sword coming out of his mouth, and his face was like the sun shining in its strength (Revelation 1:14–16).

Overwhelmed, John said:

When I saw him, I fell at his feet like a dead man. He laid his right hand on me, saying, "Don't be afraid. I am the first and the last, and the Living one. I was dead, and behold, I am alive forever and ever. Amen. I have the keys of Death and of Hades." (Revelation 1:17–18, WEB)

This scene is similar to Daniel's vision in Daniel 8–10. As biblical scholar G. K. Beale notes, there is a *fourfold pattern* between the experiences of John and Isaiah. He writes:

John's response to the vision in v 17a follows the fourfold pattern found in Daniel 8 and 10: the prophet observes a vision, falls on his face in fear, is strengthened by a heavenly being, and then receives further revelation from that being.[97]

Note how this fourfold pattern plays out the following passages:

Daniel 8:16–19 (LEB)	And he came beside where I was standing, and when he came *I became terrified and I fell prostrate on my face.* And he said to me, "Understand, son of man, that the vision is for the time of the end." *...and he touched me and made me stand on my feet.* And he said, "Look, I am making known to you what will happen in the period of wrath, for it refers to the appointed time of the end."

Daniel 10:7–12 (LEB)	And I saw, I, Daniel alone, the vision…and as a result *no strength was left in me and my complexion grew deathly pale*, and I did not retain any strength…. And look, *a hand touched me* and it roused me to my knees and the palms of my hands. And he said to me, "*You must not fear*, Daniel, for from the first day that you set your heart to understand and to humble yourself before your God, your words were heard, and I myself have come because of your words."
Revelation 1:17–19 (LEB)	And when *I saw him, I fell at his feet like a dead person, and he placed his right hand on me, saying, "Do not be afraid!* I am the first and the last, and the one who lives, and I was dead, and behold, I am living forever and ever, and I hold the keys of death and of Hades. *Therefore, write the things which you saw, and the things which are, and the things which are about to take place after these things.*"

The continued connections to the prophecies of Daniel underline the eschatological realities that Christ, the Son of Man, has been sworn in as Cosmic Ruler in these appointed "last days."

Upon placing His right hand of comfort on an overwhelmed John, Jesus says, "I am the first and the last," a clear reference to Yahweh in Isaiah.

Isaiah 41:4 (LEB)	Isaiah 44:6 (LEB)	Isaiah 48:12 (LEB)
Who has accomplished and done this, calling the generations from the beginning? I, Yahweh, am *first*; and *I am the one with the last*.	Thus says Yahweh, the king of Israel, and its redeemer, Yahweh of hosts: "*I am the first, and I am the last.*"	Listen to me, Jacob, and Israel, whom I called: I am he. *I am the first; also I am the last.*

Jesus is telling John who He is. He is to be thought of as Yahweh in every way. He is fully God, nothing less. To emphasize this, Jesus then tells John, "I am the one who lives, and I was dead, and behold, I am living forever and ever" (Revelation 1:18). Having died and risen again on the third day, Jesus is "the living God" like Yahweh is described in the Old Testament (Deuteronomy 5:26; 32:40; 1 Samuel 17:26, 36; Jeremiah 10:10; 23:36; Daniel 6:27; 12:7; Joshua 3:10; Psalm 42:2; 84:3; etc.).

What Jesus says next is the pinnacle of this present reality: "I hold the keys of Death and of Hades." This statement is loaded with many enriching and liberating truths. At the heart of this statement is an underworld battle between Christ and two demonic netherworld deities, Death and Hades.

Professor Justin Bass writes in his monograph entitled "The Battle for the Keys: Revelation 1:18 and Christ's Descent into the Underworld":

Whether a Jew or a Greek, if they heard that Christ holds the keys of Death and Hades; battle imagery would have filled their minds. Most would not see Death and Hades kindly giving away their authority over the realm of the dead, but they must have been taken forcefully. They would have understood that the two great terrors of the Greek world and the Jewish world [Death and Hades] have been defeated by Christ.[98]

In chapter 19 of my book *Gospel Over Gods*, we discovered the identity of "Death" (Hebrew: *Maveth*) was the Canaanite god Mot. I mentioned that in 1 Corinthians 15:54–55, Paul uses Hosea 13:14 to proclaim that Jesus defeated Mot (Death) and two other demonic spirits, Deber and Qeteb. Note these parallel passages:

Hosea 13:14 (ESV)	1 Corinthians 15:54–55 (ESV)
I shall ransom them from the power of Sheol [underworld]; I shall redeem them from Death [Maveth/Mot]. O Death [Maveth/Mot], where are your plagues [Deber]? O Sheol, where is your sting [Qeteb]? Compassion is hidden from my eyes.	...then shall come to pass the saying that is written: "Death [Maveth/Mot] is swallowed up in victory." "O death [Maveth/Mot], where is your victory [Deber]? O death [Maveth/Mot], where is your sting [Qeteb]?"

Here in Revelation, Jesus confirms that His battle in the underworld with "Death" (Mot) and Hades *did* occur. Perhaps Revelation's "Hades" is the demonic Deber or Qeteb of Hosea 13:14. It's certainly possible.

The *Dictionary of Deities and Demons* says this of Hades:

Hades is the Greek name for the underworld and its ruler, as is the case in the Bible. The spelling of the name sometimes varies (Aides/Hades, Aidoneus) and the etymology is debated.... Hades is a shadowy god in Greece.... His connection with the underworld makes him "horrible" and "the most hated of all the gods."... Homer mentions that he acquired the underworld through a lottery with his brothers Zeus and Poseidon.[99]

The point is Mot/Maveth (Hades in the Greek stories) was defeated by Jesus. Mot had the reputation of being an "undefeatable" god who "swallowed up" the deceased as helpless "lambs" as they entered the underworld. Here is how the Ugaritic text depicts Mot's hopeless victims:

But take care, attendants of the god,
do not draw near divine Mot,
lest he offer you up *like a lamb in his mouth*,
like a kid in the opening of his maw![100]

The irony is, it was the *Lamb of God* who defeated the underworld deity in his own "inescapable" fortress and took away his underworld keys.

Asia Minor and the rest of the ancient world are also littered with beliefs and stories of underworld deities who functioned as divine gatekeepers in the realm of the dead, such as Hekate, the key-bearer to the gate of Hades, and Persephone, who is said to command the keys to the gates of Hades in the inner earth.[101]

Our aim in this chapter is not to ferret out all of the underworld deities (there are a lot). The point is to recognize that, in the three days between His death and the Resurrection, Jesus was at war with real beings in Sheol (Acts 2:27, 31), many of whom were lauded by the nations of the world.

Again, Revelation names two enemies (from the Grecian stories) Jesus battled against for the keys—*Death* and *Hades*. These two beings are *primary* antagonists in Revelation who afflict the earth and are finally punished in the Lake of Fire for their heinous deeds. Note:

Revelation 6:8 (LEB)	Revelation 20:13–14 (LEB)
And I looked, and behold, a pale green horse, and the one seated on it was named *Death, and Hades* followed after him. And authority was granted to them over a fourth of the earth, to kill by the sword and by famine and by pestilence and by the wild beasts of the earth.	And the sea gave up the dead who were in it, and *Death and Hades* gave up the dead who were in them, and each one was judged according to their deeds. And *Death and Hades* were thrown into the lake of fire. This is the second death—the lake of fire.

As theologian and author Justin Bass puts it:

The believers of the seven churches in Revelation can rest assured
that no god or goddess or demon or Roman emperor holds their
destiny in his or her hands, but only the Lord Jesus Christ (Rev
1:18; 3:7; 9:1; 20:1).[102]

Indeed, it is *our* Lord who now holds the keys of Death and Hades
in His eternal grip.

Therefore, since the children share in blood and flesh, he also
in like manner shared in these *same things*, in order *that through
death he could destroy the one who has the power of death, that is,
the devil*, and could set free these who through fear of death were
subject to slavery throughout all their lives. For surely he is not
concerned with angels, but he is concerned with the descendants
of Abraham. (Hebrews 2:14–16, LEB; emphasis added)

Defeating the underworld was no small feat; to say it completely
shifted the landscape of the unseen world is an understatement. By the
power of the Resurrected Messiah, all netherworld gods were stunned
and defeated. As Revelation explains, this isn't to say hostile supernatural
forces are *inactive* on earth; they are indeed active. We just know how
their story will end—and so do they.

LOOKING AHEAD

In the next chapter, we will fast-forward past Christ's Ascension to the day
when the newly crowned Messiah sits down on His throne. Revelation
will reveal that the Hebrew King of promise doesn't only hold the keys
of Death and Hades, but also that He possesses the *Jewish* key of David.

4

JESUS IN HEAVEN

And to the angel of the church in Philadelphia write: "This is
what the holy one, the true one, the one who has the key of
David, the one who opens and no one can shut, and who shuts
and no one can open, says."

~REVELATION 3:7, LEB

IN A NUTSHELL

The previous chapter explored how Jesus came to possess the keys of
Death and Hades (Revelation 1:18). We learned He won these keys
by beating Death and escaping the underworld via the Resurrection.
This chapter will discuss how Jesus ascends to kingship and is given
the *key of David* (Revelation 3:7). As we will discover, this "key" is an
Old Testament concept that speaks to the Messiah's absolute authority over the entire Kingdom of God. This means the powers of darkness, plot though they may, can never overthrow the monarchy of the
Messiah.

DIGGING DEEPER

The Messiah and the Scroll of Destiny (Revelation 5:1–4)

As John is saturated with the divine presence of the Most High, He sees "in the right hand of the one who is seated on the throne a scroll, written inside and on the back, sealed up with seven seals" (LEB). In Revelation 5:1–4f and following, the Apocalypse now centers around this very mysterious scroll. Having writing on the front *and* back, and having been sealed with *seven* seals creates a bit of an enigma to be solved. In antiquity, sealed scrolls with writing on both sides were typically private contracts not accessible by the public.[103]

What could this scroll be hiding?

At this point in John's visionary experience, the sealed scroll is *hiding* its contents from all of Heaven and earth. Also, that the scroll has writing on both sides denotes that the draftsman's message is full and comprehensive.[104] There is no additional space for writing or omissions that need to be filled in.[105] The scroll is indeed *comprehensive*, as we will soon discover.

However, John's description of the scroll having writing on the front and back connects to Ezekiel 2:9–10. As Ezekiel's scroll that had writing on the front and the back was filled with "mourning," "woe," and "lamentation," the scroll in Revelation is, too.[106] This is not a coincidence. John intentionally conjures up the language of Ezekiel 2:9–10 to highlight this point.

For many, the events that will soon come to light by the unsealing of the scroll are terrifying. Indeed, Revelation contains traces of the final age of humankind, and its eschatological magnitude is off the charts.[107] It contains God's plan and purpose for the entire universe, a plan of sweet salvation and bitter judgment.[108]

Additionally, Revelation's scroll also mimics the flying scroll of Zechariah 5:1–4, which contained writing on both sides as well and functioned as a destroyer to the unrighteous. So, John's scroll should also be considered a slayer of unrighteousness.[109]

Regarding the seven seals John sees, this terminology echoes the language of Daniel 12 and Isaiah 29:[110]

Daniel 12:1, 4, 9 (LEB)	Isaiah 29:11 (LEB)
Now at that time, Michael, the great prince, will arise, the protector over the sons of your people, and it will be a time of distress that has not been since your people have been a nation until that time. And at that time your people will escape, everyone who is found written in the scroll…. But you, Daniel, keep the words secret and *seal the scroll until the time of the end*; many will run back and forth and knowledge will increase…. And he said, "Go, Daniel, for the words are secret and *are sealed up until the time of the end*."	And the vision of all this has become for you like the words of *a sealed document*. When they give it to one who knows the document, saying, "Read this now!" He says, "I am not able, *for it is sealed*."

Unbroken wax seals meant that writings had not been compromised or altered in any way. The original message of the author was still intact and authentic.[111] This is relevant in our text, because all *seven* seals remain *unbroken*.[112] So, the message the seven seals telegraph is that the content is authentic and hasn't changed. This also means the scroll was previously written—at some point prior to John's experience.

Could this be the very scroll of Daniel 12, which was to be sealed *until* the end of time when Michael, *a powerful angel*, will rise up to protect the people of God? Perhaps so, especially when considering that, next, a powerful angel proclaims with a loud voice, "Who is worthy to open the scroll and to break its seals?" (Revelation 5:2). No one in Heaven, on earth, or under the earth is able to open the scroll.

This scene screams "CRISIS!"—and that's a rare problem in Heaven![113]

Is no one truly worthy? Can none of Heaven's mighty angels, none of the Hebrew prophets from the OT, and not even God the Father open the seven-sealed scroll of destiny?[114]

When the angel's question is greeted with silence, solemn panic ensues and the Apostle John begins to weep. No scroll means no protection for Yahweh's people. No scroll means no judgments against evil.[115] Can everything humanity has hoped for and prayed for since the dawn of time come to nothing?[116] Alas, are we left without a Savior? Is there no one of Adam's race who can break the seven seals and read its judgments?[117]

One of the elders tells John that the "lion of the tribe of Judah" can unseal it and read its cosmic secrets. The descriptions of Jesus as a "lion of Judah" can be understood through Old Testament eyes. Genesis 49:8–10 calls Judah a "lion cub" and prophesies that the scepter of rulership will not depart from Judah. The passage also states all the nations will bow to, *at that time*, an ambiguous "Him" (the Messiah). Contextually, Genesis 49:8–10 was Jacob's final blessings to his sons, a line through whom the Messiah would eventually be born.[118]

Genesis 49 has undertones of conquest and victory. This is why people expected the Messiah to be a *military* juggernaut and were deranged by Jesus' observable passivity. Jewish tradition forecasted that the Hebrew Messiah would conquer his enemies "like a lion" and bring them to judgment (2 Esdras 12:31–36). The Jews of Jesus' day misunderstood. The Messiah's war is not against flesh and blood, but against spiritual rulers in high places (Ephesians 6:12). Indeed, He *is* the *mighty* warrior ("lion") prophesied to resurrect the dead "stump" of David and bring the unrighteous to judgment, but He will conquer in the form of a lamb, not a lion.[119] This is the great mystery of the Gospel: *victory through sacrifice.*[120]

The Son of Man and the Ancient of Days

How the lion of Judah becomes King is a prominent theme in Revelation. Ultimately, His ascension to kingship means Christ is God in every way. This is best understood by John's recapitulation of Yahweh's divine adjectives. That is, *what is true of Yahweh in the Old Testament is true of Jesus in Revelation*:

As we begin to unpack this concept, let's note Revelation 1:12–15:

> I turned to see the voice that spoke with me. Having turned, I saw seven golden lamp stands. And among the lamp stands was one like a son of man, clothed with a robe reaching down to his feet, and with a golden sash around his chest. His head and his hair were white as white wool, like snow. His eyes were like a flame of fire. His feet were like burnished brass, as if it had been refined in a furnace. His voice was like the voice of many waters. (WEB)

In this opening scene in the book of Revelation, John hears what's described as "the voice" (Revelation 1:12). This is a term often used as a synonym for God's name in the Old Testament (Isaiah 2:1; 13:1; Jeremiah 23:18; Amos 1:1; Micah 1:1; Habakkuk 1:1; cf. Nahum 1:1). This is a subtle clue that what John is about to see is Jesus as Most High.

In Revelation 1:13, we are introduced to the "Son of Man," whom we are first introduced to in the book of Daniel:

> I continued watching in the visions of the night, and look, with the clouds of heaven *one like a son of man* was coming, and he

came to the Ancient of Days, and was presented before him. And to him was given dominion and glory and kingship that all the peoples, the nations, and languages *would* serve him; his dominion *is* a dominion without end that will not cease, and his kingdom *is one* that will not be destroyed. (Daniel 17:13–14, LEB; emphasis added)

Clearly, the Son of Man is a *divine* figure in Daniel's vision. Throughout His earthly ministry, Jesus claimed He was this figure. In fact, Christ referred to Himself as the "Son of Man" more than He used any other messianic title. This infuriated many Jewish leaders.[121] Mark 14:62–65 states:

And Jesus said, "I am, and you will see *the Son of Man* sitting at the right hand of the Power and coming with the clouds of heaven." And the high priest tore his clothes and said, "What further need do we have of witnesses? You have heard the blasphemy! What do you think?" And they all condemned him as deserving death. And some began to spit on him and to cover his face and to strike him with their fists, and to say to him "Prophesy!" And the officers received him with slaps in the face. (LEB; emphasis added)

Clearly, the Jewish elite considered it blasphemy for Jesus to be connected with Messianic connotations; just as clearly, Jesus did not.

Additional shared descriptions from the books of Daniel and Revelation further substantiate the divinity of Christ. John sees that Jesus' "head and hair" are "white like wool, white as snow, and his eyes" are "like a fiery flame." This is precisely how the appearance of the Ancient of Days (Yahweh) is described in Daniel 7:9. Note the parallels between Daniel 7:9 and Revelation 1:14:

Daniel 7:9 (LES)	Revelation 1:14 (LEB)
I continued to watch until when thrones were set up and the ancient of days was seated, who had a robe just like *snow, and the hair of his head was like pure white wool.* His throne was like a flame of fire, his wheels a burning fire.	...and his head and *hair were white like wool, white as snow,* and his eyes were like a fiery flame.

Regarding these two passages, *The Book of Revelation* author Mounce writes:

In Dan 7:9 the Ancient of Days is described as having hair "white like wool" and clothing "white as snow." With minor modification (the hair of Christ is both "white like wool" and "as white as snow"; cf. Isa 1:18) this description is transferred in Revelation to the exalted Christ. The ascription of the titles and attributes of God to Christ is an indication of the exalted Christology of the Apocalypse.[122]

John also borrows terminology from the angelic figure of Daniel 10:6 to describe Jesus' eyes and feet.

Daniel 10:6 (LEB)	Revelation 1:14–15 (WEB)
Now his body was like turquoise, and his face was like the appearance of lightning, and *his eyes were like torches of fire,* and *his arms and his legs were like the gleam of polished bronze,* and the sound of his words was like the sound of a multitude.	*His eyes were like a flame of fire.* His feet were like burnished brass, as if it had been refined in a furnace

Fanning writes:

In this set of phrases there are clear allusions to the visions of Daniel 10:6 (the angel has arms and feet "like bronze that flashes like lightning"); and of Ezekiel 1:7 (the four celestial creatures' feet "gleamed [lit. were sparks] like bronze that flashes like lightning"). The overall effect is to add to the sense of the dazzling, heavenly glory of the son of man.[123]

John then notes that Christ's voice is "like the sound of many waters," a phrase used throughout the Old Testament to describe the sheer *volume* of God's voice (Psalm 29:3) and other divine beings (Ezekiel 1:24)

Psalm 28:3 (Brenton Lxx En)	Ezekiel 1:24 (LEB)
The voice of the Lord *is upon the waters*: the God of glory has thundered: the Lord *is upon many waters*.	And I heard the sound of their wings like *the sound of many waters*, like the voice of Shaddai, and when they moved there was a *sound* of tumult like the sound of an army; when they stood still they lowered their wings.

John's Christology is off the charts in Revelation chapter 1. His vision links Jesus Christ to the Ancient of Days and the exalted Son of Man of Daniel 7.

John's message is that Jesus *is* God; He is *not* lesser than Yahweh. He is Heaven's rightful King. In the immediate context, this fact is supported by Jesus having seven stars (angels) in His right hand (Revelation 1:16, 20). In antiquity, angels are commonly identified with heavenly bodies (stars, planets, constellations, etc.) as they are here. The message of Jesus holding the *stars* denotes Christ's authority over Heaven's army and their faithfulness to their King.

The Key Of David

As Jesus gained rights to the keys of Hades and Death via the Resurrection, His rise to kingship awarded Him the Jewish *key of David*. Revelation 3:7 states:

> And to the angel of the church in Philadelphia write: "This is what the holy one, the true one, the one who has *the key of David*, the one who opens and no one can shut, and who shuts and no one can open, says." (LEB)

This verse is saturated with Old Testament verbiage. Before we discuss the OT nuances of the key of David, let's highlight the OT titles assigned to Jesus in Revelation 3:7.

First, Christ calls Himself the "holy one." This title is used almost always exclusively to refer to Yahweh in the Hebrew Scriptures, *especially* in the writings of Isaiah, where it is used over twenty times.[124] Note the following passages:

Isaiah 40:25 (LEB)	"And to whom you will compare me, and am I equal?" says *the holy one*.
Isaiah 1:4 (LEB)	They have forsaken Yahweh; they have despised the *holy one of Israel*. They are estranged *and gone* backward.
Isaiah 37:23 (LEB)	Whom have you taunted and blasphemed, and against whom have you raised up *your* voice and lifted your eyes upward? *To the holy one of Israel!*
Isaiah 43:3 (LEB)	For I am Yahweh, your God, *the holy one of Israel*, your savior. I give you Egypt as ransom, Cush and Seba in place of you.

Jesus wants His readers and the apostate Jews in the city of Philadelphia to know *He is God*, one who is worthy of worship.[125] His use of the language of Isaiah is really setting up the reader for a more *significant* connection to the key of David (Isaiah 22), which we will soon discuss.

Second, Jesus calls Himself the "true one." This carries the idea of *genuineness*, meaning Christ is the *true Messiah* of prophecy and not a false messianic pretender the Jews claim He is.[126] God being "true" is originally an Old Testament idea:

> The Old Testament Scriptures repeatedly stress that God and his works are "true" and "faithful". The foundational presentation of the Lord's name and character in Exodus 34:6 LXX depicts him as "true" (*alēthinos*).… Moses combines the divine descriptions "true" and "faithful" in his famous song: "God—his works are true [*alēthina*], and all his ways are justice. A faithful [*pistos*] God, and there is no injustice, a righteous and holy Lord" (Deut. 32:4 LXX). Isaiah…twice refers to him as "the true God" (*ho theos ho alēthinos*) in 65:16 LXX, rendering the Hebrew phrase *'ĕlōhê 'āmēn*.[127]

Note the following passages Tabb discussed:

Exodus 34:6 (BRENTON LXX EN)	And the Lord passed by before his face, and *proclaimed the Lord God* pitiful, and merciful, longsuffering and very compassionate, *and true.*
Deuteronomy 32:4 (BRENTON LXX EN)	As for *God, his works are true,* and all his ways are judgment: God is faithful, and there is no unrighteousness in him; just and holy is the Lord.

<table>
<tr><td>Isaiah 60:14 (LEB)</td><td>...which shall be blessed on the earth; for they shall bless *the true God*: and they that swear upon the earth shall swear by the true God."</td></tr>
</table>

Next, Jesus states He is the one who has the key of David, the one who "opens and no one can shut," and who "shuts and no one can open." In Revelation 1:18, Jesus reveals He now holds the keys of Hades and Death. However, the key of David is just as cosmically important as possessing the keys to the underworld. While Jesus' keys to the underworld make Him the master of *death*, the key of David (Revelation 3:7) makes Him the master of *life* in God's Kingdom. To understand this, we need to understand this key's Old Testament backdrop.

We read in Isaiah 22:20–25:

And this shall happen: On that day I will call to my servant, Eliakim son of Hilkiah, and I will clothe him *with* your tunic, and I will bind your sash firmly about him, and I will put your authority into his hand, and he shall be like a father to the inhabitants of Jerusalem and to the house of Judah. *And I will put the key of the house of David on his shoulder, and he shall open and no one will be able to shut; and he shall shut and no one will be able to open.* And I will drive him in *like* a peg into a secure place, and he will become like a throne of glory to the house of his father. And they will hang all of the heaviness of his father's house on him, the offspring and the offshoot, all of the small vessels, from the bowls to the jars. On that day, declares Yahweh of hosts, the peg that was driven will move away into a secure place, and it will be cut down and fall, and the load that *was* on her will be cut off. For Yahweh has spoken. (LEB, emphasis added)

Isaiah reveals that God would replace Shebna (whose policies and leadership were detrimental to Hezekiah's kingdom) with another. Eliakim was made the new majordomo of God's house and given *total* control. As the *royal vizier*, nothing was beyond his jurisdiction, including the *holy sanctuary* of God. Note:

And I will place the key *of the sanctuary and the authority* of the house of David *in his hand*; and he will open, and none shall shut; and he will shut, and none shall open.[128] (Emphasis added)

In the *Word Biblical Commentary*, John D. W. Watts writes of the evolution of this powerful position in Judaism and compares it to Joseph's role in Egypt.

"Who is over the house," is the title of a ranking member of government under the king. It is used first in Solomon's list of officials (1 Kgs 4:6), where it has an unimportant position. Ahishar was apparently only the majordomo. The title is mentioned several times (1 Kgs 16:9; 18:3; 2 Kgs 15:5). By Hezekiah's time the position had grown in importance in much the same way that Joseph's grew under the pharaoh (Gen 40–44; 45:8). Shebna's position must have been very much like that of a vizier in Egypt. "All affairs of the land passed through his hands, all important documents received his seal, all the officials were under his orders. He really governed in Pharaoh's name" 2 Kgs 15:5 uses the title for Jotham, the heir of the stricken Azariah: "He was over the household, governing the people of the land."[129]

Jesus' allusion to Isaiah 22 in Revelation 3 means Eliakim is a type of Christ. Theologian, professor, and pastor Joel R. Beeke writes:

God presents Eliakim to Isaiah as a type of Christ, to whom God will commit the government of His people, saying, "The key of the house of David will I lay upon his shoulder; so he shall open, and none shall shut; and he shall shut, and none shall open" (Isa. 22:22). Isaiah's words affirm Christ as the chosen Messiah, the Son of David, who has absolute power over entry into the kingdom of heaven. He says that when He opens, no one can shut, and when He shuts, no one can open. Christ has the key to salvation and controls the door of the kingdom of God.[130]

As Beeke aptly notes, Christ having the key of David means *only He decides* who may enter His household.[131]

This is *cosmically* significant.

That members of Hell's army cannot obstruct the entrance to the Kingdom of God is the lynchpin to Satan's defeat. As wielding the keys of the *underworld* makes Jesus the master of death, possessing the key to the *overworld* (Heaven) makes Jesus the master of life. Through Jesus, anyone who wants to change their allegiance from darkness to light can do so because the Messiah possesses the key of David.

There are additional typological layers worth noting between Eliakim (Isaiah 22) and Jesus (Isaiah 9) that help anchor our discussion. Beale writes:

The key (the government of the house of Judah) is set on Eliakim's shoulder (Isa. 22:22); compare "The government will rest upon His [Jesus] shoulders" (9:6).

Isaiah 22:22 (Brenton Lxx En)	Isaiah 9:6 (Brenton Lxx En)
I will give him [Eliakim] the key of the house of David *upon his shoulder.*	For a child [Jesus] is born to us, and a son is given to us, whose government *is upon his shoulder.*

Eliakim will become a father to those in Jerusalem and Judah (22:21); compare "His name [Jesus] will be called…'Eternal Father'" (9:6).

Isaiah 22:21 (BRENTON LXX EN)	Isaiah 9:6 (DEAD SEA SCROLLS BIBLE)
…and I will put on him [Eliakim] thy robe, and I will grant him thy crown with power, and I will give thy stewardship into his hands: and *he shall be as a father* to them that dwell in Jerusalem, and to them that dwell in Juda.	For a child is born to us, a son is given to us. The government will be on his shoulders. He [Jesus] is called Wonderful Counselor, Mighty God, *Everlasting Father*, the Prince of Peace.

Eliakim will become a throne of glory to his father's house (22:23); compare "There will be no end to the increase of His [Jesus'] government…on the throne of David" (9:7).

Isaiah 22:23 (BRENTON LXX EN)	Isaiah 9:7 (LES)
And I will make him [Eliakim] a ruler in a sure place, and *he shall be for a glorious throne of his father's house.*	His [Jesus'] leadership is great, and *there is no limit* to his peace on *the throne of David* and his kingdom, to establish and take hold of it by justice and by righteousness, now and forever.

Eliakim was appointed to his royal position by God (22:21), as would be the coming Messiah (9:6–7).

Isaiah 22:21 (Brenton Lxx En)	Isaiah 9:6–7 (Brenton Lxx En)
...and I will put on him thy robe, and I will grant him thy crown with power, and *I will give thy stewardship into his* [Eliakim] *hands:* and he shall be as a father to them that dwell in Jerusalem, and to them that dwell in Juda [sic].	...*for I will bring peace upon the princes,* and health to him [Jesus]. *His government* shall be great, and of his peace there is no end.[132]

In the immediate context, Jesus' retooling of Isaiah 22 in Revelation 3 ("the one who has the key of David, the one who opens and no one can shut, and who shuts and no one can open") means the apostate Jews of Satan's synagogue in the city of Philadelphia *cannot* forbid them entrance into the true Kingdom, for *the Messiah*, not the apostate Jews, holds the key of David.[133] In the broader context of the book of Revelation, the message is that *powerful* entities are *powerless* to reclaim those marked with the seal of Christ, including Babylon the Great, whom we will soon discuss.

LOOKING AHEAD

In the next chapter, we will examine Jesus on a white horse. This word picture ultimately describes Jesus at war with Babylon. We will discover that, although the powers of darkness are legally defeated, they are not yet finally defeated; they wage war with the Messiah and the twelve tribes of Israel—and will continue to do so until the end of time.

5

JESUS IN ARMAGEDDON

And I saw heaven opened, and behold, a white horse, and the one seated on it was called "Faithful" and "True," and with justice he judges and makes war."

~REVELATION 19:11, LEB

IN A NUTSHELL

Though the Messiah's victory is certain, the nations' gods have yet to relinquish the fight. This chapter explores the Battle of Armageddon and how Revelation frames this conflict with consistent Old Testament imagery.

DIGGING DEEPER

Revelation 1:7–8 begins by declaring that "He is coming." Though the referent of "He" is ambiguous in this passage, later in the book of Revelation (14:14–16) "He" is identified as the "He" is the Son of Man.

The *coming* of Jesus is a prominent theme throughout Revelation and is mentioned seven times (2:5, 16; 3:11; 16:15; 22:7, 12, 20), and

"I will come" is mentioned twice (3:3 and 3:20).[134] The imminent return of the Lord should not be thought of as some far-off event we will never see or experience. John doesn't want the seven churches to have this mindset, for the end of the world has already begun. Indeed, we are in "the last days," and the end is at hand.[135]

In His ministry, Jesus described His future return to earth as being "on the clouds" (Matthew 24:30; Matthew 26:64; Mark 13:26; Mark 14:62; Luke 21:27).

Interestingly, the book of Acts also states that when Jesus *left* earth, a "cloud" received Him (Acts 1:9). As Scripture reveals, Jesus was emphatic about returning to earth in/on/with the clouds, but why? This description is loaded with Old Testament theology and pagan lingo. Both Jews and Gentiles knew the implications of Jesus' eschatological claim.

He was articulating that He is *deity*.

Riding on the clouds is associated with the *divine presence* in antiquity (Exodus 13:21; 16:10; Psalm 68:4, 33; Isaiah 19:1).[136] In the minds of the ancients, it's what the gods do. It's how deities travel as *divine warriors* and *divine judges*.[137] Satan (Baal) is called the "rider of the clouds" in ancient writings from Ugarit, and he begged to take his everlasting kingdom by his cosmic supporters.[138]

Over two thousand years ago, Jesus arrived and began telling people He was the true rider of the clouds. This was strange, even to Gentiles. It pummeled pagan ideologies for a living *man* to be "the cloud rider," and Jesus knew it. However, our Lord was aiming for more than a polemic against Baal and pagan thought. His sights were set on the calloused hearts of the covenant people of Yahweh.

His claim to be the rider of the clouds was primarily designed to send shockwaves through Jerusalem and its Jewish leaders. They would have understood that Jesus was claiming to be the *Son of Man* who "cometh with the clouds" of Daniel's prophecy. Note the parallels between Daniel 7:13 and our verse, Revelation 1:7.

Daniel 7:13 (LEB)	Revelation 1:7 (LEB)
I continued watching in the visions of the night, and look, *with the clouds of heaven* one like a son of man was coming, and he came to the Ancient of Days, and was presented before him.	Behold, *he [the Son of Man] is coming with the clouds*, and every eye will see him, even every one who pierced him, and all the tribes of the earth will mourn over him. Yes, amen.

Sadly, as the Gospels reveal, many Jews refused to accept Jesus' *divine* status as the Son of Man of Daniel 7. However, to the seven churches of Asia, this meteorological promise to "return on the clouds" is very assuring. The divine King *is* coming!

John's use of Daniel 7 is one of *many* allusions He makes in this remarkable chapter of prophecy in the book of Revelation. Note the following:

Revelation	Daniel	Parallel
1:4	7:9a	God enthroned
1:4	7:10b	Heavenly beings around the throne
1:4	7:13–14	Dominion of Christ/Son of Man
1:6, 9	7:18, 22, 27a	Saints constituted/given a kingdom
1:7a	7:13	Son of Man coming with the clouds
1:11	7:10	Book associated with judgment
1:12–16	7:9–10	Description of a heavenly figure
1:17a	7:15	Seer's reaction
1:17–20	7:16ff.	Interpretation of the vision [139]

Grasping the cosmic significance of the return of Jesus "on the clouds" is not only incredibly comforting to believers, it's quite illuminative in Christ's battle against evil forces. The Cloud Rider is coming, and He is coming to wage war.

Jesus on the White Horse

Jesus is depicted as riding on a white horse in Revelation 19:11–16:

And I saw heaven opened, and behold, a white horse, and the one seated on it was called "Faithful" and "True," and with justice he judges and makes war. Now his eyes were a flame of fire, and on his head were many royal headbands having a name written that no one except he himself knows. And he was dressed in an outer garment dipped in blood, and his name is called the Word of God. And the armies that are in heaven, dressed in clean, white fine linen, were following him on white horses. And out of his mouth came a sharp sword, so that with it he could strike the nations. And he will shepherd them with an iron rod, and he stomps the winepress of the wine of the furious wrath of God, the All-Powerful. And he has a name written on his outer garment and on his thigh: "King of kings and Lord of lords." (LEB)

Most Christians know this account as describing the Battle of Armageddon. Armageddon is *the battle to end all battles*. It's the final war between the forces of light and the armies of the powers of darkness. To say it's the most important battle in human history is an understatement. It's important to realize that, in Revelation, there is *not* one Armageddon passage; there are actually three (Revelation 16:12–16; 19; 20:7–10). (Note to readers: Please read these three passages before moving forward.)

Consequently, the appearance of these passages in three different places in Revelation dismantles the argument for a *linear* reading of the book. Each narrative describes the same event—but from a different camera angle.

Many believers assume the subject of Armageddon is original to Revelation, but it's not. It actually has roots in ancient Judaism. For example, Armageddon is discussed in the Dead Sea Scrolls. To get a flavor of the Jewish expectation of Armageddon around the time of Jesus Christ, let's read a small portion from the War Scroll (1QM).

> On the day when the Kittim fall there shall be a battle and horrible carnage before the God of Israel, for it is a day appointed by Him from ancient times as a battle of annihilation for the Sons of Darkness. On that day the congregation of the gods and the congregation of men shall engage one another, resulting in great carnage. The Sons of Light and the forces of Darkness shall fight together to show the strength of God with the roar of a great multitude and the shout of gods and men; a day of disaster. It is a time of distress fo[r al]l the people who are redeemed by God. In all their afflictions none exists that is like it, hastening to its completion as an eternal redemption. On the day of their battle against the Kittim, they shall g[o forth for] carnage in battle. In three lots the Sons of Light shall stand firm so as to strike a blow at wickedness, and in three the army of Belial shall strengthen themselves so as to force the retreat of the forces [of Light. And when the] banners of the infantry cause their hearts to melt, then the might of God will strengthen the he[arts of the Sons of Light.] In the seventh lot the great hand of God shall overcome [Belial and al]l the angels of his dominion, and all the men of [his forces shall be destroyed forever.][140]

The translators of this text summarize the entirety of the War Scroll in the excellent resource, *The Dead Sea Scrolls: A New Translation*. They write:

Armageddon: the war to end all wars. These words stir up images of inevitable conflict, the final focus on the dark side of human nature, the ultimate catharsis that ushers in an age of peace. All of these issues come to a head in the War Scroll, a text that describes the eschatological last battle in gory detail, as righteousness is fully victorious and evil is forever destroyed. This vivid account gives us insight into how, at about the time of Jesus, some Jews conceived of Armageddon…. Although this war is said to extend over forty years, the writer of the scroll was particularly concerned with the details of the very final day of battle. After six bloody engagements during this last battle, the Sons of Light and Sons of Darkness are deadlocked in a 3–3 tie. In the seventh and final confrontation "the great hand of God shall overcome [Belial and al]l the angels of his dominion. (1QM 1:14–15)[141]

That Jews were writing about Armageddon long before John discusses it means some of the prophet's readers are not surprised by the Armageddon event being described in Revelation.

The reason there is Jewish expectation of an Armageddon event is because of Ezekiel 38–39. *These prophetic chapters are the bones of Armageddon.* Many of Ezekiel's elements are present in Revelation 16:12–16, 19:11–21, and 20:7–10. John's Armageddon passages must be analyzed against the context of Ezekiel 38–39. When done so, it's apparent that John continually recycles concepts from Ezekiel: the great antagonist Gog/Magog, the "assembling" armies, the battle at the mountain(s) of Jerusalem, the great eschatological meal, the birds of prey—all of it.

Ezekiel's prophecy speaks of Gog from the land of Magog assembling an army from the north and marching on the mountainous city of God. There have been many attempts to identify Gog throughout history. In some scholarly camps, Gog is the biblical giant Og, the last of the Rephaim who reigned over Bashan in the north. Though dead, many think Og will return as a demonic influencer recruiting for Armageddon. This interpretation has biblical merit. Since Og's origin can be linked to the Nephilim and Genesis 6, his spirit would be categorized as *demonic*. Revelation 16:14 says three demonic spirits will perform signs to the world's kings to gather them for the battle.

Others look to the annals of history for names and countries similar to Gog and Magog, such as the city prince Gagi mentioned in Babylonian records as dwelling north of Assyria. Others nod to the ancient country Gaga, which is mentioned in the *Amarna Letters* of ancient Egypt. Others have perceived Gog to be a more contemporary figure, such as Hitler or Napoleon. More recently, prophecy analysts associate Gog/Magog with Russia because the LXX transliterates the Hebrew word *ros* ("chief") by calling him the "ruler of Rosh. The argument is that *Rosh* etymologically links to Russia; therefore, Armageddon involves Russia."[142] Incidentally, the same etymological argument once led many to connect "Rosh" with "Rome." This approach can lead one down many roads that lead to several supposed "Gogs." Simply put, *there is no consensus about who Gog is.*

However, one thing is sure: Gog perfectly symbolized the eschatological enemy of darkness, which plots in the cosmic "north" as outlined in Scripture (Isaiah 14).[143] That's what really matters.

According to Ezekiel 39:21–29, the outcome of Ezekiel's Gog/Magog battle would prove that Israel once fell into Babylonian captivity not because God was weak and Babylon was strong, *but because Israel sinned with other gods.* Therefore, Christ's victory at Armageddon publicly delegitimizes Babylon's former claims of victory and reverses their effect.

The depiction of Jesus riding on a horse in Armageddon underlines that we are still at war today—not with flesh and blood, but against principalities and powers in the heavenly places (Ephesians 6:12).

The Messianic Army

As military leader, Jesus has full command of His army; believers are part of that army. With great subtlety, Revelation 7 compares the Church to the *military* of the twelve tribes of Israel:

> And I heard the number of the ones who were sealed, one hundred forty-four thousand sealed from every tribe of the sons of Israel: from the tribe of Judah, twelve thousand sealed, from the tribe of Reuben, twelve thousand, from the tribe of Gad, twelve thousand, from the tribe of Asher, twelve thousand, from the tribe of Naphtali, twelve thousand, from the tribe of Manasseh, twelve thousand, from the tribe of Simeon, twelve thousand, from the tribe of Levi, twelve thousand, from the tribe of Issachar, twelve thousand, from the tribe of Zebulun, twelve thousand, from the tribe of Joseph, twelve thousand, from the tribe of Benjamin, twelve thousand were sealed. After these things I looked, and behold, a great crowd that no one was able to number, from every nation and tribe and people and language, standing before the throne and before the Lamb, dressed in white robes and with palm branches in their hands. (Revelation 7:4–9, LEB)

John employs Old Testament language here in his list of the tribes of Israel. However, identifying the 144,000 creates a hotbed of controversy. Candidates *typically* include the faithful remnant of Israel, Jewish Christians, Christian martyrs, spiritual Israel (consisting of Jews and Gentiles; see Ephesians 2:11–19), and Gentile Christians since the Jews have rejected their place.[144]

Is it possible John uses OT tribal language to describe those of *Jewish* descent? Yes, especially when one considers how he *next* sees "a great crowd that no one was able to number, from every nation and tribe and people and language, which stood before the throne and before the Lamb, dressed in white robes and with palm branches in their hands" (Revelation 7:9). The two groups seem juxtaposed for contrast. However, when we dig deeper into this *seemingly* "second group" of believers, there is *no distinction* when one considers the language of the Abrahamic promise. The phrase "a great multitude which no one was able to number" reminds one of the promise made to Abraham that God would multiply their descendants, "which shall not be numbered for multitude" (see especially Genesis 16:10; 32:12; also see Genesis 13:16; 15:5; 22:17; 26:4; Hosea 1:10; Jubilees 13:20; 14:4–5; Hebrews 11:12). In Revelation, the promise to Israel is applied to the Church from all nations.[145]

So, the 144,000 *and* the "crowd that no one could number" are most likely *two complementary pictures* of the same reality—the redeemed children of God.

> The first picture of the sealed 144,000 stresses that God protects and preserves the complete number of the people who belong to him. The second picture, of the great crowd, stresses that God saves his people from every nation, tribe, people and language, accomplishing a new-exodus deliverance by the blood of the Lamb.[146]

John's conflation of Israel with the Church fits within the framework of Revelation as Judeo-Christian literature.[147] Let's dig into the numbers in John's list.

Numbers are important in Revelation and are best understood *symbolically*. The numerical value of believers in Revelation 7:4–9 is described as 144,000. In his book, *All Things New*, Tabb writes:

> Numbers in Revelation are typically symbolic, and the number 144,000 is twelve squared and multiplied by a thousand, which stresses completeness and perfection.[148]

The number twelve is used frequently throughout Revelation, as the following chart demonstrates:

The Number Twelve in Revelation	
144,000 believers sealed (12 × 12 × 1000)	7:4–8; 14:1, 3
12 stars in the woman's crown	12:1
12 gates and pearls in the holy city Jerusalem	21:12, 21
12 angels	21:12
12 tribes of the sons of Israel	21:12
12 foundations for the city's walls	21:14
12 apostles	21:14
12,000 stadia for the city's dimensions (12 × 1000)	21:16
144 cubits for the walls' height (12 × 12)	21:17
12 kinds of fruit from the tree of life	22:2[149]

While John is likely repeating the pattern of twelve in the 144,000, reading Revelation through the eyes of the OT prophets reveals clear connections to the *military census* of Numbers chapters 1 and 26. The following chart organizes the *military numbers* from the tribes of Israel before and after the wilderness wanderings.

Tribe	Before Wanderings	After Wanderings	Gains	Losses
Reuben	46,500	43,730		2,770
Simeon	59,300	22,200		37,100
Gad	46,650	40,500		5,150

Tribe	Before Wanderings	After Wanderings	Gains	Losses
Judah	74,600	76,500	1,900	
Issachar	54,400	64,300	9,900	
Zebulun	57,400	60,500	3,100	
Ephraim	40,500	32,500		8,000
Manasseh	32,200	52,700	20,500	
Benjamin	35,400	45,600	10,200	
Dan	62,700	64,400	1,700	
Asher	41,500	53,400	11,900	
Naphtali	53,400	45,400		8,000
	603,550	601,730	59,200	61,020[150]

While many get caught up in the formulation of the number itself (144,000 = twelve squared and multiplied by a thousand), they are overlooking the main thing—that the *style* of John's tribal list mirrors Israel's military census.

Furthermore, John reveals in Revelation 14:4 that the 144,000 are *adult male* Israelites. This is no coincidence. A military census in the OT was a tally of *males* of military age—twenty years and over (Numbers 1:3, 18, 20, etc.; 26:2, 4; 1 Chronicles 27:23; cf. 1 Samuel 24:9; 1 Chronicles 21:5).[151] Like Numbers 1 and 26, it's clear from the form of Revelation 7:4–8 that this is a *military census* that highlights the strength of the eschatological nation of God.[152]

Bauckham convincingly argues that it would be natural to think of an Israelite army assembled for a messianic war, especially since the reunion of the tribes was part of a Jewish eschatology (see Isaiah 11:11–12, 15–16; 27:12–13; Jeremiah 31:7–9; Ezekiel 37:15–23; Sir 36:11; Tobit 13:13; 2 Baruch 78:5–7; cf. Matthew 19:28).[153]

The primary textual evidence to which Bauckham referred is Isaiah 11:12–14. There, Isaiah prophesied a future military operation with all the dispersed tribes:

…and he will raise a signal for the nations. And he will gather the outcasts of Israel, and he will gather the scattered ones of Judah together from the four corners of the earth. And the jealousy of Ephraim shall depart, and the enemies of Judah shall be cut off. Ephraim shall not be jealous of Judah, and Judah shall not be an enemy of Ephraim. But they shall swoop upon the Philistine shoulder, westward. Together they shall plunder the sons of the east. Edom and Moab will be under their command, and the sons of Ammon will be their subjugated people. And Yahweh will divide the tongue of the sea of Egypt, and he will wave his hand over the river with his scorching wind; and he will strike it into seven streams, and he will make it passable by foot. So there shall be a highway from Assyria for the remnant of his people that remains, as there was for Israel when it went up from the land of Egypt. (Isaiah 11:12–16, LEB)

Before the days of Christ, Jews at Qumran viewed Isaiah 11:12–16 (as well as others) as the model for the eschatological Israel who would reassemble in the wilderness to reconquer the same land in the messianic war.[154] Like many Kingdom motifs, the fulfillment of Isaiah 11 is *already, but not yet*. Revelation 7 is playing on this principle.

At the top of John's military census is the tribe of Judah (Revelation 7:5). Leading a tribal list with Judah is puzzling if it's not ancillary to its structure, and I argue that it is. Typically, Judah is listed fourth. Moving Judah to number one purposefully reflects its ascension as *tribal head* of God's people.[155] Genesis 49:8–10 discusses Judah's prominence and strength.

Judah, as for you, your brothers shall praise you. Your hand shall be on the neck of your enemies. The sons of your father shall bow down to you. Judah is a lion's cub. From the prey, my son, you have gone up. He bowed down; he crouched like a lion and as a lioness. Who shall rouse him? The scepter shall not depart from Judah, nor the ruler's staff between his feet, until Shiloh comes. And to him shall be the obedience of nations. (Genesis 49:8–10, LEB)

Ezekiel also prophesied that a latter-day *Davidic king* from the tribe of Judah would unite all tribes and reign over them forever (Ezekiel 37:15–25). This, of course, is Jesus.

So, John lists Judah as the *head* of the military census because Jesus, the Lion of the Tribe of Judah, leads God's covenant people into battle, and His victory is *already, but not yet* (Revelation 5:5).

An overlooked phrase regarding the 144,000 is that they "have not defiled themselves with women" (Revelation 14:1–4). This is an unmistakable allusion to 1 Enoch 12:3–6:

Revelation 14:1–4 (ESV)	1 Enoch 12:3–6
Then I looked, and behold, on Mount Zion stood the Lamb, and with him 144,000 who had his name and his Father's name written on their foreheads. And I heard a voice from heaven like the roar of many waters and like the sound of loud thunder. The voice I heard was like the sound of harpists playing on their harps, and they were singing a new song	And I Enoch was blessing the Lord of majesty and the King of the ages, and lo! the Watchers called me—Enoch the scribe—and said to me: "Enoch, thou scribe of righteousness, go, declare to *the Watchers of the heaven* who have left the high heaven, the holy eternal place, and *have defiled themselves with women*, and have done as the children of

<table>
<tr><td colspan="2">Revelation 14:1–4 (ESV)   1 Enoch 12:3–6</td></tr>
<tr>
<td>before the throne and before the four living creatures and before the elders. No one could learn that song except the 144,000 who had been redeemed from the earth. It is these who have not defiled themselves with women, for they are virgins. It is these who follow the Lamb wherever he goes. These have been redeemed from mankind as firstfruits for God and the Lamb.</td>
<td>earth do, and have taken unto themselves wives: 'Ye have wrought great destruction on the earth: And ye shall have no peace nor forgiveness of sin: and inasmuch as they delight themselves in their children, The murder of their beloved ones shall they see, and over the destruction of their children shall they lament, and shall make supplication unto eternity, but mercy and peace shall ye not attain.'"[156]</td>
</tr>
</table>

[Olson] argues that the redeemed 144,000 "virgins" (Rev. 14:4a) stand in radical opposition to the defiled fallen angels mentioned in 1 Enoch 1–36, who were engaged in sexual practices with the daughters of men (cf. Gen. 6:1–4). According to Olson (1997:500), the 144,000 virgins of Revelation 14 are an anti-image to, not only of the followers of the beast mentioned in the preceding chapter and Rev. 14:6–20 (cf. Rev. 17–18), but to the fallen angels of 1 Enoch 1–36. He also argues that by contrasting the Redeemed with the Watchers, John is actually giving the 144,000 the role of good angels (1997:501ff.).[157]

John's usage of 1 Enoch is a dead giveaway that John sees the 144,000 as displacing and replacing the *Watchers* (fallen angels) in Yahweh's heavenly host. Furthermore, Revelation 14 has the "anti-Watchers" (the 144,000) standing in allegiance on Mount Zion with the Lord, branded with His name. This is incredibly powerful when juxtaposed with the

Watchers who descended to Mount Hermon in rebellion and, for all intents and purposes, bear the mark of the beast. Another one of John's subtle tie-ins to 1 Enoch is that he omits the tribe of Dan from the census list in Revelation 7:4–9. The late Dr. Michael S. Heiser explains why this is conspicuous:

> Dan had a checkered history. The tribe forsook its allotted inheritance in the south of Canaan and migrated north, appropriating the priest of Micah the Levite, who kept household gods and an idol in his house (Joshua 19:40–48; Judges 18). The Danites eventually conquered the city of Laish and renamed it Dan (Judges 18:27, 29). This city became a cult center to Baal in later Israelite history. Earlier in Israel's history, instead of receiving a blessing from the dying Jacob like his brothers, the patriarch pronounced, "Dan shall be a serpent in the way, a viper by the path, that bites the horse's heels so that his rider falls backward" (Genesis 49:17). Deuteronomy 33:22 contains the cryptic note that "Dan is a lion's cub that leaps from Bashan."
>
> These failures and passages associate Dan with rebellion against God, the region of Bashan, whose name in Canaanite would have been bathan ("serpent"), and Baal worship at a location at the foot of Mount Hermon. It is no wonder that some early church writers believed that the reason Dan was omitted from Revelation 7 was because the Antichrist—the enemy of the 144,000—would come from the tribe of Dan.[158]

John's omission of the tribe of Dan speaks *volumes*; no tribe associated with Baal worship *at the foot of Mount Hermon*, the invasion site of the Watchers, will fight on Team Jesus. Soldiers of the Messianic King must be loyal, brave, and true, and Dan is surely not that.

LOOKING AHEAD

In the next chapter, we will turn our attention to *God's cosmic enemy in the book of Revelation* and connect the dots from Babel to Babylon. Understanding a bit of ancient history and biblical geography will help us identify Babylon the Great and why Jesus is at war with her.

6

BABEL IS BABYLON

He cried with a mighty voice, saying, "Fallen, fallen is Babylon the great, and she has become a habitation of demons, a prison of every unclean spirit."

~Revelation 18:2, web

IN A NUTSHELL

This chapter will prove that Babylon the great cannot be limited to Rome and that Old Testament Babylon is what's *primarily* in view. We will discover how Babylon traces back to the Tower of Babel and why it matters. We will also note how John adopts a *Babylonian framework* in Revelation 17–18, which brings into focus why chaos is sown among the nations.

DIGGING DEEPER

Nimrod and the Fallen Angels of Babel

In my book, *Gospel Over Gods*, I discuss in great detail how the Tower of Babel event in Deuteronomy 32:8 explains the origins of national gods.

At Babel, God divorced the nations and allotted them to angelic sons of God (Deuteronomy 32:8–9). Note:

Deuteronomy 32:8 (ESV)	Deuteronomy 32:8 (LES)	Deuteronomy 32:8 (THE MESSAGE)
When the Most High gave to the nations their inheritance, when he divided mankind, he fixed the borders of the peoples according to the number of the *sons of God*.	When the Most High distributed nations as he scattered the descendants of Adam, he set up boundaries for the nations according to the number of the *angels of God*.	When the High God gave the nations their stake, gave them their place on Earth, He put each of the peoples within boundaries under the care of *divine guardians*.

These "gods" did not walk according to their divine instructions, but led the nations into chaos and utter darkness, just as Psalm 82 explains:

God stands in the divine assembly; he administers judgment in the midst of the gods. "How long will you judge unjustly and show favoritism to the wicked? Selah. Judge on behalf of the helpless and the orphan; provide justice to the afflicted and the poor. Rescue the helpless and the needy; deliver them from the hand of the wicked." They do not know or consider. They go about in the darkness, so that all the foundations of the earth are shaken. I have said, "You are gods, and sons of the Most High, all of you. However, you will die like men, and you will fall like one of the princes." Rise up, O God, judge the earth, because you shall inherit all the nations. (LEB)

This passage is a preview into the courtroom of Heaven. Asaph, the psalmist, describes a scene where the gods of the nations are judged for their crimes; they have led the nations astray—away from Yahweh's light, deep into the darkness—and now they must die like men.

How does all of this relate to Babylon? The linguistic leap from Babel to Babylon is obvious; the two are phonetically linked. However, more than that, they are *historically* linked. To understand how, we need to revisit ancient history.

The Bible credits Nimrod (the builder of the Tower of Babel) with building the ancient cities of Mesopotamia (Genesis 10:10–11). Mesopotamia was a fertile region between the Tigris and Euphrates.

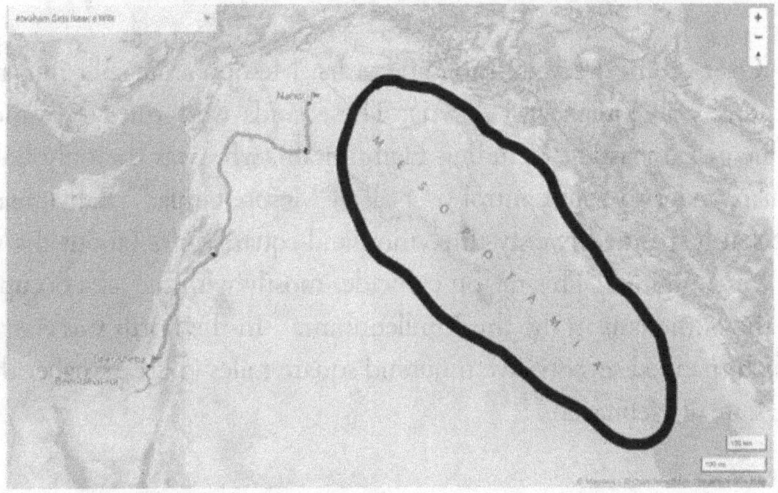

Nimrod built Babel, Erech, Akkad, and Calneh (which literally means "the place of Anu," one of the three chief gods of Sumerian religion). These cities were in southern Mesopotamia in the region of Shinar, commonly known as Sumer. The people inhabiting Sumer were known as the Sumerians.

Scripture also credits Nimrod with the early development of the northernmost part of Mesopotamia called Ashur, which eventually became Assyria. The point is the entirety of Mesopotamia can be traced back to Nimrod, the leading architect behind the tower of Babel.

Over the next several thousand years, Mesopotamia split into two sections, Babylonian and Assyria. These lands were ruled by various influential dynasties, including Hammurabi, who was the only Babylonian leader to gain control over all of Mesopotamia.[159] Babylonia in the south spanned twenty-three thousand square miles (about the size of West Virginia). This region coincides mostly with the area occupied by the Sumerians in the third millennium.[160] In the north was Assyria, which spanned seventy-five thousand square miles (a little smaller than the state of Nebraska).[161]

Babylon was the capital city of Babylonia and in the same neighborhood as the infamous and much older Tower of Babel. *Babylon's writings, religion, and deities are therefore inseparable from the Babel event.* That John sees OT Babylon as the harbinger of cosmic evil in Revelation is not figurative.

Chaos and evil hatched from Babylon. The following timeline is a helpful reference to grasp Mesopotamia's many dynasties and time periods:

Timeline for Ancient Mesopotamia
(Sumer, Babylonia, and Assyria)

Early Periods [Sumer]
Halaf 6100–5400
Ubaid 5300–3800
Uruk 4100–2900
Jemdet Nasr 3100–2900
Early Dynastic I 2900–2800
Early Dynastic II 2800–2600
Early Dynastic III 2600–2334 (Rise of Sargon)
Akkad
Sargon 2334–2279
Rimush 2278–2270
Mainshtushu 2269–2255
Naram-Sin 2254–2218
Sharkalisharri 2217–2193
Period of Confusion 2192–2190
Ur III
Ur Namma 2112–2095
Shulgi 2094–2047
Amar-Sin 2046–2038
Shu-Sin 2037–2029

Ibbi-Sin 2028–2004
Isin/Larsa Period 2017–1835
Ishbi-Irra 2017–1985
Old Babylonian
Hammurabi 1792–1750
Samsuiluna 1749–1712
Abi-eshhuh 1711–1684
Ammiditana 1683–1647
Ammisaduqa 1646–1626
Samsuditana 1625–1595
Assyrian
Shamshi-Adad 1813–1781
Ishme-Dagan 1780–?
Mari
Yasmah-Addu 1795–76
Zimri-Lim 1775–1762
Kassite Babylonia
Agum II 1602–1585
Brunaburiash II 1380–1350
Khashtiliash IV 1232–1225
Assyria
Assur-uballit I 1363–1328
Shalmaneser I 1273–1244
Tukulti-Ninurta I 1243–1207
Babylonia
Nebuchadnezzar I 1124–1103
Nabu-apla-iddina 885–828
Nabopolassar 626–605
Nebuchadnezzar II 604–562
Evil-Merodach 561–560
Neriglissar 559–556

Labashi-Marduk 556

Nabonidus 555–539

Assyria

Tiglath-Pilesar I 1114–1076

Adad-Nirari II 911–891

Assurnasirpal II 883–859

Shalmaneser III 858–824

Shamshi-Adad IV 823–811

Tiglath-Pilesar III 744–727

Shalmaneser V 726–722

Sargon II 721–705

Sennacherib 704–681

Esarhaddon 668–627

Assurbanipal 668–627

Assyria overthrown by 609[162]

Surveying Babylon's history is extremely helpful in understanding how Babylon traces back to the Tower of Babel.

The Trial of the Nations

Revelation 1–3 has Jesus conducting *forensic investigations* among the seven churches of Asia Minor. Essentially, the letters to the saints are legal speeches wherein Jesus condemns and commends based upon His findings. This judgment setting is preparing the way for the more obvious courtroom proceedings in John's second vision in Revelation 4:1–16:21, in which the Messiah puts the nations and their gods on *trial*.[163]

Understanding this divine court setting in the book of Revelation is imperative in parsing much of John's language.

The Divine Court of Heaven

As stated, the setting for much of the book of Revelation is the throne room of God, where the divine council meets to make decrees and judgments. The *Lexham Bible Dictionary* describes this council as a term for the heavenly host or the assembly of divine beings who aid Yahweh in administering the affairs of the cosmos.[164]

The divine council has discussions, determines resolutions, makes decisions, and takes action. It's referred to in various ways throughout the OT, such as "El's council" (Job 15:8), the "council of Eloah" (Psalm 82:1), the "council of Yahweh" (Jeremiah 23:18), and the "council of the holy ones" (Psalm 89:5[6], 7[8]).[165]

Understanding the OT backdrop to God's heavenly court is necessary to grasping what is happening in Revelation. John suddenly finds himself amid this council and identifies some of its participants:

John identifies both the setting of the heavenly council, as well as the members. The four living creatures and the twenty-four elders point to the ongoing role of the heavenly court through their appearance at significant junctures throughout the book. The fact that the elders are mentioned as seated around the throne before John mentions the four living creatures that are in the midst of the throne, highlights their importance (4:4). They participate in the heavenly worship (4:10–11; 5:9–10, 14; 11:16–18; 19:4), are involved with the prayers of God's people (5:9), and act as interpretative guides (5:5; 7:13). Throughout Revelation's storyline, the elders lay down the symbols of their authority by either casting off their crowns or falling down in worship, thus removing themselves from their position on their thrones (4:10; 5:8, 14; 11:16; 19:4).[166]

The heavenly court convenes in Revelation 4–5 to install an eschatological judge worthy enough to prosecute the nations and their gods.[167] They conclude that only the Lamb of God is found worthy for this judicial office.

The Genre of Prophetic Lawsuit

An added layer to Revelation's judicial framework is its *literary style*. The heavenly court scenes of Revelation have traits of an OT genre scholars call "prophetic lawsuit" (Hebrew: *rîb*; "quarrel, dispute, lawsuit").[168] Heiser writes:

This literary genre presents God as judge, prosecutor, and jury in the context of bringing an indictment against his people for covenant violations. These scenes are at times presented in a heavenly courtroom scene, where members of God's council bear witness to the indictment, participate in deliberations, and assist in carrying out the sentence against the guilty.[169]

Prophetic lawsuit passages typically follow the same pattern: 1) preliminary remarks, 2) interrogation, 3) indictment, 4) declaration of guilt, 5) ultimatum/punishment. Entire prophetic books such as Malachi follow this pattern.[170] In her 2020 book, *Trying Man, Trying God: The Divine Courtroom in Early Jewish and Christian Literature*, Meira Z. Kensky explains:

One of the most important ways in which the divine courtroom appears in the Hebrew Bible is through its invocation in the so-called "prophetic lawsuit," or "*rîb*-pattern" form of prophetic speech. Throughout the prophetic literature, the prophets indict the people of Israel for various crimes against God, all of which ultimately lead up to breach of covenant. For the prophets, this justifies God's intention to punish the people for their misdeeds. This form of prophetic address, therefore, is an explanation of why God's actions are just. The prophets use the legal language as a means of expressing God's formal complaints and rights as a litigant, an injured party, and show through the mechanisms of human justice how God's actions are themselves functions of divine justice, even though on the surface they may not seem so.[171]

Alan S. Bandy, in *The Prophetic Lawsuit in the Book of Revelation*, writes:

The letters to the seven churches constitute lawsuit speeches whereby Jesus conducts a forensic examination of his covenant people. The form of the letters generally distinguishes them as prophetic oracles similar to the OT prophets, and more specifically as covenant lawsuit speeches. As such, the Book of Revelation follows the pattern of the OT prophetic lawsuit that begins with the people of God. The judgments and promises announced for the churches in the seven letters remains contingent upon what they do in response to these oracles. In this sense the remaining vision, especially the interludes, relates to how the churches respond (i.e., faithfully endure as witnesses) during the heightened state of persecution. Once the Lord deals with his people he turns his attention to the surrounding nations with oracles of judgment…the judgment of the nations is closely tied to the theme of vengeance for their treatment of the saints.[172]

Recovering the OT background of prophetic lawsuit speeches frames much of Revelation's language as *judicial.* It helps the reader unravel many of John's elements, such as the scroll with seven seals, which is to be understood as a legal document of judgment.[173]

Revelation 17–18 and OT Babylon

Yahweh's OT prophets decried Babylon's wickedness and prophesied their doom. Revelation 17–18 frequently alludes to their writings by parroting OT messaging. John's not doing this because he *doesn't* want his readers to think about historical Babylon; he's doing it because he *does*. Tethering Revelation 17–18 to the OT is evidence that John adopts a true Babylonian framework in the Apocalypse. Note the following chart.

Shared Concept	OT Babylon	NT Babylon
The destruction of Babylon that "sits on many waters" definitely refers to the Euphrates and its many waterways. These waters represent the effects that Babylonian society had on the ancient world overall. Its many channels of influence perpetrated like darkness.[174]	For his [God's] wrath is against Babylon, to destroy it utterly (Jer. 51:13)… against the inhabitants of Babylon dwelling upon many waters. (Jeremiah 28:11–13 LXX)[175]	Come, I will show you the judgment of the great prostitute who is seated on many waters. (Revelation 17:1, LEB). And he said to me, "The waters that you saw, where the prostitute is seated, are peoples and crowds and nations and languages. (Revelation 17:15, LEB)
John's being transported "into the wilderness" in Revelation 17:3 alludes to Isaiah's vision against Babylon, "coming from the wilderness."[176]	The oracle of the wilderness of the sea: As storm winds passing over in the Negev, it comes from the desert, from a frightful land. (Isaiah 21:1–2, LEB)	And he carried me away into the wilderness in the Spirit. (Revelation 17:3, LEB)

Shared Concept	OT Babylon	NT Babylon
St. John describes Babylon as a place full of demons and sinister creatures. This is a clear allusion to Isaiah 13:21, which describes foul entities residing in the aftermath of the destruction of Babylon.[177]	And Babylon, which is called glorious by the king of the Chaldeans, shall be as when God overthrew Sodoma and Gomorrha. It shall never be inhabited.... But wild beasts shall rest there; and the houses shall be filled with howling; and monsters shall rest there, and devils shall dance there, and satyrs shall dwell there; and hedgehogs shall make their nests in their houses. It will come soon, and will not tarry. (Isaiah 13:19–22, Brenton LXX En)	And he cried out with a powerful voice, saying, "Fallen, fallen is Babylon the great, and it has become a dwelling place of demons and a haunt of every unclean spirit and a haunt of every unclean bird and a haunt of every unclean and detested animal." (Revelation 18:2, LEB)
Babylon's sins have "reached as high as the heavens, and lifted up to the skies." This expression is figurative. However, it may loosely carry literal undertones that point to the tower of babel built in lower Mesopotamia.	We tried to heal Babylon, and she was not healed. Forsake her and let us go each one to his country, for her judgment has reached to the heavens, and it has been lifted up to the skies. (Jeremiah 51:9, LEB)	And I heard another voice from heaven saying, "Come out from her, my people, so that you will not participate in her sins, and so that you will not receive her plagues, because her sins have reached up to heaven, and God has remembered her crimes." (Revelation 18:4–5, LEB)

Shared Concept	OT Babylon	NT Babylon
God told OT Babylon that He would "pay back" their iniquities. John leverages this OT language as ammunition against cosmic Babylon in Revelation 18:6.[178]	O daughter of Babylon, about to be devastated, happy shall be he who pays back to you what you paid out to us. (Psalm 137:8, LEB) Summon archers against Babylon, all those who bend the bow. Encamp all around her, there must not be for her an escape. Take revenge on her according to her deeds." (Jeremiah 50:29, LEB)	Pay back to her as she herself also paid out, and pay back double according to her deeds; in the cup that she mixed, mix double for her. (Revelation 18:6, LEB)
Babylon's arrogance as a lady/queen/princess in luxury is mentioned in Isaiah 47:8 and Revelation 18:7.[179]	...and saidst, I shall be a princess for ever: thou didst not perceive these things in thine heart, nor didst thou remember the latter end. But now hear these words, thou luxurious one, who art the one that sits at ease, that is secure, that says in her heart, I am, and there is not another; I shall not sit a widow, neither shall I know bereavement. (Isaiah 47:7–8, Brenton LXX En)	As much as she glorified herself and lived in luxury, give to her so much torment and mourning, because in her heart she said, "I sit as a queen, and am not a widow, and I will never see mourning!" (Revelation 18:7, LEB)

Shared Concept	OT Babylon	NT Babylon
That "lady Babylon" will get plagues in "one day" and die in Revelation 18:8 derives from Isaiah 47:9. This typifies Babylon's swift destruction.[180]	And these two shall come to you in a moment, in one day: the loss of children and widowhood shall come on you completely, in spite of your many sorceries, in spite of the power of your great enchantments. (Isaiah 47:9, LEB)	Because of this her plagues will come in one day—death and mourning and famine—and she will be burned up with fire, because the Lord God who passes judgment on her is powerful! (Revelation 18:8, LEB)
That earthly kings will mourn at the destruction of Babylon (Revelation 18:9) derives from Jeremiah 50–51. They will despair because their lover has died.[181]	Suddenly Babylon has fallen and she is shattered. Wail over her. (Jeremiah 51:8, LEB)	And the kings of the earth will weep and mourn over her, those who committed sexual immorality and lived sensually with her, when they see the smoke of her burning. (Revelation 18:9, LEB)
That the faithful of Revelation 18:20 will "rejoice" over Babylon's defeat is based on the language of Jeremiah 51:48.[182]	Then the heaven and the earth and all that is in them will shout for joy over Babylon, for from the north the destroyers will come to it," declares Yahweh. (Jeremiah 51:48, LEB)	Rejoice over her, heaven and the saints and the apostles and the prophets, because God has pronounced your judgment on her! (Revelation 18:20, LEB)

Shared Concept	OT Babylon	NT Babylon
Tossing Babylon as a "stone" into the sea derives from Jeremiah 51:63. [183]	And Jeremiah said to Seraiah, "At your coming to Babylon, then you must see that you read aloud all these words. And you must say, 'Yahweh, you yourself spoke against this place, to destroy it.... And then when you finish reading aloud this scroll, you must tie a stone on it, and you must throw it into the middle of the Euphrates.' And you must say, 'Thus shall Babylon sink, and she will not rise, because of the face of the disasters that I am bringing on her, and they will grow weary.'" Thus far the words of Jeremiah. (Jeremiah 51:61–64, LEB)	And one powerful angel picked up a stone like a great millstone and threw it into the sea, saying, "In this way Babylon the great city will be thrown down with violence, and will never be found again!" (Revelation 18:21, leb)

These links prove John adopts a true Babylonian framework. I suggest that while Rome was as *a* latter-day Babylon, it *is not* in view here. Here, the spotlight is on the archetype (Babylon), not the type (Rome). Babylon is positioned on the "many waters" of the Euphrates, enthroned over peoples, crowds, nations, and languages (Revelation 17:15). Babylon controls "all the kings of the earth," making them drink the wine of sexual immorality (Revelation 17:2). "Babylon's" sorcery deceived "all the nations" (Revelation 18:23).

As noted at the beginning of this chapter, the backdrop to Babylon's cosmic control described in the book of Revelation began at the Tower of Babel.[184] Understanding this is imperative in following the trajectory of the rest of this book.

LOOKING AHEAD

This chapter established that Babel = Babylon because Babylon is inseparable from the Babel event. We also established that the gods of Babel/Babylon are to blame for sowing chaos among the nations. Fittingly, in the next chapter, we study how the Messiah brings judgment against the nations through four Babylonian gods referred to as the "four horsemen of the Apocalypse."

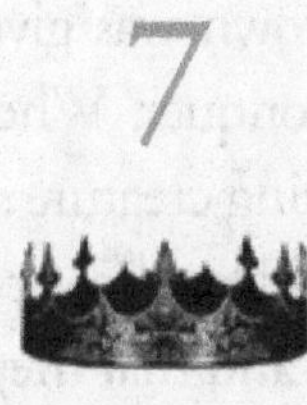

THE WAR IN THE STARS

Then a white horse appeared, and he who sat on it had a bow.
A crown was given to him, and he came out conquering, and to
conquer.

~REVELATION 6:2, WEB

IN A NUTSHELL

The chapter explores John's astronomical passages and links them to
Babylonian astrology and Babylonian gods.

DIGGING DEEPER

The Four Horsemen and Babylonian Astrology

In Revelation 6, John sees the four horsemen of the Apocalypse being
summoned by the four living creatures. Their mission is simple: destroy
the world.

I saw that the Lamb opened one of the seven seals, and I heard
one of the four living creatures saying, as with a voice of thunder, "Come and see!" Then a white horse appeared, and he who

sat on it had a bow. A crown was given to him, and he came out conquering, and to conquer. When he opened the second seal, I heard the second living creature saying, "Come!" Another came out, a red horse. To him who sat on it was given power to take peace from the earth, and that they should kill one another. There was given to him a great sword. When he opened the third seal, I heard the third living creature saying, "Come and see!" And behold, a black horse, and he who sat on it had a balance in his hand. I heard a voice in the middle of the four living creatures saying, "A choenix of wheat for a denarius, and three choenix of barley for a denarius! Don't damage the oil and the wine!" When he opened the fourth seal, I heard the fourth living creature saying, "Come and see!" And behold, a pale horse, and the name of he who sat on it was Death. Hades followed with him. Authority over one fourth of the earth, to kill with the sword, with famine, with death, and by the wild animals of the earth was given to him. (Revelation 6:1–8, WEB)

While some suggest the rider on the white horse in Revelation 6 is benevolent and the other three riders are malevolent, the consensus among most scholars is that the four horsemen are seen as *one group of demonic agents*.[185] In part, this is because they have a background in the horsemen of Zechariah 1:8–15 and the four chariots drawn by horses of different colors in Zechariah 6:1–8. It is apparent for several reasons. Both contexts describe colored "horses" and convey judgment and war. Dr. Michael Heiser writes:

The horses in Zechariah…are actually chariot teams, and chariots were instruments of war, so the judgment idea is not absent in Zechariah. The chariot teams are sent out to punish the nations that are oppressing God's people. By analogy, in Revelation 6, the Lamb is unleashing judgment on the world (the "four corners of the earth") via the four horsemen to avenge the oppression of those who follow him.[186]

Like the *four* groups of horse-drawn chariots were commissioned to patrol the earth and punish those nations oppressing Yahweh's people in the OT, the *four* horses and their riders in Revelation 6 are commissioned to judge the unbelievers. John is intentionally drawing on the language of Zechariah 6 (see also Zechariah 1:8–15) in Revelation 6 to make this corresponding point. John's usage of Zechariah means all four horsemen in Revelation 6, including the rider on the white horse, *play for the same evil team.*

While our focus has been on John's OT connections in Revelation 6:1–8, understanding his *astronomical portrait* gets us closer to identifying the four horsemen.

Indeed, we must look to the stars.

Planets and constellations have represented specific figures, gods, and ideas for eons. Thus, asterisms and stars have been a *universal language* for thousands of years. The *Lexham Bible Dictionary* (LBD) notes the landmark discovery of the *Enuma Anu Enlil,* the ancient world's lexicon of the celestial revelation of the gods:

Babylonians believed that gods communicated with the earth through the sky. The task of astrologers was to learn that "language" so that they could interpret it for their constituents…. Priests and scribes functioned as the astrologers of Babylon, reading the sky for setting calendars and predicting the future…. The observations of the priests and scribes were codified in the Enuma Anu Enlil. There are roughly 7,000 scenarios in 70 tablets that detail what celestial phenomena signify. The 70 tablets deal first with the moon and then the sun, followed by the weather; they conclude by addressing the appearance of stars and planets. The text is a means of standardization…. The Enuma Anu Enlil became the "lexicon" of the celestial revelation of the gods.[187]

So, to the Babylonians, the heavens were a tablet on which their gods wrote messages.[188] Their belief can be traced back to Sumerian literature from the third millennium BC, when the gods themselves used a tablet called *dub.mul.an*, "Tablet Stars of Heaven."[189] Since recovering collections of interpretations on heavenly phenomena, some scholars see bridges between the Babylonian divination manual *Enuma Anu Enlil* and Revelation 6 (Zechariah chapters 1 and 6).[190] The colors of Revelation's horses and the action taken by their riders do, in fact, correlate to four corresponding planets, four demonic Babylonian gods, four cardinal directions, and four constellations per the manual.[191]

Color	Planet	Deity/Demon	Constellation	Direction
White	Jupiter	Marduk	Taurus	East
Red	Mercury	Nabu	Aquarius	North
Black	Saturn	Ninurta	Scorpio	West
Pale/Speckled	Mars	Nergal	Leo	South

Regarding this chart, *Star of Bethlehem* author Dag Kihlman says:

That the colours are connected to the constellations can be shown. The clearest example is black/Scorpio. "I looked, and there was a black horse, and he who sat on it had a pair of scales in his hand." Since the two claws of Scorpio were seen also as the balances of Libra, the connection is obvious.[192]

Per the manual, the rider on the black horse is the Babylonian god Ninurta.

Color Horse	Deity/Demon	Constellation
White	Marduk	Taurus
Red	Nabu	Aquarius
Black	Ninurta	Scorpio
Pale/Speckled	Nergal	Leo

Next, Kihlman writes:

South is connected with Leo, Nergal, who was the king of the Netherworld, connected with wild animals, death, and pestilence: "there was a pale horse, and the name of him who sat on it was Death and Hades followed him. Power over a fourth of the earth was given to them, to kill with the sword, with hunger, with death, and by beasts of the earth."[193]

Color Horse	Deity/Demon	Constellation
White	Marduk	Taurus
Red	Nabu	Aquarius
Black	Ninurta	Scorpio
Pale/Speckled	Nergal	Leo

Kihlman then discusses the rider on the red horse:

North, Aquarius is linked to Nabu, the main war-god at the time, and thus a sword was given to him.[194]

Color Horse	Deity/Demon	Constellation
White	Marduk	Taurus
Red	Nabu	Aquarius
Black	Ninurta	Scorpio
Pale/Speckled	Nergal	Leo

And what of the rider on the *white* horse? Marduk is associated with white, Jupiter, Taurus, and the east, per the divination manual.[195] Note:

Color	Planet	Deity/Demon	Constellation	Direction
White	Jupiter	Marduk	Taurus	East
Red	Mercury	Nabu	Aquarius	North
Black	Saturn	Ninurta	Scorpio	West
Pale/Speckled	Mars	Nergal	Leo	South

Marduk's ascension to *kingship* status in the Babylonian pantheon can explain what John saw: "And I looked, and behold, a white horse, and the one seated on it had a bow, and a crown was given to him" (Revelation 6:2, LEB). Marduk was crowned king of the gods by defeating Tiamat, the chaotic deity of the sea, with an *arrow that split her into two halves.* This victory solidified Marduk as head of the pantheon and ousted An from "heaven's" throne. An was the original creator and bestower of royal insignia in the earliest Sumerian texts, but now even he yielded to Marduk's newfound supremacy.[196]

The picture would then paint Marduk, king of the gods at Babylon, riding from the east as a demonic equestrian set on conquering. Marduk, or *Bel,* is a known supernatural nemesis of Yahweh, as cited in Jeremiah 50:1–2 and 51:44. In the Babylonian Exorcistic Incantation, *Marduk-Ea*, the god Marduk is framed as the "liberator of the possessed," a savior to the downtrodden. Truly, this is dark deception at its finest. Marduk (the rider on the white horse) is neither benevolent nor a savior; he is malevolent.

If John penned Revelation 6 with ancient astronomical standardization in mind, seals 1–4 depict four demonic *Babylonian* deities attacking from four cardinal directions. The first deity is Marduk, the director of the evil Babylonian gods.[197] This, of course, is meaningful because Babylon is the name of evil in the book of Revelation (Revelation 14:8; 16:19; 17:5; 18:2, 10, 21).

What's the point?

We have already established that John has used Zechariah 1 and 6 in his description of the four horsemen in Revelation 6. Zechariah's vision described four supernatural horsemen who presaged God's *revival of the city of Jerusalem* after its destruction during the Babylonian exile. It's easy to see the polemic power behind God's strategy in Zechariah. Yahweh would force Babylonian deities to act as agents of goodwill for the Jewish people—only twenty years removed from using them to incarcerate Judah in Babylon. In Revelation, the four horsemen repeat these actions with a twist; they bless Yahweh's people by *harming* eschatological "Babylon."

The Four Horsemen as the Gods of the Euphrates

Prophetic images of the four horsemen continue elsewhere in Revelation, though they are a bit ambiguous. In Revelation 7, the "four winds of the earth" are described as being held back by four of God's angels so they don't destroy typological Babylon prematurely. Note:

After this, I saw four angels standing at the four corners of the earth, holding the four winds of the earth, so that no wind would blow on the earth, or on the sea, or on any tree. I saw another angel ascend from the sunrise, having the seal of the living God. He cried with a loud voice to the four angels to whom it was given to harm the earth and the sea, saying, "Don't harm the earth, the sea, or the trees, until we have sealed the bondservants of our God on their foreheads!" (Revelation 7:1–3, WEB)

These four wind deities aren't just normal wind; they're to be associated with spiritual beings, the four horsemen. These Babylonian gods are also described as spirits "bound" (held back) at the Euphrates in Revelation 9:14–21:[198]

...saying to the sixth angel who had the trumpet, "Free the four angels who are bound at the great river Euphrates!" The four angels were freed who had been prepared for that hour and day and month and year, so that they might kill one third of mankind. The number of the armies of the horsemen was two hundred million. I heard the number of them. Thus I saw the horses in the vision and those who sat on them, having breastplates of fiery red, hyacinth blue, and sulfur yellow; and the horses' heads resembled lions' heads. Out of their mouths proceed fire, smoke, and sulfur. By these three plagues, one third of mankind was killed: by the fire, the smoke, and the sulfur, which proceeded out of their mouths. For the power of the horses is in their mouths and in their tails. For their tails are like serpents, and have heads; and with them they harm. The rest of mankind, who were not killed with these plagues, didn't repent of the works of their hands, that they wouldn't worship demons, and the idols of gold, and of silver, and of brass, and of stone, and of wood, which can't see, hear, or walk. They didn't repent of their murders, their sorceries, their sexual immorality, or their thefts. (WEB)

Readers who insist on a linear reading of Revelation struggle to make the connections between the four winds, the four horsemen, and the four angels/spirits. Like much of Revelation, John utilizes progressive parallelism to describe his vision(s).

Even still, some may ask, "Why are the four angels at the *Euphrates River* in Revelation 9 and *not* at the four corners of the earth like they were in Revelation 7"?

That the four angels of 9:14 are at the Euphrates and not at the four corners of the earth is a mixing of metaphors: the river sums up the end-time expectations concerning the direction from which the final onslaught of the Satanic enemy against the whole world will come.[199]

Commentators G. K. Beale and Sean M. McDonough drill down deeper into end-times expectations surrounding the Euphrates River, which, ultimately, geographically points to a terrifying upriser and defiler, a dreaded army from the north, who opposes wayward Israel and the rebellious Gentile nations. They note how the four (presumably wicked) angels held back at the "great river Euphrates" conjure up the OT prophecy of a northern upriser beyond the Euphrates whom God would bring to judge Israel (Isaiah 7:20; 8:7–8; 14:29–31; Jeremiah 1:14–15; 4:6–13; 6:1, 22; 10:22; 13:20; Ezekiel 38:6, 15; 39:2; Joel 2:1–11, 20–25).[200]

Indeed, Jeremiah's portrait of destruction on the bank of the Euphrates continually pings back to John's prophecy of the angels' being released there. Note the language of Jeremiah 46:

Concerning Egypt: Concerning the army of Pharaoh Neco, the king of Egypt, which was by *the Euphrates River* at Carchemish, which Nebuchadnezzar the king of Babylon defeated in the fourth year of Jehoiakim the son of Josiah, the king of Judah.… "Harness the horses and mount the steeds! And take your stand with helmets! Polish the spears! Put on the body armor!"… "The swift cannot flee, and the warrior cannot escape. In the north by *the bank of the Euphrates River*, they have stumbled and they have fallen."…"For that day is to the Lord Yahweh of hosts a day of retribution, to take revenge on his foes. And the sword will devour and be satisfied, and it will drink its fill of their blood, for a sacrifice is for the Lord Yahweh of hosts in the land of the north *by the Euphrates River*." …"Her sound is like a snake that glides away, for they march in force. And with axes they come to her like those who chop trees. They will cut down her forest," declares Yahweh, "for it is impenetrable. Yes, they are more numerous than locusts, and they are without number." (Jeremiah 46: 2, 4, 6, 10, 22–23, 22–23, LEB)

It should not be lost on the modern reader that the Euphrates was no ordinary river to the ancients. It was viewed as a personified river god or snake god in the Babylonian milieu.[201] However, most significant to our text is that the river was viewed as a *gateway* to the netherworld. The Euphrates had an overall importance in the cosmology of ancient people in that it was seen as the frontier between earth and the underworld.[202]

In *The Dictionary of Deities and Demons,* it's noted:

In Rev 16:12, the dried-up bed of the Euphrates functions as a highway for "the kings from the east", perhaps a designation of the rulers of the nether world. In Rev 9:14, the river is the boundary between the world of the living and the realm of the dead: four death-dealing angels were kept in check on the Euphrates. According to 2 Esd 13:39–45, finally, the Israelites, whom Shalmaneser took captive, found refuge in Arzareth, "a region where no human being had ever lived", which they reached by the narrow passages of the Euphrates. This "Other Land", as Arzareth can be rendered (Hebr ʾereṣ ʾaḥeret), stands for the nether world, from which the dispersed Israelites would return in the end of time. On their way back, "the Most High will stop the channels of the river again" (2 Esd 13:47), so that they might pass the river of death.…

To some extent, then, the view of the later Biblical writings reflects Babylonian mythology. To the Mesopotamians of the first millennium BCE, the Euphrates is divine inasmuch as it is an aspect of the primeval river linking the earth with the underworld. Though the Euphrates never has divine status in the Biblical texts, it does have a mythological significance inasmuch as it is considered to be a branch of the Primeval River and marks the line of transition between the world of the living and the regions beyond: that is, the kingdom of the dead.[203]

John's mention of the Euphrates would have immediately conjured up netherworld imagery in the minds of his readers.

So, the Euphrates doesn't just link to OT prophecies about an eschatological army *crossing* the dried-up river; it also points to the four angel gods *released* there. John clearly links the two. These supernatural beings are the "gods of the Euphrates," as they are called in the greeting formula of a Middle Babylonian letter.[204]

We can speculate that perhaps the army and its kings are either embodied by these underworld deities or led by them into battle. The language of Revelation 16:12, a parallel account to ours, certainly hints at this:

And the sixth poured out his bowl on the great river Euphrates, and its water was dried up, in order that the way would be prepared for the kings from the east. (LEB)

Releasing the four angels at the Euphrates means they are given full authority to now lead a united attack against typological Babylon, the very nation(s) that deified them as gods.

In summary, the four horsemen, the four winds, and the four angels are all the same entities, and the overarching progress of John's Apocalypse continues to build as he narrates the story from different lenses and perspectives.

The Four Living Creatures

While our attention thus far has primarily been on the four horsemen and the four colored horses, the "four living creatures" who summoned the demonic riders in Revelation 6 are also important in seeing Babylonian connections. The creatures in Revelation 6 derive from Ezekiel 1:5 and 10:

Also out of the midst thereof came the likeness of four living creatures. And this *was* their appearance; they had the likeness of a man…. As for the likeness of their faces, they four had the face of a man, and the face of a lion, on the right side: and they four had the face of an ox on the left side; they four also had the face of an eagle. (Ezekiel 1:5,10, KJV 1900)

In both Revelation 6 and Ezekiel 1, the living creatures' faces are described as being *similar* to those of a lion, an ox, a man, and an eagle. Notice that these faces match the constellations in Kihlman's chart: Leo = "like a lion," Taurus = "like an ox," Aquarius = "like a man."[205]

Color	Planet	Deity/Demon	Constellation	Direction
White	Jupiter	Marduk	Taurus	East
Red	Mercury	Nabu	Aquarius	North
Black	Saturn	Ninurta	Scorpio	West
Pale/Speckled	Mars	Nergal	Leo	South

The only outlier appears to be Scorpio. It *appears* to not match the face of an eagle. However, it is often forgotten that Scorpio (a scorpion) is a depiction of the constellation's infant stage; the clawed scorpion morphs into a clawed *eagle* and then a clawed phoenix. So, there is a pattern in all four instances after all.

Like Zechariah did with the colored horses and the four winds (cardinal directions), the prophets Ezekiel and John signified the chart's four constellations through the faces of the four living creatures. This picture is powerfully polemic to Ezekiel's audience: Babylonian deities must submit to the throne of God, too. That John also sees the faces of the four living creatures *appear* as constellations associated with Babylonian deities dismantles Babylon's religious prowess and foreshadows their eschatological defeat. While some may struggle to believe John and his first-century readers could have understood Babylonian astrology and its conations of other gods, the sacred teachings of Babylon survived well into the fourth century AD.[206]

The Birth of Messiah and September 11, 3 BC

John sees another astronomical story play out in the stars. In Revelation 12, he sees a conflict between an astronomical woman and a dragon:

A great sign was seen in heaven: a woman clothed with the sun, and the moon under her feet, and on her head a crown of twelve stars. She was with child. She cried out in pain, laboring to give birth. Another sign was seen in heaven. Behold, a great red dragon, having seven heads and ten horns, and on his heads seven crowns. His tail drew one third of the stars of the sky, and threw them to the earth. The dragon stood before the woman who was about to give birth, so that when she gave birth he might devour her child. She gave birth to a son, a male child, who is to rule all the nations with a rod of iron. Her child was caught up to God and to his throne. The woman fled into the wilderness, where she has a place prepared by God, that there they may nourish her one thousand two hundred sixty days. (Revelation 12:1–6, WEB)

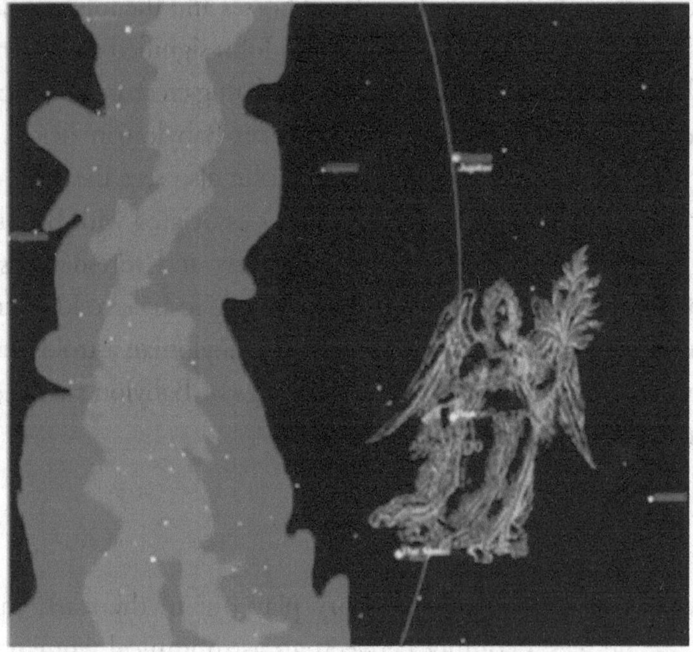

Virgo

John specifies that this part of his vision is depicted in the heavens (the stars). John, the astral prophet, sees a *literal* alignment of known constellations in the night sky. He sees Virgo and Hydra/Scorpio. Heiser writes:

Revelation 12:1 gives us clear details: the woman is "clothed" with the sun, there are twelve stars around her head, and the moon is at her feet. She is an astronomical (heavenly) sign. The idea that the woman is a constellation is made plausible when one looks closely at the text. The description that the woman was "clothed" with the sun is stock astronomical language for the sun being in the midst of a constellation. While the sun is in the woman, the moon is at her feet. For this situation to occur, the constellation of the woman must be, in astronomical language, on the ecliptic, the imaginary line in the sky that the sun and moon follow in their journey through the zodiac constellations....

The detail that the moon was located under the feet of the woman (Virgo) must not be forgotten in all this. The sun must be in the Virgin constellation while the moon is simultaneously at her feet for John's vision to be accurately interpreted astronomically. Because of the moon's "behavior" relative to the ecliptic and Virgo in any given year, the twenty-day window narrows to a roughly ninety-minute period in which to astronomically pinpoint the birth of the child.[207]

That John sees the constellation "Virgo" as the woman is apparent. Additionally, he sees "the dragon" standing before the woman to "devour" her child at birth. The seven-headed dragon is either the constellation Hydra or Scorpio.

Hydra has the advantage of matching the description of the seven heads atop the dragon in Revelation 12:3 (see also 13:1; 17:3, 7, 9).

Hydra was also conceived as a sea serpent, imagery that matches descriptions in Revelation (13:1), which, in turn, come from the Leviathan material of the Old Testament (Isaiah 27:1). However, Hydra is not precisely on the ecliptic; it is adjacent and only slightly below the woman. In other words, Hydra is not positioned directly under the feet of the woman, waiting to devour the child as soon as it emerges from the woman. The ecliptic problem is resolved if ancient Scorpio is John's referent, but that said, the text of Revelation 12 only has the dragon present ("stood before the woman"), not directly under her feet. Both options are possible correlations.[208]

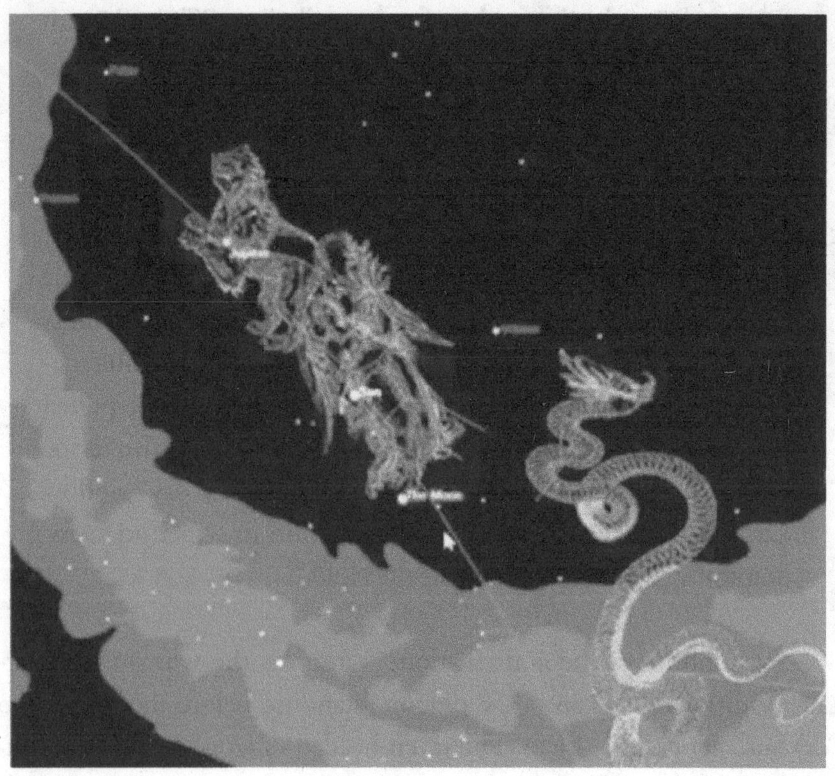

Hydra

As Heiser notes, plugging John's details into an astronomy program reveals an eighty- to ninety-minute window during which all of this aligns. This brief period falls on September 11, 3 BC, a realistic birthdate of Jesus.

> Incredibly, the astronomical reconstruction of the circumstances of Revelation 12:1–7 that produces a birth date for the Messiah of September 11, 3 B.C., was also the beginning of the Jewish New Year in 3 B.C. (Rosh ha-Shanah)—Tishri 1, the Day of Trumpets. The Feast of Trumpets/Tishri 1 was also the day that many of the ancient kings and rulers of Judah reckoned as their inauguration day of rule. This procedure was followed consistently in the time of Solomon, Jeremiah, and Ezra. This is a powerful piece of evidence for the astronomical reading of Revelation 12:1–7 as celestial signs of the birth of the messianic king.[209]

Christ being born on September 11, 3 BC, isn't just significant regarding the Jewish calendar. It is also significant in Babylon.

Tishri, Marduk, and the Gods of Babylon

While viewing Christ's birth from a Jewish perspective is incredibly insightful, *it's only half of the picture.* We must look at this passage from a Babylonian perspective, too. From the Sumero-Babylonian tablets *Enuma Elish* and *Astrolbe B*, pieces of John's astronomical image are mentioned, namely the constellations of Virgo or *"Bēlet-ilī"* (the woman in labor) and Libra (the limbs of Scorpio), often called "the scales." Note:

> In the month of Tašrītu the constellation of Bēlet-ilī, the woman in labor, becomes visible…. The month of Tašrītu (belongs)

to Šamaš, the "warrior" (= Iqqur īpuš §105). In the month of Tašrītu the "Scales" (= Libra) becomes visible.[210]

The Babylonian month *Tašrītu* is the Hebrew month *Tishri*. In fact, the Jewish calendar is based on the Babylonian calendar, as indicated by the following chart.[211]

	Babylonian	Jewish
I	Nisannu	Nisan
II	Ajaru	Iyyar
III	Simanu	Sivan
IV	Du'ûzu	Tammuz
V	Âbu	Ab
VI	Ulûlu	Elul
VII	Tašrîtu	Tishri
VIII	Arahsamna	Marheshvan
IX	Kislîmu	Kislev
X	Tebêtu	Tebeth
XI	Šabatu	Shebat
XII	Addaru	Adar

Astronomy in Mesopotamia usually concerns the gods, the king, or the country.[212] That John sees Jesus born in *Tishri* is more than a mere poke in the eye to Babylon; it completely dismantles their cultish existence.

In *Tishri*, the very month Revelation 12 has Mary birthing the Messiah, the Babylonians worshiped Shamash. The month of *Tašrîtu* was dedicated to this deity.[213] Shamash fits the messianic profile to a "T." He was deemed the judge, the king, and the shepherd. He is said to give light to the world, loosen the bonds of the imprisoned, grant health to the sick, and even revive the dead.[214]

Sound familiar?

That Jesus, the Great Judge, the King of Kings, and the Good Shepherd would be born in *Tishri*, or *Tašrîtu*, dethrones Shamash.

Most damning of all, Babylon celebrated its New Year festival during *Tishri*. The *Akitu* festival, as it was officially called, was celebrated for eleven consecutive days in the months *Tashritu* (the opening of the religious year) and *Nisan* (the opening of the civil year).[215] Like ancient Israel, the Mesopotamians maintained two calendars—civil and religious.[216]

The *Akitu* festival was a time for the gods to decree fates and for the reign of earthly kings to be renewed or struck down.[217] It was also a momentous festival for Marduk (Bel), king of the gods at Babylon. As we discovered in our study of the four horsemen, Marduk was the rider on the white horse. Ancient texts reveal that for the *Akitu* festival in Babylon, Marduk left his temple and convened in the holy *Akitu* chapel outside the city's walls with his band of lesser gods.[218] On the fourth day of the festival, the priests recited the *Enuma Elish*, which describes Marduk's victory over the chaos monster Tiamat.[219] On day five, the cultic priests reenacted the *Enuma Elish* to reinforce the mythical "victory" of their lord.[220] When the festival was completed, Marduk went back to his temple where he was re-enthroned as the patron deity. His renewed subjects then sang a celebratory hymn to acknowledge him as *king of the gods* at Babylon.

It is no coincidence that Marduk, Babylon's king deity, and Jesus, the Jewish King of promise, both ride on white horses in the book of Revelation (Revelation 6:2; 19:11). They are leading their armies into battle against one another, vying for cosmic superiority. Their longstanding struggle is illustrated in the very themes of Babylon's New Year festival. The festival can be divided into five primary categories: 1) combat; 2) victory; 3) creation; 4) divine enthronement; and 5) judgment. These elements are present in the Bible's description of Jesus Christ. Christ arrested the waters, created the universe, ascended on high, and is, of course, the Judge on the Great Day.

This cosmic struggle comes into focus when one considers that the Babylonian magi, or wise men from the East, *left* Babylonia to bring gifts and offerings to the Christ child (Matthew 2:1–12). The westerly visit of the Babylonian magi telegraphed to those in Babylonia that the boy born in Bethlehem was just more important than Marduk and the starting lineup of the gods of Babylon. Despite a full calendar organized around their gods, the stargazers from the east abandoned their deities to visit *the Child*. That many of John's original readers *also* saw the arrival of the Christ child in *Tishri* as theologically powerful and polemic is certain.

Furthermore, according to the ancient tablets of *Enuma Elish* and *Astrolbe B, Tishri* (Tašrîtu) was also the month of the annual offerings to the Annunaki. Note the text(s):

Month Tašrītu, the "Hitched Yoke," Enlil. The divine emblems are sanctified, the oath of the people and prince is cleared. *The pure annual offering of the lands is made to the Anunnaki.* The gate at the Apsu is opened.[221]

The Annunaki is a group of evil demons (often *seven* in number) who are wandering spirits of the earth. It is believed their name means "strong ones" or "gods of the watery habitation."[222] Nebuchadnezzar II dedicated an altar at the walls of Babylon to the Annunaki, which he called an altar of "joy" and "rejoicing." On the festival of Marduk, sacrifices were offered to these gods.[223]

In the great temple of Marduk there was a fountain in which the gods and the Anunnaki, according to a Babylonian hymn, "bathe their countenance"; and when to this notice it be added that another hymn praises them as the "shining chiefs" of the ancient city of Eridu, it will be apparent that the conceptions attached to this group span the entire period of Babylonian-Assyrian history.[224]

From Babylonian holidays to the epics and omens of early Mesopotamia, Jesus' birth in *Tishri*, or *Tašrītu*, would have sent shockwaves across the biblical landscape and utterly irritated the powers of darkness.

LOOKING AHEAD

This chapter articulated the *astronomical* threads woven into the tapestry of Revelation, which, ultimately, depicts Babylonian gods being active and present in the last days. In the next chapter, we will discover that John's vision of the bottomless pit points to the release of the Babylonian *apkallu*, commonly referred to in the Judeo-Christian contexts as the "Watchers."

THE RELEASE OF THE APKALLU

The fifth angel sounded, and I saw a star from the sky which had fallen to the earth. The key to the pit of the abyss was given to him. He opened the pit of the abyss, and smoke went up out of the pit, like the smoke from a burning furnace. The sun and the air were darkened because of the smoke from the pit. Then out of the smoke came locusts on the earth.

~REVELATION 9:1–4, WEB

IN A NUTSHELL

The chapter investigates Revelation 9 and uncovers how the demonic locusts that come out of the abyss are the "Watchers" of Genesis 6, also known as the *apkallu* in Babylonian texts.

DIGGING DEEPER

The Watchers and the Apkallu

The Babylonians boasted that their knowledge of the stars was transmitted by *seven* pre-Flood gods called the *apkallus*.[225] This is wildly important. Biblical scholar J. C. Greenfield writes:

> In Mesopotamian religion, the term apkallu (Sumerian: abgal) is used for the legendary creatures endowed with extraordinary wisdom. Seven in number, they are the culture heroes from before the Flood.… In the myth of the "Twenty-one Poultices" the "seven apkallu of Eridu," who are also called the "seven apkallu of the Apsu," are at the service of Ea (Enki).… A variety of wisdom traditions from the antediluvian period were supposedly passed on by the apkallu.… The seven sages were created in the river and served as "those who ensured the correct functioning of the plans of heaven and earth." Following the example of Ea, they taught mankind wisdom, social forms and craftsmanship. The authorship of texts dealing with omens, magic and other categories of "wisdom" such as medicine is attributed to the seven apkallu.[226]

The Jewish book of 1 Enoch reorients the Babylonian *apkallu* narrative by assigning blame to a particular classification of fallen angels known as the "Watchers" for sharing forbidden knowledge with humanity. This, of course, becomes an expansion of Genesis 6:1–4 and illuminates why the world became so corrupt before the Flood and also afterward.[227] To better grasp this, let's read 1 Enoch 6–8:

> And it happened that when the sons of men multiplied in those days, they begat good and beautiful daughters. And the angels,

the sons of heaven, saw them and longed for them and said to one another, "Come let us choose for ourselves women from among the people and bring forth for ourselves children." And Semiaza, who was their ruler, said to them, "I fear you may not wish to do this deed and I alone will be responsible for a great failure." Therefore they all answered him, "Let us all swear by an oath, and devote one another to mutual destruction, not to turn back from this decision until we complete it and do this deed." Then they all made a vow together and put each other under a curse in regard to this. These are the names of their rulers: Semiaza (this was their ruler *of all the angels*), Arathak, Kimbra, Sammane, Daniel, Arearos, Semiel, Iomiel, Chochariel, Ezekiel, Batriel, Sathiel, Atriel, Tamiel, Barakiel, Ananthna, Thoniel, Rhamiel, Aseal, Rhakiel, Touriel. These are the chiefs of tens among them. Then they took for themselves women, each of them choosing a woman for themselves. They began to go to them and defile them. And they taught them sorcery and enchantments and cutting of roots and explained herbs to them. But those who became pregnant brought forth great giants from three thousand cubits. These *giants* ate up the produce of the men. When the men were not able to provide for them, the giants had courage against them and ate up the men. And they began to sin against birds and wild animals and reptiles and fish, and each one of them ate up the flesh and drank the blood. Then the earth brought up charges against the lawless ones. **Azael** taught the humans to make swords and weapons, shields and breastplates—the lessons of the angels; and they showed to them their mining and craftsmanship, anklets and adornment, powders and painted eyes, and all kinds of chosen stones and dying. Much ungodliness and prostitution happened and they were led astray and ruined in all their ways. **Semiaza** taught enchantments and cutting of roots; **Armaros**, spells of healing;

Rhakiel, astrology; **Chochiel,** the science of symptoms; **Sathiel,** watching the stars; **Seriel,** the course of the moon. Therefore the cry of the utterly destroyed people went up unto heaven. (Enoch 6:1–8:4, LES)

That 1 Enoch assigns blame to *seven* fallen angels for bringing higher knowledge in the days of Jared is extremely illuminating. Obviously, these are meant to denote the *seven* pre-Flood *gods* called the *apkallus,* through which the Babylonians received higher knowledge. *Reversing Herman's* author, Dr. Michael Heiser, writes:

It is no understatement that, for Mesopotamians, the entire repository of knowledge that was to prove indispensable for civilization—and thus their own greatness—"was traced back to the wisdom of apkallus in its entirety." This role is a precise parallel to the Watchers of 1 Enoch, who taught humanity forbidden knowledge by which they became wicked and depraved (1 Enoch 8:1–4; 10:7–8).[228]

Fragments of 1 Enoch (4Q208–4Q211), including Astronomical Enoch (chapters 72–82) were recovered in the Dead Sea Scrolls (DSS). Studying these Second Temple texts have led many scholars to assert that Jewish scribes show dependence and trained familiarity with the *Enuma Anu Enlil* and Mesopotamian scribal lore.[229] Amar Annus, the brilliant Estonian scholar, notes the clear connections between Babylonian writings and 1 Enoch. He states:

When one considers this list of forbidden crafts from the point of view of Mesopotamian priests and scholars, almost everything looks familiar. "Spells and the cutting of roots" are relevant to Babylonian medicine (asûtu). The skills taught by Hermani are crafts used in exorcism, āšipūtu. Baraqel's expertise, whose name means "lightning of God," involves the "signs of Adad," the meteorological omens on the tablets 37–49 in the series Enuma Anu Enlil. The first two long sections of this celestial omen series, the "signs of Sin" (tablets 1–22) and the "signs of Shamash" (tablets 23–36), are taught to humankind in the Book of Watchers by the angels with appropriate names, Shamsiel and Sahriel. The "signs of the stars" taught by Kokabel must be a lore related to Enuma Anu Enlil's tablets 50–70, where the planetary omens are dealt with.… Finally, the "signs of the earth," taught by the angel Arteqoph, are probably not related to geomancy, but to the terrestrial omen series Šumma ālu.… In any case, many important Babylonian "antediluvian" sciences are well represented in the above catalogue, which can be taken as pars pro toto of all important Mesopotamian sciences. If the list is of independent origin, it may be illuminative to note that it contains seven names, in accordance with the seven antediluvian sages.[230]

With Babylonian teachings transcending into all cultures and scribal circles, including Jewish, the astronomical portions of Revelation would have been especially digestible for John's ancient audience. Noted theologian and professor Matthew Neujahr agrees. He writes:

Suffice it to say that the work on the Aramaic Astronomical Book and corresponding material in 1 Enoch is extremely technical, not merely philologically but even mathematically. Consensus has emerged that the specific ideas about the movement of celestial bodies, and their use for calendrical calculation, can be traced directly to Mesopotamian scribal lore, particularly ideas present in the astronomical compendium MUL.APIN and the omen series Enūma Anu Enlil.[231]

As Annus and Neujahr articulate, 1 Enoch's interaction with Babylonian space omens is undeniable. Understanding this helps to bridge the cultural gaps between the *apkallu* and the Watchers. It also helps us comprehend John's demonic creatures of the Abyss, as we will soon discuss.

Archeologists have discovered small *apkallu* figurines buried in boxes under ancient Mesopotamian ruins. These ancient "action figures" were used to ward off evil.[232] What's most telling is that, according to Akkadian ritualistic texts, the *apkallus* are also referred to as *maṣṣarē*, meaning "watchers." The Aramaic equivalent of this term is *ʿyryn*, "the wakeful ones," a word used of the evil Watchers.[233] All of this is evidence that 1 Enoch was written to reorient the Babylonian *apkallu* narrative and assign blame to these fallen angels for their crimes against God and humanity.

The Watchers are not the only sinister beings from Jewish literature accounted for in Mesopotamian tablets. The Enochic giants are also accounted for in the Mesopotamian tradition where they are called the *utukku-s*. Scholar Ida Fröhlich writes:

> The Enochic Giants have the same characteristics as the Mesopotamian demons; they are tall and obtrusive beings, roaming in bands, attacking their victims indiscriminately. They ravage the work of humans, devour the flesh of animals and humans, and consume their blood. They are born from a sexual union of heavenly and earthly beings, considered in the Enochic story to be impure.[234]

Another tie-in between 1 Enoch and Mesopotamian records is Enmeduranki. According to the *Sumerian King List*, Enmeduranki (the king of Sippar) was the *seventh* antediluvian (pre-Flood) king. He was special because he was granted access to the heavenly realm, where he received higher knowledge from the gods Adad and Shamash. Enmeduranki is the equivalent to the man Enoch in 1 Enoch, who is also labeled as the *seventh* pre-Flood patriarch (from Adam) and was taken to the higher realm where he, too, was given access to divine knowledge.[235] Conflating Enoch, "the seventh," with Enmeduranki, "the seventh," points to the Jewish writer's agenda to link the geologies in Genesis 4–5 and the *Sumerian King List* together in 1 Enoch.

The plot thickens.

Henry Drawnel, a researcher and teacher mostly interested in Qumran studies and Jewish apocalyptic literature, has written at length of how 1 Enoch 6–11 parrots the literary patterning of the Babylonian exorcistic incantation *Marduk-Ea* (noted in the last chapter). The following chart is based on Drawnel's work and further demonstrates that 1 Enoch was likely crafted, at least in part, as a polemic against Babylonian writings.[236]

Marduk-Ea Literary Pattern		1 Enoch 6–11	
I/1. Introduction— present tense verbal forms	General description of the demonic activity; cosmic birth of the exorcised evil	Birth of demons; demonic attack on humanity, animals, and nature	6:1–2; 7:la–b; 7:2–5
		Sinful character of the sexual union, oath, descent, list of names, pollution, teaching, accusation	6:3–8; 7:lc–e; 8:1–3; 7:6+8:4
I/2. Introduction— preterite verbal forms	Attack on a man and description of the symptoms	Omitted	
II. Marduk-Ea dialogue	Marduk sees the demonic attack	The angels see the demonic attack	9:1
	He enters the house (= the temple)	They enter (the house = the sanctuary)	9:2

Marduk-Ea Literary Pattern		1 Enoch 6–11	
	----------	The angelic report about the accusation of dying humanity	9:3, 10
	My father!	Praise of God	9:4–5
II. Marduk-Ea dialogue	Marduk reports to Ea (repetition of 1/1 and 1/2)	Angelic report to God (repetition of 8:1; 6:1–2; 7:1a–c; 7:2; 7:1d–e; 8:3)	9:6–9
	Marduk: "I do not know what to do."	Angels: "You know everything, but do not tell us what to do."	9:11
	Ea equates his knowledge with that of Marduk.	Omitted	
	Narration	Narration	10:1
	Commissioning formula, "Go, my son, Marduk."	Commissioning formula, "Go, Sariel…, Raphael…, Gabriel…, Michael."	10:2,4, 9, 11
	----------	Message to Noah	10:2–3
III. Ritual instruction	Ea's speech: Healing ritual	God's speech: Healing and elimination procedures (verbs in imperative and imperfect)	10:4–8, 9–10, 11–14
	----------	God's speech: instruction (verbs in imperative)	10:15–16, 20
	----------	God's speech: blessing of humanity and nature (verbs in imperfect)	10:17–19
	Ea's speech: Expected positive results: purification of the patient, protection of the personal god (verbs in precative).	God's speech: Future positive results: purification of the earth, conversion, and blessing (verbs in imperfect).	10:21–11:2

Marduk-Ea Literary Pattern		1 Enoch 6–11	
IV. Conclusion	Ea's speech: Demons or ill-ness should leave the man (verbs in precative).	Omitted	

If Drawnel is correct about Enoch's use of *Marduk-Ea*, it's quite illu-minating. The literary arrangement of 1 Enoch 6–11 would then be based on the Babylonian Incantation text in order to link the two nar-ratives together.

Now, why is this important regarding the book of Revelation?

If John is shooting at historical Babylon and the repository of Meso-potamian literature in the book of Revelation (as we have established that he is), one shouldn't be surprised that he often loads his weapon with Enochian bullets. Being familiar with 1 Enoch helps one track John's shots better in all the various firing lanes throughout the book.

The Watchers Locked in the Abyss

The *apkallu* are said to have originally emerged from the primeval deep known by Mesopotamians as the *Apsu* or *Abzu* (a watery habitation). This was considered underworld territory, just as the sea often is in Scrip-ture.[237] According to the *Erra Epic* and other cuneiform tablets, after being heralded as culture heroes, the *apkallu* violated created order by their cohabitation among humans. Their real transgression was that they reproduced with women and fathered hybrid offspring.[238] This angered Marduk, the high god of Babylon. So, the story goes that he punished them by sending a flood into the world. They were then judged and forced to return as prisoners to the *Apsu* from whence they came.

Sound familiar?

It should. It's the same story 1 Enoch and the Bible tells about the angels who sinned in the days of Noah.

With that backdrop in mind, let's study Revelation 9. The chapter begins with a "star" falling to the earth where a very important key is given to him. This "star" is an angelic figure, not a hot rock or ball of gas. Note:

> The fifth angel sounded, and I saw a star from the sky which had fallen to the earth. The key to the pit of the abyss was given to him. (Revelation 9:1, WEB)

However, for centuries, the debate has raged on about whether this angel is a rebel or loyalist to Heaven. Regardless of which team the "star" or "angel" plays for in Revelation 9:1, as John states, the key this angel is given could open the shaft to the "abyss" (Greek: *abussos)* or "bottomless pit." This is very important, because this is where the punished Watchers/*apkullu*, are being held. Heiser writes:

> In 1 Enoch 10:12–13, the abyss (*abussos*) is the place where the offending Watchers (=sons of God of Gen. 6:1–4) are imprisoned "for seventy generations." The partially synonymous relationship between the Abyss and the realm of the dead is indicated by the fact that some members of the abyss are imprisoned, unable to leave (the Watchers) whereas others (Satan, demons) are not so imprisoned. This may be what is behind the fear of the demons in Luke 8:31 ("And they begged him not to command them to depart into the abyss"; cf. Matt 8:29).[239]

Both Peter and Jude confirm the Watchers' tradition, which puts the angels who sinned in the days of Noah in the *lowest* chamber of the Abyss, Tartarus. Note:

2 Peter 2:4 (LEB)	Jude 6 (LEB)
For if God did not spare the angels who sinned, but held them captive in Tartarus with chains of darkness and handed them over to be kept for judgment.	And the angels who did not keep to their own domain but deserted their proper dwelling place, he has kept in eternal bonds under deep gloom for the judgment of the great day.

Peter also revealed in 1 Peter 3:18–21 that the slain Lord Jesus visited these imprisoned spirits upon His death and descent into the underworld to reiterate their eternal doom.

According to 1 Enoch and other Second Temple texts, the sons of God of Genesis 6 were responsible for the precipitous decline of morality before the Flood, not just for procreating with human women, but for an *array* of evil. They are considered *the most sinister beings in existence*. While many modern Christians attempt to explain away Peter and Jude's use of 1 Enoch, Dr. Justin Bass considers it folly.

> I believe that the disobedient angels in Genesis 6:1–4 are the "spirits" that Peter had in mind and this designation would have been familiar to his audience. Moreover, 1 Enoch seems to have played a very important role for the authors of 1 Peter, 2 Peter, Jude and the early Christian community. France says, "To try to understand 1 Peter 3:19–20 without a copy of the Book of Enoch at your elbow is to condemn yourself to failure." The parallels between 1 Peter 3:19–20 and 1 Enoch are striking. For example, Enoch is sent to pronounce a message of condemnation to disobedient angels called pneumata [spirits]! The angels that Enoch preached to had "transgressed the commandment of the Lord" and were thus disobedient (1 Pet 3:20). Lastly, Enoch

condemned them eternally through the proclamation: "you will have no peace."[240]

Dr. Bass' assessment is correct; the Watchers' transgression and punishment are clearly embedded in Peter and Jude's writing.

It is most interesting that, in the Aramaic *Targum Pseudo-Jonathan*, two of the Watchers are named in its rendition of Genesis 6:4:

Shamhazai and Azael fell *from heaven and* were on earth in those days, and also after the sons of *the great ones* had gone in to the daughters of men, who bore them children; *these are called* the heroes of old, the men of renown.[241]

Recalling that the sons of God (the Watchers) of Genesis 6 were put in the Abyss for their transgressions is paramount in understanding what John sees next—their *release* from the Abyss.

The Watchers as Locusts

John writes:

The fifth angel sounded, and I saw a star from the sky which had fallen to the earth. The key to the pit of the abyss was given to him. He opened the pit of the abyss, and smoke went up out of the pit, like the smoke from a burning furnace. The sun and the air were darkened because of the smoke from the pit. Then out of the smoke came locusts on the earth, and power was given to them, as the scorpions of the earth have power. (Revelation 9:1–3, WEB)

Here, the Watchers are described as hybridized demonic locusts. It will become more apparent in subsequent verses that these locusts aren't *ordinary* locusts. John calling the Watchers "locusts" is meant to pull several OT threads, primarily the Exodus plagues, which he repeatedly retools. Of these verses, Beale writes:

> Demonic-like beings portrayed as locusts arise from the smoking abyss and go out to the earth. "Authority was given to them" (ἐδόθη αὐταῖς ἐξουσία), which means that they were commissioned by someone to execute a task. Either God or Christ commissioned them, as we can see from use of the same authorization clause in 6:2–8; 8:2 and elsewhere in the Apocalypse (see further on 6:2–8 and esp. on 13:2–7). The model of the exodus plagues here confirms that God is the one who has absolute sovereignty over the plagues. The authority of the locusts is likened to the power that scorpions have over their prey…. The victims of these locusts are people on the earth, as the following verses reveal.[242]

Notice the language of Exodus 10:12–15:

> And Yahweh said to Moses, "Stretch out your hand over the land of Egypt with *the locusts* so that they may come up over the land of Egypt, and let them eat all the vegetation of the land, all that the hail left behind." And Moses stretched out his staff over the land of Egypt, and Yahweh drove an east wind into the land all that day and all night. The morning came, and the east wind had brought the locusts. And the locusts went up over all the land of Egypt, and they settled in all the territory of Egypt, very severe. Before it there were not locusts like them, nor will there be after it. And they covered the surface of all the land, *and the land was dark with them*, and they ate all the vegetation of the land and all the fruit of the trees that the hail had left, and no green was left in the trees nor in the vegetation of the field in all the land of Egypt. (LEB)

Like the locusts darkened the sky in Exodus 10, the smoke from the Abyss and the demonic locusts darken the sun in Revelation 9. *Power* is given to these demonic locusts to inflict the pain of scorpions upon the unbelievers of earth. This picture, by the way, is a *reversal* of Jesus' promise to the disciples in Luke 10:18–20.[243]

John continues:

> They were told that they [the demonic locusts] should not hurt the grass of the earth, neither any green thing, neither any tree, but only those people who don't have God's seal on their foreheads. They were given power, not to kill them, but to torment them for five months. Their torment was like the torment of a scorpion when it strikes a person. In those days people will seek death, and will in no way find it. They will desire to die, and death will flee from them. (Revelation 9:4–6, WEB)

It's interesting that the locusts of Exodus 10:15 destroyed "the land, and they devoured the vegetation, and all the fruit of the trees…[and] there was no green thing left on the trees." In Revelation 9, the demonic locusts are tasked with not harming the grass of the earth nor any green thing nor any tree, only unbelievers, who do not have the seal of God upon their foreheads. As the plagues did not harm the Israelites, true believers are spiritually protected from the fifth plague.[244] As the locusts tormented the Egyptians (Wisdom 16:1), so these demonic locusts will torment those found among spiritual Egypt.

Furthermore, the unbelieving Jews are prophesied to be among those who will endure the eschatological plagues of Egypt, as Beale explains:

> Deuteronomy 28 also predicts that "in the latter days" (so 32:20; 4:30) Israel will suffer the plagues of Egypt (vv 27, 60), including the plague of locusts (vv 38–39, 42), because of idolatry

(e.g., v 14; 29:22–27; 30:17; 31:16–20). This latter-day affliction includes "plagues" (v 61) of "madness [LXX "insanity"] and … bewilderment of heart, and groping at noon, as the blind man gropes in darkness" (vv 28–29), "being driven mad" (v 34), "trembling heart … despair of soul" (v 65); their "life will hang in doubt" and they will have "dread of heart" (vv 66–67)…. The parallels with Wisdom and Deuteronomy show that the Egyptian plagues are still in the background of Rev. 9:4–6.[245]

Next, John further describes the demonic locusts:

The shapes of the locusts were like horses prepared for war. On their heads were something like golden crowns, and their faces were like people's faces. They had hair like women's hair, and their teeth were like those of lions. They had breastplates like breastplates of iron. The sound of their wings was like the sound of many chariots and horses rushing to war. They have tails like those of scorpions, with stingers. In their tails they have power to harm men for five months. (Revelation 9:7–10, WEB)

The apostle's description of the locusts is rooted in Joel 1–2, which in turn is rooted in the locust plague of Exodus 10.[246] For example, John's locusts having men's faces and the appearance of horses prepared for battle derives from Joel 2:4–7, which describes the locusts there as "like the appearance of horses, and like war horses, so they run…like a mighty people arranged for battle…like mighty men…like soldiers."[247] The locusts having teeth like lions derives from Joel 1:6:

Because a nation has invaded my land, strong and beyond counting. Its teeth are the teeth of a lion, and its fangs are those of a lioness. (LEB)

Jewish tradition even describes the locusts that devoured Egypt as having the teeth of lions. Louis Ginzberg writes in his book, *Legends of the Jews*:

> Therefore God brought the locusts into the Egyptian border, to eat the residue of that which was escaped, which remained unto them from the hail, for the teeth of the locust are the teeth of a lion, and he hath the jaw teeth of a great lion.[248]

Furthermore, the sound of the wings of the demonic locusts as that of horse-drawn chariots derives from the description in Joel 2:4–5:[249]

> Like the appearance of horses is their appearance, and like horsemen they run; [5] like the sound of chariots on the tops of the mountains, they leap about; like the sound of a flame of fire devouring stubble; like a strong army arranged in rows for battle. (LEB)

Describing the Watchers who come out of the Abyss as a "destroying swarm of demonic locusts" makes perfect sense against an OT backdrop. As Dr. Heiser writes, in no way does it…

> …undermine their identification as the fallen Watchers. Hybridized theriomorphic ("animal-shaped") descriptions applied to demonic spirits are common in ancient Jewish and classical literature. If one wishes to understand Revelation 9 in its ancient literary context, the passage describes the release of the fallen Watchers before their ultimate destruction with Satan.[250]

Additionally, releasing the Watchers from their prison in Revelation does not contradict Peter and Jude's writings, which have these spirits imprisoned *until* judgment. In fact, it *fulfills* their prophecy. It confirms "until" has finally come to past. Beale writes:

Consequently…the judgment formerly limited to the demonic realm is being extended to the earthly realm. As a result of Christ's death and resurrection, the devil and his legions have begun to be judged, and now the effect of their judgment is about to be unleashed on unbelieving humanity, who give their ultimate allegiance to the devil.[251]

Eschatological judgment involves more than going to Heaven or Hell; it also entails global destruction. So, their release from the Abyss in Revelation 9 means cosmic judgment is officially here. Indeed, in the words of Dr. Heiser:

There is clearly a textual relationship between Revelation 9 and Enochian and other 2nd temple Jewish material that has the original offending Watchers imprisoned in the pit to await final judgment (1 En[och] 10:4–14; 18:11–16; 19:1; 21:7; 54:1–6; 88:1–3; 90:23–26; Jubilees 5:6–14; 2 Pet[er] 2:4; cf. 4 Ezra 7:36; Prayer of Manasseh 3).[252]

Abaddon, the King of the Watchers

In Revelation 9:11, John reveals the demonic locusts (the Watchers) have over them as king the angel of the Abyss, and His name in Hebrew is "Abaddon," but in Greek, he has the name "Apollyon."

Like Hades and Death (Revelation 1:18), Abaddon is both a *place* and a *proper name* that means "Destruction" or "Destroyer." Let's first consider Abaddon, the location:

[Hell and Abaddon] shall open
[and all] the flying arrows of the Pit.
shall send out their voice to the Abyss.
And the gates [of Hell] shall open

[on all] the works of Vanity;
and the doors of the Pit shall close
on the conceivers of wickedness;
and the everlasting bars shall be bolted
on all the spirits of Naught.[253]

This citation associates it with Hell and the Abyss and has "flying arrows" coming out of it (think locusts with stingers). Another portion of the DSS[254] locates Abaddon and the great Abyss as part of earth's cosmological structuring, described as the "deep places" of the earth.

Give thanks…
    [Bless] His holy Name always
    …all the angels of the holy firmament
    …[above] the heavens,
    the earth and all its deep places,
    the great [Abyss] and Abaddon
    and the waters and all that is [in them.]
    [Let] all His creatures [bless Him] always
    for everlasting [ages. Amen! Amen!]
    …bless His holy Name.
    Sing to God.[255]

Furthermore, the DSS[256] has Belial (Satan) being uprooted from Abaddon, his home of destruction, in a final battle between the evil spirits and God's holy angels.

[Come,] strengthen yourselves for the battle of God, for this day
is an appointed time of battle [for G]od against all the n[ations,
… judgm]ent upon all flesh. The God of Israel is about to raise

His hand in His wondrous [streng]th [against] all the spirits of wick[edness … m]ighty ones of the gods are girding themselves for battl[e, and] the formation[s of the] h[o]ly ones [are rea]dying themselves for a day of [vengeance …] the God of I[srae]l […] to remove Bel[ial …] in his place of destruction (Abaddon).[257]

Associating Abaddon with Sheol and the realm of the dead is consistent with the OT (Job 26:6; 28:22; Psalm 88:11; Proverbs 15:11; 27:20).[258] So, Abaddon is a place.

Abaddon is also *personified* in the OT and the DSS. Abaddon, the angel of the Abyss, is cursed without forgiveness in the following:[259]

Then [they shall continue and say, "Cursed are you, O ange]l of the pit, O spir[it of Aba]ddon, for al[l] the purposes of your guilty desire, [and for all your abomina]ble [purposes] and [your] wicked counsel, [and da]mned are you for [your unjust domi]n[ion] [and your guilty] and [wicked] authority with all [the] de[filements of Sheo]l and w[ith the reproaches of the pi]t, [with the disgra]ces of destruction wi[thout remnant and without] forgiveness by the fierce anger of [Go]d [for all eternit]y. Amen. A[men.][260]

It is essential to understand that Satan had various names and aliases in Second Temple Judaism, such as "Belial," "Mastema," and even "Abaddon." Jubilees, the Jewish book known as the "Little Genesis," describes Satan/Mastema as being over evil spirits, including the imprisoned Watchers.[261] Undoubtedly, John's Jewish audience would have read the book of Jubilees and other Second Temple texts and knew Abaddon = Belial = Mastema = Satan. He is the king to the bottomless pit.

LOOKING AHEAD

This chapter established that John sees the imprisoned Watchers (*apkallu* in Babylonian writings) being released from the Abyss. In the next chapter, we will study the horrendous beasts of Revelation and make Old Testament and Mesopotamian connections.

9

THE BEASTS AND ENUMA ELISH

Then I stood on the sand of the sea. I saw a beast coming up out of the sea, having ten horns and seven heads. On his horns were ten crowns, and on his heads, blasphemous names.

~REVELATION 13:1, WEB

IN A NUTSHELL

In this chapter, we will discover that the two beasts in Revelation 13 are a *blend* of the beasts cited in Daniel 7 (which represent evil kingdoms) and their Ancient Near Eastern antecedents, Tiamat and Leviathan of the sea and Behemoth/Rahab of the land. These vile creatures are mythological beasts found in Mesopotamian and Canaanite creation myths and in the Old Testament. In Scripture, they are postured as God's enemies and represent the ongoing struggle between order and chaos, good and evil. The overall message is that God's rivals will oppress God's people and amass faithful followers *until* they are finally slain at the end of time.

DIGGING DEEPER

The Beasts of Daniel 7 and Revelation 13

Revelation 13 follows John's vision of the "two witnesses" that describes the Church's witness amid Daniel's "great tribulation" period and their ongoing battle with the beast. It also comes on the heels of John's vision in Revelation 12 involving a cosmic struggle between a woman (the Church/Israel) and a dragon.

In Revelation 13, John now sees yet another fight-or-flight storyline involving God's distressed people and dreaded chaos monsters. He writes:

> Then I stood on the sand of the sea. I saw a beast coming up out of the sea, having ten horns and seven heads. On his horns were ten crowns, and on his heads, blasphemous names. The beast which I saw was like a leopard, and his feet were like those of a bear, and his mouth like the mouth of a lion. The dragon gave him his power, his throne, and great authority. (Revelation 13:1–2, WEB)

The description of this beast is a conglomerate of the details in Daniel 7, where John describes four beasts that represent four evil kingdoms, the last of which is Rome. In his and Campbell's *Shorter Commentary* on Revelation, Beale writes:

> The first agent of the devil is a beast coming up out of the sea. Vv. 1–2 are a creative reworking of Dan. 7:1–7. The beast with ten horns and seven heads is based on Dan. 7:2–7, 19–24. This beast is like a leopard, a bear, and a lion. The seven heads are a composite of the heads of the four beasts Daniel saw, one like

a leopard, one like a bear, one like a lion, and a fourth with ten horns. Other features of the Danielic beasts are also applied to the one beast in v. 2. In addition, the ten diadems on the ten horns are a reference to Daniel's fourth beast, whose "ten horns" are interpreted as "ten kings" (Dan. 7:24). Likewise, the blasphemous names on his heads are connected with the blaspheming figure of Dan. 7:8, 11, who is also associated with the fourth Danielic kingdom (see on vv. 5–6 below). That the monster in vv. 1–7 is modeled primarily on Daniel 7 is supported by the above analysis of the similar portrayal of the dragon in 12:3–4 (on which see), which was predominantly taken from Daniel 7–8.[262]

That John sees the attributes and ferocity of all four beasts funneled into one single beast in Revelation 13 is evident. The mighty beast, who in the first century was thought by many to be Rome, is said to speak blasphemies for forty-two months (3.5 years). John writes:

They worshiped the dragon because he gave his authority to the beast; and they worshiped the beast, saying, "Who is like the beast? Who is able to make war with him?" A mouth speaking great things and blasphemy was given to him. Authority to make war for *forty-two months* was given to him. He opened his mouth for blasphemy against God, to blaspheme his name, his dwelling, and those who dwell in heaven. It was given to him to make war with the saints and to overcome them. Authority over every tribe, people, language, and nation was given to him. All who dwell on the earth will worship him, everyone whose name has not been written from the foundation of the world in the book of life of the Lamb who has been killed. If anyone has an ear, let him hear. If anyone is to go into captivity, he will go into captivity. If anyone is to be killed with the sword, he must be killed. Here is the endurance and the faith of the saints. (Revelation 13:4–10, WEB)

This forty-two month/3.5 years/1,260-day period keeps coming up in Revelation 11–13. As we've noted, it's Daniel's "great tribulation" period in which the Church must suffer *until* Christ's return. Forty-two is commonly associated with tribulation throughout the biblical narrative, particularly with Israel. Beale states:

> The reason for the exact number of "forty-two" here and in 13:5 is likely to recall the same time of Elijah's ministry of judgment (Luke 4:25; Jas. 5:17; see on 11:6) and Israel's entire time of wilderness wandering after the Exodus, which encompassed a total of forty-two encampments (so Num. 33:5–49). This is reinforced by possibly reckoning forty-two years for the Israelites' total sojourn in the wilderness, since it appears they were in the wilderness for two years before incurring the penalty of remaining there for forty years until the death of the first generation.[263]

It makes sense for John's readers to comprehend that their persecution is part of Daniel's vision, and it mirrors the suffering of OT Israel during this symbolic 42-month/1,260-day period.

Today, the Roman Empire is no more, yet the Beast of Revelation 13 continues to speak blasphemies against God in Heaven and war with the saints in every nation (Revelation 13:7). Therefore, *limiting* the beasts of Revelation 13 to Rome is nearsighted and wrong.

Truthfully, the scene of evil beasts coming from the sea *predates* Rome (and the book of Daniel, for that matter) and is the foundation of the Bible's cosmic war. To understand why, we need to revisit the ancient literary genre of *Chaoskampf.*

The Written War of Chaos

God's *war* with the nation's gods (fallen angels) isn't just contentious; it is also *literarily* combative. This means the two powers vie for *written* superiority in various thematic categories. This is commonly referred to as "polemic theology." As John D. Currid notes in his book, *Against the Gods*:

> Polemical theology is the use by biblical writers of the thought forms and stories that were common in ancient Near Eastern culture, while filling them with radically new meaning. The biblical authors take well-known expressions and motifs from the ancient Near Eastern milieu and apply them to the person and work of Yahweh, and not to the other gods of the ancient world....
>
> The primary purpose of polemical theology is to demonstrate emphatically and graphically the distinctions between the worldview of the Hebrews and the beliefs and practices of the rest of the ancient Near East.[264]

One literary battleground is an ancient motif commonly referred to as *Chaoskampf*. This is an ancient motif or recurring storyline deep in earth's past in which a deity battles a chaos monster, serpent, or dragon from the seas. Beating the sea serpent always brings order into the cosmos and elevates the deity as god of gods.

Mythological Creatures and Revelation 13

The Sea Beast and the Ancient Near Eastern Context

The earliest known tale of this cosmic struggle involving a deity and a sea monster is preserved in the seven tablets of creation known as the

Enūma eliš. In this story, Marduk, the god of Babylon, defeats the water dragon Tiamat to earn supremacy in the Babylonian pantheon. We will say more concerning the *Enūma eliš* later in this section.

A similar story is preserved in Caananite mythology, where, in the Baal Cycle, Baal (the god of thunder) defeats Yamm/Leviathan of the sea. His heroics also elevate amid the gods. After his victory, Baal ruled over Mount Zaphon, where, supposedly, lesser gods built his palace.

Scholar Eric Ortlund discusses how Isaiah 27:1 interacts with the Baal's victory over Leviathan (Yamm). This is polemic theology at its finest. He writes:

> With regard to the Baal Epic, Mot, the god of death, makes reference to a prior victory of Baal over Lotan (claiming it will not help Baal when he fights with Death). Mot describes Lotan, the "fleeing" and "twisting" serpent (brḥ and qltn); the identical description of YHWH'S eschatological enemy in Isaiah 27:1 prevents any confusion about the identity of Leviathan in the Old Testament.[265]

Note the similarities between Isaiah 27:1 and the Ugaritic text:

KTU 1.5:1:1–8 (Ugaritic Text)	Isaiah 27:1 (LEB)
Though you smote Litan [Leviathan] *the fleeing serpent, finished off the twisting serpent*, the encircler with *seven heads*, you burned him up, and thus you brightened the heavens.	On that day, Yahweh will punish with his cruel, great and strong sword Leviathan, *the fleeing serpent*, and Leviathan, *the twisting serpent*, and he will kill the sea monster that is in the sea."

This is significant. Both Ugaritic texts and biblical texts use Leviathan (*lītānu/liwyātān*) as a proper name when discussing the seven-headed mythical water dragon.[267] Isaiah 27:1 is a polemic punch against Baal's victory over Leviathan in that it deems Yahweh as the eschatological victor over the foul beast.

Elsewhere, the OT pulls this same thread to describe Israel's crossing of the sea.

Isaiah 51:9–10 (ESV)	Psalm 74:12–15 (ESV)
Awake, awake, put on strength, O arm of the LORD; awake, as in days of old, the generations of long ago. Was it not you who cut Rahab in pieces, who *pierced the dragon*? Was it not you who dried up the sea, the waters of the great deep, who made the depths of the sea a way for the redeemed to pass over? (Isaiah 51:9–10, ESV)	Yet God my King is from of old, working salvation in the midst of the earth. You divided the sea by your might; *you broke the heads of the sea monsters on the waters. You crushed the heads of Leviathan*; you gave him as food for the creatures of the wilderness. You split open springs and brooks; you dried up ever-flowing streams."

Did Israel defeat a *literal* swimming sea dragon in the Red Sea? No. Slaying the dragon represented Israel's victory over Pharaoh, the chaos nation of Egypt, and the *chaotic gods of Egypt* (Exodus 12:12).

Chaos water dragon

Now, back to the *Enūma eliš*.

Austen Henry Layard

Many scholars believe Genesis 1 (and some elements in Genesis 2–3) was, in part, *stylistically* written as a polemic response to the seven tablets of creation known as *Enūma eliš*, which predate the book of Genesis by well over a thousand years.[268] That God was not only interested in telling the account of Creation, but also shooting at His "competition" makes total sense.

The wedge-shaped cuneiform tablets were found by Austen Henry Layard (1817–1894), a real-life Indiana Jones, in 1849 in Mesopotamia in ancient ruins of the city Nineveh. The seven tablets were found in the library ruins of the Assyrian king, Ashurbanipal. The *Baker Encyclopedia of the Bible* notes:

> The words enuma elish mean "when on high" and are the first two words of the epic, introducing the reader to a time when the heavens "on high" had not been named and the earth did not yet exist.[269]

Assuming you're not familiar with the mythical struggle between Marduk and Tiamat, an epical creation story with which Israel and her neighbors were aware, you will find it difficult to see how this all connects. The *Dictionary of Deities and Demons* summarizes:

> In the Babylonian creation epic Enūma eliš, Tiāmat (also called Mummu) is the personified primeval ocean that was defeated by Marduk, whose supremacy over the Babylonian pantheon was established through battle. *Marduk defeated Tiāmat* [the sea] *in single combat, using the winds* and a huge net as his weapons. The

body of the dead Tiāmat [the sea] was split like a fish to be dried into two halves, one of which became the sky. Having positioned the celestial bodies, Marduk used Tiāmat's spit for clouds, placed a mountain on her head, and made an outlet from her eyes for the waters of the Euphrates and the Tigris (Enūma eliš IV 93–V 66; emphasis added).[270]

The Bible seems to interact with the Babylonian creation story (*Enūma eliš*) in the Genesis Creation account where it takes polemic jabs at the Babylonian deities by asserting it was the *Spirit* (wind) of God, not Marduk, who "hovered" or "brooded" over the face of the waters and willed "Deep" (Hebrew: *Tĕhôm*; Akkadian: *Tiāmat*) into submission (Genesis 1:2–7).[271] Notice I wrote "deep" and *not* "the deep," as most English translations read. Hermann Gunkel writes:

The Babylonian form of the monster, Ti'āmat, actually corresponds in the Hebrew to the technical term for the primordial sea, תהום [*tĕhôm*]. The invariable use of this term without the definite article [the] allows us to conclude that it was once a proper name and hence designated a mythical figure.[272]

God's victory over the chaotic waters (*Tiamat*) is further evidenced in the Greek OT where the English Septuagint uses *epipherō* for "hovers" over the face of the primordial sea (Genesis 1:2). The Greek term *epipherō* means:

1. to bestow something on someone;
2. bring something over and put it on someone;
3. to cause someone or something to undergo something adverse, bring (on/about), inflict;
4. to add something on top of something add trouble; or
5. to bring charges or make accusations, bring, pronounce.[273]

This lends to the idea that the Spirit (Hebrew: *Rûwach*, "wind") of God is *inflicting, arresting, binding, and bringing charges against* the chaotic sea (*Tiāmat*). In *Against the Gods*, John Currid emphasizes that most scholars agree with this assessment:

[German theologian Franz] Delitzsch and others also contend that the word tehom ("deep") in Genesis 1:2 is a remnant of Mesopotamian myth. Supposedly it relates to Tiamat, the goddess of the deep sea…. In the Babylonian creation account Marduk defeats her, divides her, and forms her into the earth, sea, and heavens. Lying behind the account of God's creation in Genesis 1, therefore, is the Mesopotamian myth that he conquered the chaos deity Tiamat and then created the universe. All the evidence, say many scholars, suggests that the biblical writer was merely demythologizing the pagan world-order. This suggestion has become fact in much recent literature.[274]

Yahweh subduing the sea is one of Moses' many possible jabs toward the creation epic of Marduk and Tiamat. As *Lexham Bible Dictionary* points out, the Babylonian creation story does seem to parallel the Genesis Creation account(s) in several places.[275]

The following chart includes some of the possible parallels.[276]

Babylonian Creation Epic	Genesis Creation Account
The Lord [Marduk] *rested*, and inspected her corpse.	And on the seventh day *God* finished his work…and *he rested*….
He [Marduk] divided the monstrous shape and created marvels (from it)…. *Her waters he arranged* so that they could not escape….	and God divided the light from the darkness…let it separate the waters from the waters… And God said, "Let the waters under the heavens be gathered together into one place, and let the dry land appear."

Babylonian Creation Epic	Genesis Creation Account
The Lord [Marduk] measured the dimensions *of Apsû* [primordial waters]... which he had *created as the sky*....	And God called the expanse Heaven....
As for the *stars*, he [Marduk] set up constellations corresponding...... to them.	And God made the two great lights... and the stars.
He [Marduk] designated *the year and marked out its divisions*...apportioned three stars each to the twelve months....	And God said...and let them be for signs, and for *seasons, and for days, and years*:
He opened the *Euphrates and Tigris* from her eyes	And the name of the third river is the *Tigris*.... And the fourth river is the *Euphrates*.
"I [Marduk] shall make *a house to be a luxurious dwelling* for myself... and shall found his cult centre within it... and I shall establish my private quarters... and confirm my kingship	The Lord God took the human that he formed, and he placed him *in the paradise* to work and to keep it.... So the Lord God sent him away from *the paradise of luxuriousness* to work the land from which he was taken.
"I hereby name it Babylon, 'home of the great gods'."	And the Lord God planted a garden in *Eden*, in the east, and there he put the man whom he had formed.... and *you will be as gods* who know good and evil."

While the similarities between the *Enūma eliš* and the Genesis Creation may be unsettling to many modern Christians, it appears that Yahweh met the Babylonian epic *head-on* and set the record straight on who the true Creator of the cosmos is. As I wrote earlier, similarities do not require the reader to dismiss the historical genuineness of the Genesis 1 account. In *From Chaos to Cosmos*, Sidney Greidanus states:

The narrator in Genesis 1 is setting out an authentic and distinctive creation theology, but in so doing is willing to use familiar mythological imagery to present important ideas that might not easily be expressed in other ways.[277]

Truthfully, a *literal* and *historical* reading of Genesis 1 can remain intact *even* with Moses responding to the *Enūma eliš*. The Bible reveals that the angelic sons of God witnessed Yahweh create the world:

Where wast thou when I founded the earth? tell me now, if thou hast knowledge, who set the measures of it, if thou knowest? or who stretched a line upon it? On what are its rings fastened? and who is he that laid the corner-stone upon it? When the stars were made, all my angels praised me with a loud voice. And I shut up the sea with gates, when it rushed out, coming forth out of its mother's womb. (Job 38:4–8, Brenton Lxx En)

It's plausible, therefore, that Babel's angels (Deuteronomy 32:8; Psalm 82) kept elements of the true story and inserted them into their own creation epics as propaganda. That God wants to sink these stories and win the written war seems only logical. What is definite is that early readers of Genesis would have identified Moses' polemic features and read them as verbal jabs against Marduk and Baal.

Moses and the other biblical writers knew one of the best ways to address the established creation epics was to hijack their elements and hand them to Yahweh. Their deities' power becomes Yahweh's power. Their monsters become Yahweh's monsters. Their victory becomes Yahweh's victory. Again, the goal was total dethronement of pagan ideology and total enthronement of Yahweh. That's what Moses and the other biblical writers occasionally did. When necessary, they let their "pens" do the fighting:

Inspired by the Holy Spirit, the biblical authors stripped the ancient pagan literatures of their mythological elements, infused them with the sublimities of their God, and refuted the pagan myths by identifying the holy Lord as the true Creator and Ruler of the cosmos and of history.[278]

Ultimately, this style of writing was designed to increase Israel's faith in Yahweh and deter them from serving other gods.

When reading about the seven-headed monster who comes out of the sea in Revelation 13, if your mind does not go back to Babylon, the *Enuma Elish*, and Marduk's victory over Tiamat, you are missing much of John's framework. While this cluster of ideas does link to Daniel 7, as we have set forth in this chapter, its antecedent is much older. Ultimately, John's sea beast swims back to Babylon, ancient Sumer, and the region of Mesopotamia. Divorcing the ancient Near East context from the text in this instance only dilutes God's victory over Babylon the Great in the book of Revelation.

The Land Beast and the Antichrist

While our attention has centered on the sea beast in Revelation 13, its counterpart, the land beast, also contributes to the discussion. Next, John sees the dreaded counterpart to the sea dragon, the land beast.

I saw another beast coming up out of the earth. He had two horns like a lamb and it spoke like a dragon. He exercises all the authority of the first beast in his presence. He makes the earth and those who dwell in it to worship the first beast, whose fatal wound was healed. He performs great signs, even making fire come down out of the sky to the earth in the sight of people. He deceives my own people who dwell on the earth because of the signs he was granted to do in front of the beast, saying to those who dwell on the earth that they should make an image to the beast who had the sword wound and lived. It was given to him to give breath to the image of the beast, that the image of the beast should both speak, and cause as many as wouldn't worship the image of the beast to be killed. He causes all, the small and the great, the rich and the poor, and the free and the slave, to be given marks on their right hands or on their foreheads; and that no one would be able to buy or to sell unless he has that mark, which is the name of the beast or the number of his name. Here is wisdom. He who has understanding, let him calculate the number of the beast, for it is the number of a man. His number is six hundred sixty-six. (Revelation 13:11–18, WEB)

This land beast is connected to the Antichrist, whose number is 666. Many commentators assume it's Nero due to gematria and the fearful rumors that he would return from the dead (as in "fatal wounds would heal"). Gematria is a counting system wherein numerical values are assigned to letters. The sum of the letters then equals a number. Multiple ancient languages, including Greek and Hebrew, adopted this coded language. Variant spellings of Nero in Greek add up to 666, as well as 616, which is found in several alternate manuscripts of Revelation 13:18. Surprisingly, In *Against Heresies 5.30.3*, Irenaeus doesn't even so much as nod at in Nero's direction, but believes the word "titan" (the Grecian version of the Genesis 6 "giants") is most convincing. Note:

It is therefore more certain, and less hazardous, to await the fulfilment of the prophecy, than to be making surmises, and casting about for any names that may present themselves, inasmuch as many names can be found possessing the number mentioned; and the same question will, after all, remain unsolved. For if there are many names found possessing this number, it will be asked which among them shall the coming man bear…. Teitan too, (TEITAN, the first syllable being written with the two Greek vowels and), among all the names which are found among us, is rather worthy of credit. For it has in itself the predicted number, and is composed of six letters, each syllable containing three letters; and [the word itself] is ancient, and removed from ordinary use; for among our kings we find none bearing this name Titan, nor have any of the idols which are worshipped in public among the Greeks and barbarians this appellation. Among many persons, too, this name is accounted divine, so that even the sun is termed "Titan" by those who do now possess [the rule]. This word, too, contains a certain outward appearance of vengeance, and of one inflicting merited punishment because he (Antichrist) pretends that he vindicates the oppressed. And besides this, it is an ancient name, one worthy of credit, of royal dignity, and still further, a name belonging to a tyrant. Inasmuch, then, as this name "Titan" has so much to recommend it, there is a strong degree of probability, that from among the many [names suggested], we infer, that perchance he who is to come shall be called "Titan." We will not, however, incur the risk of pronouncing positively as to the name of Antichrist; for if it were necessary that his name should be distinctly revealed in this present time, it would have been announced by him who beheld the apocalyptic vision. For that was seen no very long time since, but almost in our day, towards the end of Domitian's reign.[279]

Irenaeus (AD 130–203) of Gaul was a disciple of Polycarp, *who was a disciple of the Apostle John*, the penman of Revelation. Given his close ties to John, Irenaeus' theory should be given considerable weight. Dr. Heiser writes:

The point being made here is not that the Antichrist will be a giant. No biblical or Enochic text draws such a conclusion. Rather, the material indicates that Second Temple Jewish readers of Revelation may have parsed the Antichrist as having a direct association with the fallen Watchers, the classical Titans, and the giants. Given the evidence that Second Temple Jews thought of the great end-times enemy as a man in league with Satan (Belial), and that they had a propensity to see Satan as leader of the Watchers, perceiving the Antichrist as an embodied Watcher-spirit (demon) is understandable.[280]

So, both the sea beast and land beast connect to the activity of chaotic angels. This understanding makes sense in the overarching theme of Revelation: spiritual war.

The Temple of Marduk and the Bronze Sea

The ocean symbolized chaos in the ancient world. Eric Ortlund summarizes in his excellent book, *Piercing Leviathan*:

The ocean is a recurring symbol for cosmic chaos in the ANE, the Old Testament and the book of Job specifically (see 7:12; 26:12). Modern Western cultures do not tend to make this connection, but it is not hard to imagine why ancient Semites would have found the ocean a suitable symbol for that relentless, unorganizable force that would swallow and drown the fertile order of creation if not contained by the Creator. After all, the watery depths cannot be mapped or divided or tilled, as the earth can; no human can impose any boundary on them. Consider as well how ancient Semites would have known only as much about the sea as they could have learned from swimming in it. To them, it would have felt bottomless, murky, the opposite of fruitful and ordered creation.[281]

We can better understand how the sea symbolizes chaos in the book of Revelation by looking at the ancient temples of King Solomon and Marduk, the patron deity of Babylon. Twin handcrafted seas (reservoirs) sat in the both structures. From spoils acquired by King David (1 Chronicles 18:8; 2 Samuel 8:8), Hiram of Tyre was hired to construct this thirty-ton reservoir that held twelve thousand gallons of water.[282] The Bronze Sea (also called "Molten Sea") was displayed in the courtyard of the Temple (1 Kings 7:23–26).[283] Due to its great height, most scholars agree that it had no *practical* purpose, but held a purely *symbolic* role.[284] What did it symbolize? German scholar Hermann Gunkel wrote in 1895:

> In Babylon such a "Sea" was placed in the shrine of Marduk. Thus was symbolized the power of Marduk over Ti'âmat.... Accordingly, the cultic symbol of the "Sea" in the Temple is classified together with the concept of the "World Sea" and the Chaos Myth.[285]

In David Shapira's excellent journal article, entitled, "The Molten Sea Revisited," he summarizes how several other scholars view the symbolism of the Bronze Sea in light of its twin in Babylon. He writes:

> [Samuel] Terrien surmises that, since the temple was thought to be the hub of the world, the Sea held a cosmic significance linked to the mythic notion of tehom (Tiamat)—i.e., the "abyss."
>
> [John] Gray… adds that a similar water vat existed at the Marduk temple in Babylon, where it was known as ta-am-tu—in apparent allusion to Marduk's mythological battle and

triumph over Tiamat. Water, according to Gray, symbolizes the triumph of the cosmos over chaos.

Ernest Wright sees the Sea as a Canaanite theological reference.[286]

Carol Meyers agrees with these scholars' consensus and acknowledges the significance of the artificial sea discovered in Babylon. She writes:

The temple of Marduk at Babylon, for example, had an artificial sea (ta-am-tu) in its precincts; and some Babylonian temples had an apsû- sea, a large basin. Such features symbolize the idea of the ordering of the universe by the conquest of chaos…. Ancient Israel shared in this notion of watery chaos being subdued by Yahweh and of the temple being built on the cosmic waters. The great "molten sea" near the temple's entrance would have signified Yahweh's power and presence. Furthermore, the bronze courtyard furnishings (including the large pillars Jachin and Boaz [1 Kings 7:21]) were the only temple appurtenances visible to the public, which included both Israelites and foreigners in the cosmopolitan days of Solomonic reign. The role of these elaborate objects in providing visual messages about Yahweh's availability and power thus helped establish the legitimacy of the monarchy.[287]

As the molten sea symbolized Yahweh's power over chaos, the Babylonian's *artificial sea* celebrated the victory of their god Marduk over Tiamat, the personified primeval ocean of chaos.[288]

Marduk, the patron deity of Babylon, was often cosmic enemy number one. He is addressed with the following titles in ancient tablets: "Bel," "the director of the gods," "the counselor of the gods," "the lord of the gods," and "chiefest among the great gods."[289] Marduk is mentioned by name in Jeremiah 50:1–2 and 51:44.

So, it's easy to see why God wanted Israel to have a *visual reminder* (the Molten Sea) displayed in the courtyard of Solomon's Temple, which represented Yahweh's power over primeval waters and His superiority over Marduk, the chief god of the Sumerians, Babylonians, and Assyrians.[290]

But there is more.

Meyers writes of the unique *base* upon which the Bronze Sea rested:

Most amazing of all was the way it [the Bronze Sea] was supported on four sets of bronze oxen, with three oxen in each set. Each set of oxen faced a direction of the compass, with their "hinder parts" facing inward and supporting the basin.[291]

The bronze oxen add yet another layer to this supernatural puzzle. Gentile gods such as Osiris, Baal, and El were often described with bovine terminology in the ancient Near Eastern world.[292] *Eerdmans Dictionary of the Bible* states:

In Egypt the Apis bull, a personification of the Nile, was the sacred animal of Osiris. A bull with a sun disk and ankh between its horns, similar to bulls found in Egypt, has been discovered in Tyre. This could suggest Egyptian influence in the use of the bull in Syria-Palestine. The Bull of Heaven appears in Mesopotamian mythology as a vehicle for the gods' judgment. In Canaanite religious practice the bull was often used as a symbol for either Baal or El. In Hazor a pair of bulls has been found with feet on their backs, interpreted as a representation of Baal. Similar depictions exist of Adad, often seen as a Mesopotamian representation of Baal.[293]

The psalmist prophesied that the bulls of Bashan would surround the cross of Jesus in His final moments. Notice the bovine terminology in Psalm 22:12–13.[294]

> Many bulls have compassed me: Strong *bulls* of Bashan have beset me round. They gaped upon me with their mouths, As a ravening and a roaring lion. (Psalm 22:12–13, KJV 1900)

The point is that heavenly powers in ancient literature, including the Old Testament, were often linked to bovines (oxen, bulls, cows, calves, etc.).

Could God be laying blame and punishment on the bullish powers of the heavenly realm by decreeing that twelve oxen statues be tasked with bearing the Bronze Sea on their backs? Or, perhaps, since the sea contained still water, was it God's way of demonstrating He would subdue the chaotic deities in the unfolding of time? One can only speculate.

However, the Bible implicitly insists the bronze oxen were meant to denote other gods, such as the Canaanite god El.[295] In the reign of King Ahaz (743–727 BCE), the evil king of Judah removed the oxen and placed the Bronze Sea on a pavement of stones (2 Kings 16:37). Sadly, his motive was to not offend the pagan king of Assyria with the blatant iconography that slammed his bovine gods (2 Kings 16:17–18).

Still, there is more.

Another important detail the Bible gives of the Bronze Sea is that its rim was like that of a cup, "like a lily blossom." Shapira writes:

> The Hebrew word for lily (shushan)—means a lotus flower, and is a transliteration of the Egyptian term sšn (שושן Solomon's choice of lotuses as an ornamentation of the pillars and the Sea is indicative of Egyptian influence. The lotus held political and religious significance as one of the in-carnations of the sun god,

Khafre—who rises every morning from the primordial waters in Egypt.[296]

Could the lily-shaped rim on the Bronze Sea be an intentional jab against an Egyptian god who is thought to arise from the *primordial* sea? It's certainly possible. The lotus plant is mentioned in Job 40:20–21 where Behemoth is said to lie down under the lotus plants, which cover him with shade.[297] Behemoth is considered by many scholars a chaos creature, which we will soon note. Could the lilies on the Molten Sea echo back to primeval chaos monsters like Behemoth? Perhaps.

One thing is sure: Housing the Bronze Sea in Solomon's Temple is God's way of placing blame on Israel's supernatural enemies for causing chaos around the world. It's also God's way of demonstrating that He brings order amid chaos.

The biblical record notes that the Solomon's Bronze Sea was eventually broken and carried off by the Chaldeans to be used in the temples of Babylon (2 Kings 25:13, LEB), the geographical place-name of evil in the book of Revelation (14:8; 16:19; 17:5; 18:2, 10, 21). Undoubtedly, the Babylonians would have considered capturing Israel's artificial sea a *victory* for Marduk.

No More Sea: The Beginning Is the Ending

It should not be lost on the reader that the book of Revelation ends the way Genesis 1 began: God *conquers* chaos and the sea. In the new Creation, there will be no more sea:

> I saw a new heaven and a new earth, for the first heaven and the first earth have passed away, and *the sea is no more*. (Revelation 21:1, WEB)

Vanquishing the sea in Revelation speaks to the defeat of God's cosmic enemies, the cessation of their chaos, and the absence of evil.[298] This storybook ending will not be subverted by the Devil and his angels. They will not slay the Creator God like in the Babylonian epic of creation. Rather, they will "die like men" (Psalm 82). Their death will come at the eschaton, wherein they will be "brought up from the *sea*" and "cast into the *lake* of fire" (Revelation 21:13–14).

That Revelation contains echoes associated not only with Genesis but also the *Enuma Elish* is not surprising. The creation myth gave legitimacy to the rise of Babylon and Marduk, the patron deity of the city, and it's precisely that city that gets destroyed in the Apocalypse.[299] Though the *Enuma Elish* is millennia older than John's readers, the story has lived on through many ancient manuscripts, including Greek.[300]

We have already noted Isaiah 27:1. At second glance, it speaks of God punishing the twisting serpent Leviathan on the Day of Yahweh (the end of time):

> On that day, Yahweh will punish with his cruel, great and strong sword *Leviathan*, the fleeing serpent, and Leviathan, the twisting serpent, and he will kill *the sea monster that is in the sea*. (LEB)

That Yahweh will kill Leviathan, the twisting serpent of Canaanite religion, plays into John's point in Revelation 11–13; when Daniel's "great tribulation" is over (forty-two months), the sea dragon will die, and God's people will be delivered. This grand celebration happens at the divine banquet also known as the "marriage supper of the Lamb" (Isaiah 55:1–3; 62:8–9; 65:13, 17–18; Zechariah 9:11–12, 16–17).[301] The Jewish book of 2 Baruch has the most detailed description of this end-times supper; God's people will eat the flesh of Leviathan and Behemoth in celebration (2 Baruch 29–30). Note 2 Baruch 29:3-4, 6a:

And it will happen that when all that which should come to pass in these parts has been accomplished, the Messiah will begin to be revealed. And Behemoth will reveal itself from its place, and Leviathan will come from the sea, the two great monsters which I created on the fifth day of creation and which I shall have kept until that time. And they will be nourishment for all who are left. Those who have hungered will rejoice. (2 Baruch 29:3–4, 6a)

Behemoth

This thought is also echoed in 1 Enoch 60:7–9, 24:

On that day, *two monsters* will be parted—one monster, a female named Leviathan, in order to dwell in the abyss of the ocean over the fountains of water; and (the other), a male called Behemoth, which holds his chest in an invisible desert whose name is Dundayin…. And the angel of peace who was with me said to me, "These two monsters are prepared for the great day of the Lord (when) they shall turn into food. So that the punishment of the Lord of the Spirits should come down upon them in order that the punishment of the Lord of the Spirits should not be issued in vain.[302]

In his book, *Jesus and the Last Supper*, Brant Pitre notes the odd dish served on the Day of the Lord.

Fourth, and quite memorably, the righteous can also expect to feed on the flesh of Leviathan and Behemoth. It is not clear whether this image is hyperbolic and figurative or is intended as a literal description of the viands of the banquet. Either way, it seems to represent the triumph of the righteous over the destructive powers of this world.[303]

The two beasts of Jewish tradition, one by land and one by sea, are especially profound since Revelation 13 depicts exactly that (a sea beast and land beast). These two beasts are described in tandem in Job 40–41 as being incomparable to God's power, though evidence of His majesty. So, John's ancient audience would have viewed the beast of the sea as a symbol of cosmic chaos during the Great Tribulation, whose roots are not only founded in Scripture but also in Mesopotamian and Canaanite mythology.[304]

LOOKING AHEAD

Our study thus far has laid the groundwork for the eschatological fall of Babylon. In the next chapter, we will pull more of John's typological threads as we seek to witness Babylon the Great unravel before our eyes.

THE FALL OF BABYLON

Another, a second angel, followed, saying, "Babylon the great
has fallen, which has made all the nations to drink of the wine of
the wrath of her sexual immorality."

~REVELATION 14:8, WEB

IN A NUTSHELL

In this chapter, we will explore the passages in Revelation that contribute
to the prophetic fall of Babylon. Most of these passages seem slightly
ambiguous on the surface, but underneath lie clear Old Testament
threads John sews into the fabric of Revelation to describe the end of
the dark empire.

DIGGING DEEPER

The Two Witnesses and the Seed of Babylon (Revelation 11:1–12)

In chapter 2 of this book, we were introduced to the mighty angel of
Revelation 10. John's description reveals that this mighty messenger is
Jesus. As we discussed, Christ is the angel in the passage *functionally*, not
ontologically (in other words, He's still the Creator, not a created being).

Revelation 11 opens with this angel still presumably present, speaking with John, and a description of two mysterious witnesses who build the Kingdom of God, only to be slain by a beast. This unthinkable action triggers final judgment and cements Babylon's eternal doom.

A reed like a rod was given to me. Someone said, "Rise and measure God's temple, and the altar, and those who worship in it. Leave out the court which is outside of the temple, and don't measure it, for it has been given to the nations. They will tread the holy city under foot for forty-two months. I will give power to my two witnesses, and they will prophesy one thousand two hundred sixty days, clothed in sackcloth." These are the two olive trees and the two lamp stands, standing before the Lord of the earth. If anyone desires to harm them, fire proceeds out of their mouth and devours their enemies. If anyone desires to harm them, he must be killed in this way. These have the power to shut up the sky, that it may not rain during the days of their prophecy. They have power over the waters, to turn them into blood, and to strike the earth with every plague, as often as they desire. When they have finished their testimony, the beast that comes up out of the abyss will make war with them, and overcome them, and kill them. Their dead bodies will be in the street of the great city, which spiritually is called Sodom and Egypt, where also their Lord was crucified. From among the peoples, tribes, languages, and nations, people will look at their dead bodies for three and a half days, and will not allow their dead bodies to be laid in a tomb. Those who dwell on the earth will rejoice over them, and they will be glad. They will give gifts to one another, because these two prophets tormented those who dwell on the earth. After the three and a half days, the breath of life from God entered into them, and they stood on their feet. Great fear fell on those who saw them. I heard a loud voice from heaven saying to them, "Come up here!" They went up into heaven in a cloud, and their enemies saw them. (Revelation 11:1–12, WEB)

In an instant, John is told to measure the heavenly Temple. This command seems to be related to Ezekiel 40–48, in which an angel is depicted as measuring various features of the Temple as a picture of its future glory. It also conjures up the language of Zechariah 1. John's Temple talk is setting the groundwork for the work and growth of the Kingdom in the Church Age and the global presence of the Temple at the end of time.[305]

Even though the courtyard outside the Temple isn't really fit for pagans, it will be overrun by them, meaning God's opponents will, at least for a season, persecute God's elect.

It will seem like evil is winning.

That evil will tread/trample the holy city (sacred space) is an abomination and consistently fits into the biblical framework associated with the rise of the Antichrist(s). This passage taps into Daniel's famous prophecy of the Tribulation period wherein God's faithful will suffer prior to earth's end. This is evident by John citing certain time periods, such as forty-two months (1,260 days) to describe the duration of suffering (Daniel 7:25; 12:7, 11–12). Beale writes:

For Daniel, this [period of suffering] lay far off in the future, but for John it has begun, starting with the resurrection of Christ and continuing until His return (see on Rev. 1:1, 7).[306]

Forty-two is commonly associated with tribulation throughout the biblical narrative, particularly with Israel. Beale continues:

The reason for the exact number of "forty-two" here and in 13:5 is likely to recall the same time of Elijah's ministry of judgment

(Luke 4:25; Jas. 5:17; see on 11:6) and Israel's entire time of wilderness wandering after the Exodus, which encompassed a total of forty-two encampments (so Num. 33:5–49). This is reinforced by possibly reckoning forty-two years for the Israelites' total sojourn in the wilderness, since it appears they were in the wilderness for two years before incurring the penalty of remaining there for forty years until the death of the first generation.[307]

It makes sense for John's original readers to comprehend that their persecution is part of Daniel's vision and mirrors the suffering of OT Israel. During this symbolic forty-two-month/1,260-day period, the angel tells John, "his *two witnesses* will prophesy."

Just who are the two witnesses?

The identity of this pair of witnesses in Revelation 11 is steeped in Zechariah 3–4. However, before we dive deeper into the language of the two witnesses in Zechariah, we must understand the framework of that prophet's writing. Having been in Babylon, the Jews are set to return to the holy city of Jerusalem and *rebuild* God's Temple (the Second Temple). However, this endeavor will not happen without leaders. The book reveals that Joshua (the high priest) and Zerubbabel (the prince/king) will lead God's elect to restore the city's former glory. Restoring the glory of Jerusalem, the holy city, is at the heart of Revelation 11, though on a global scale. (Though space does not allow here, to appreciate what John sees and understands about the two witnesses and how this illuminates Revelation 11, read Zechariah 1:12–4:14 in its entirety). Zechariah 1:12–4:14 reveals that Zerubbabel, which means "the seed of Babylon," will restore Jerusalem.[308] That Zerubbabel, *a Babylonian Jew*, would leave Babylon the Great to restore Jerusalem, the great city of God, fits in nicely with John's Babylonian agenda. It's also prophetic that Joshua (Yeshua) will lead the spiritual restoration of the city.

Together, Joshua and Zerubbabel, the anointed leaders, are "the sons of fresh oil," "the "glorious ones," and "the two witnesses" of Yahweh.

The "oil" language may also denote their role in laying the foundation of the Second Temple:

Given the context of laying the foundation of the temple, it may be important that the ceremonial laying of the foundation often featured mortar mixed with oil rather than water. If this connection is valid, it would again identify Joshua and Zerubbabel as the ones carrying out the building project. Sennacherib claims that he sprinkled a foundation with oil as if it were river water.[309]

Zechariah's vision of the lampstand and olive trees encourages them:

…to trust not in financial or military resources but in the power of God's Spirit working through them. As is often the case in the Old Testament, God's Spirit is represented by the oil (see Isa. 61:1–3).[310]

Should we conclude that John sees Joshua and Zerubbabel in Revelation 11? Are they the two witnesses? It's doubtful. Most scholars assert that although the two witnesses in Revelation 11 are based on Zechariah 3–4, John's two witnesses denote the "faithful church" that labors to build the Kingdom in the face of opposition—like Joshua and Zerubbabel did in the OT. The two witnesses as the faithful church may be in the background of the two churches (lampstands) who escaped Christ's accusations earlier in the book. Beale writes:

Above all, only two of the seven churches in chs. 2–3 escaped Christ's accusations of unfaithfulness (Smyrna and Philadelphia). That these two churches as representative of the faithful church are in mind is apparent from the identification of the "prophetic witnesses" here as "lampstands." Thus there is pictured here the faithful remnant church who witnesses.[311]

It's significant that Jesus (the mighty Angel) "grants authority to the two witnesses." The New Testament records Jesus commissioning His disciples with shared authority to preach and teach in His name (Matthew 28:18–20). The *power* of the Church is demonstrated in what John says in Revelation 11:5–6:

> If anyone desires to harm them, fire proceeds out of their mouth and devours their enemies. If anyone desires to harm them, he must be killed in this way. These have the power to shut up the sky, that it may not rain during the days of their prophecy. They have power over the waters, to turn them into blood, and to strike the earth with every plague, as often as they desire. (WEB)

This description conjures up language that makes the reader think of another dyad—Moses and Elijah. Elijah withheld rain from the earth (1 Kings 17–18) and Moses turned water to blood (Exodus 7:17–25). These two were legal witnesses of Jesus' Transfiguration at Mount Hermon, the site that hatched Watchers. There, the Father announced Jesus as His Son (Mark 9:4–7).

What John reveals next is the harsh reality of witnessing in the heart of Babylon:

> When they have finished their testimony, the beast that comes up out of the abyss will make war with them, and overcome them, and kill them. Their dead bodies will be in the street of the great city, which spiritually is called Sodom and Egypt, where also their Lord was crucified. From among the peoples, tribes, languages, and nations, people will look at their dead bodies for three and a half days, and will not allow their dead bodies to be laid in a tomb. Those who dwell on the earth will rejoice over them, and they will be glad. They will give gifts to one another,

because these two prophets tormented those who dwell on the earth. (Revelation 11:7–10, WEB)

If John's vision stopped here, these witnesses would have no hope. But, when all hope is lost, they are resurrected and brought to Heaven (Revelation 11:11–12). That the witnesses will rise again (and that Babylon will not) is a subtle dig against Yahweh's supernatural rivals. The gods of Babel will have no resurrection.

The City of Tyre and the Fall of Babylon (Revelation 18:9–24)

Another word picture that describes the fall of Babylon is found in Revelation 18:9–24. Without explicitly naming the city, John conflates the ancient city of Tyre with Babylon and sees it as the prototype for its fall. Before we discuss why and investigate John's Tyrian template in Revelation 18:9–24, let's review the history of Tyre.

The prophet Isaiah declares that its foundations are from the days of old (Isaiah 23:7). Established around 3000 BC on the Phoenician coast, Tyre is often intertwined with the biblical narrative, especially during the reigns of David and Solomon. Israel and Tyre became allies shortly after David slew the Philistines, who were geographical enemies of the Tyrians (the people of Tyre). The city of Tyre was the main source for the building materials and laborers for David's palace and Solomon's Temple (2 Samuel 5:11; 1 Kings 5–7). They also collaborated in other business ventures in which Tyrian sailors were sent to help operate King Solomon's fleet of ships (1 Kings 9:26–27).[312]

Later, Jezebel, the daughter of Tyrian/Sidonian king, Ethbaal, resolidified the Judeo/Tyrian alliance by marrying King Ahab (1 Kings 16:31). Consequently, the longstanding partnership soon dissolved following Jehu's *coup d'état* and Jezebel's murder.[313] Decades later, the prophet Amos accused Tyre of "forgetting the covenant of brotherhood":

Thus says Yahweh: "For three transgressions of Tyre and for four I will not revoke the punishment, because they delivered up a whole community to Edom and they did not remember the covenant of brotherhood!" (Amos 1:9, LEB)

So, what does all of this have to do with Revelation 18?

John uses Ezekiel's prophecy (which predicted Tyre's destruction) to depict the fall of Babylon *typologically*. That is, John copies and pastes numerous elements from Ezekiel 26–27 into Revelation 18 to portray Babylon's pending defeat. Let's note a few of these shared elements:

Shared Concept	OT Tyre	NT Babylon
In Ezekiel, the princes/kings of the nations would mourn the fall of Tyre because of their economic loss. In Revelation, the kings of the earth would weep over the loss of their sensual lover.	*And all the princes of the nations of the sea* shall come down from their thrones, and shall take off their crowns from their heads, and shall take off their embroidered raiment: they shall be utterly amazed; they shall sit upon the ground, and fear their own destruction, and *shall groan over thee. And they shall take up a lamentation for thee,* and shall say to thee, How art thou destroyed from out of the sea, the renowned city,that brought her ter-	*And the kings of the earth will weep and mourn over her,* those who committed sexual immorality and lived sensually with her, when they see the smoke of her burning, standing far off because of the fear of her torment, saying, "Woe, woe, the great city, Babylon the powerful city, because in one hour your judgment has come!" (Revelation 18:9–10, LEB)

Shared Concept	OT Tyre	NT Babylon
	city,that brought her terror upon all her inhabitants. And the isles shall be alarmed at the day of thy fall." (Ezekiel 26:16–18, Brenton lxx En)	
Ezekiel lists the goods and services that Tyre traded to the many nations of the biblical landscape. Their "merchants" would miss these items when Tyre was destroyed. John mentions 15 out of the 29 items from Ezekiel 27 in Revelation 18. As was the trickle effect from the fall of Tyre, John notes that this list of traded items would cease when Babylon falls.	See Ezekiel 27:7–25 at length for complete list of goods.	And the merchants of the earth weep and mourn for her, since no one buys their cargo anymore, cargo of gold, silver, jewels, pearls, fine linen, purple cloth, silk, scarlet cloth, all kinds of scented wood, all kinds of articles of ivory, all kinds of articles of costly wood, bronze, iron and marble, cinnamon, spice, incense, myrrh, frankincense, wine, oil, fine flour, wheat, cattle and sheep, horses and chariots, and slaves, that is, human souls. "The fruit for which your soul longed has gone from you, and all your delicacies and your splendors are lost to you, never to be found again!" The merchants of these

Shared Concept	OT Tyre	NT Babylon
	Fine linen with embroidery from Egypt became your bed-spread to put glory around you, and *to cover you with blue and purple from the islands of Elishah, and they became your clothing.* (Ezekiel 27:7, LES)	in fear of her torment, weeping and mourning aloud, *"Alas, alas, for the great city that was clothed in fine linen, in purple* and scarlet, adorned with gold, with jewels, and with pearls!"* (Revelation 18:11–16, ESV)[314]

As Ezekiel prophesied that turncoat Tyre would fall by the power of Babylon, in Revelation, John prophesies that Babylon the betrayer will fall by the King in Heaven. Like Tyre, who "abandoned the covenant of brotherhood," the angels over the nations betrayed Yahweh's trust by leading their allotted people into spiritual darkness. Asaph prophesied that this act of rebellion would *not* go unpunished. These spirits' tranquil immortality and posture of pride will evaporate when they die like men (Psalm 82:6–7) in the Lake of Fire (Matthew 25:41).

Babylon and the Valley of Decision (Revelation 14:6–8)

In plain language, Revelation 14:6–8 depicts the judgment of Babylon as *falling* from power:

I saw an angel flying in mid heaven, having an eternal Good News to proclaim to those who dwell on the earth—to every nation, tribe, language, and people. He said with a loud voice, "Fear the Lord, and give him glory, for the hour of his judgment has come. Worship him who made the heaven, the earth, the sea, and the springs of waters!" Another, a second angel, followed, saying, "*Babylon the great has fallen*, which has made all the nations to drink of the wine of the wrath of her sexual immorality." (WEB)

Again, the evil John sees *falling* in Revelation 14 isn't just Rome; it's Babylon. As we discussed, Babylon = Babel. To ignore John's Babylonian framework in this passage would be catastrophic to seeing the long-anticipated reversal of the Babel event.

Like a war-torn soldier longing for peace, the angel flying in mid-Heaven is tasked with carrying this good news to *every* nation, tribe, language, and people over which the gods of Psalm 82 have long reigned. Babylon the Great will meet her *final* doom on the great Day of Yahweh. Undoubtedly, this would be a part of the good news the angel carries. This context seems to also carry an "already, but not yet" undertone. If so, as the light of the Gospel spreads toward the eschaton, the darkness diminishes and the gods of Babylon are cosmically crushed.

The "fallen" language surrounding Babylon in Revelation 14:8 is borrowed from Isaiah 21:9:

> "And look at this! A man's chariot is coming, a pair of horsemen!" Then he responded and said, "It has fallen! Babylon has fallen! And all the images of her gods are smashed on the ground!" (LEB)

The smashing of the "images of her gods" should be noticed. When Babylon falls, the message is this: so do her gods. John goes on to describe the *harvest* of all things Babylon in Revelation 14:14–20:

> I looked, and saw a white cloud, and on the cloud one sitting like a son of man, having on his head a golden crown, and in his hand a sharp sickle. Another angel came out of the temple, crying with a loud voice to him who sat on the cloud, "Send

your sickle and reap, for the hour to reap has come; for the harvest of the earth is ripe!" He who sat on the cloud thrust his sickle on the earth, and the earth was reaped. Another angel came out of the temple which is in heaven. He also had a sharp sickle. Another angel came out from the altar, he who has power over fire, and he called with a great voice to him who had the sharp sickle, saying, "Send your sharp sickle and gather the clusters of the vine of the earth, for the earth's grapes are fully ripe!" The angel thrust his sickle into the earth, and gathered the vintage of the earth and threw it into the great wine press of the wrath of God. The wine press was trodden outside of the city, and blood came out of the wine press, up to the bridles of the horses, as far as one thousand six hundred stadia. (WEB)

This section of Scripture is based on Joel 3:11–14, which prophesies God's punishment of evil nations (which would include their angelic hosts) in the Valley of Jehoshaphat:

Hurry and come, all the nations, from all around, and gather yourselves there. Bring down your mighty warriors, O Yahweh! Let the nations be roused and let them come up to the valley of Jehoshaphat, for there I will sit to judge all the nations from all around. Send forth the sickle, for the harvest is ripe! Go tread, for the winepress is full! The vats overflow, because their evil is great! Commotion, commotion in the valley of decision! For the day of Yahweh is near in the valley of decision!" (LEB)

"Jehoshaphat" means "Yahweh will judge."[315] Since John constructs this section of Scripture from Joel 3:11–14, the Valley of Jehoshaphat should be viewed as the *location of judgment* in Revelation 14. The *actual* location of this valley is debated. Options include the following:

- The Valley of Beracah (2 Chronicles 20:26), where King Jehoshaphat won a tremendous victory
- The King's Valley (2 Samuel 18:18), where Absalom built a monument
- The Tyropoeon Valley, which runs north-south through Jerusalem
- The Kidron Valley

The *Anchor Yale Bible Dictionary* notes the Kidron Valley is the most popular location among many groups, and that it has been viewed by Christians, Muslims, and Jews as the location of final judgment.[316]

Interestingly, Zechariah 14:4–5 talks of a supernaturally widened valley at *the same site* where the Lord left the earth—the Mount of Olives. Though space doesn't allow us to explore that subject further here, to get the *full flavor* of the OT prophecies that John is tapping into in Revelation 14, I recommend reading Joel 3 and Zechariah 14 before moving forward in our study.

Harvesting the nations with their gods is consistent with Isaiah 24:21–23, in which the prophet Isaiah sees the hosts of Heaven and the kings of the earth punished together as prisoners at the end of time:

And this shall happen on that day: Yahweh will punish the *host of heaven in heaven*, and *the kings of the earth on the earth*. And they will be gathered in a gathering, like a prisoner in a pit. And they will be shut in a prison and be punished after many days. And the full moon will be ashamed and the sun will be ashamed, for Yahweh of hosts will rule on Mount Zion and in Jerusalem, and before his elders in glory. (Isaiah 24:21–23, LEB; emphasis added)

No matter the precise location of the valley of decision, the point is that every wicked nation and its god(s) will be gathered together and punished in a pit of destruction.

The Seven Trumpets and Walls of Babylon
(Revelation 8 and following)

Revelation 8 discusses the seventh seal and introduces the seven trumpet judgments of the Apocalypse. This fascinating chapter screams "typology." Like the city of Tyre in Revelation 18:9–24, in Revelation 8 and following, John sees Jericho as a *prophetic type* of the fall of the "great city" of Babylon. Thus far, the seals have contained terrifying images of Babylonian demons and the dissolution of the cosmos. Strangely, seal seven contains none of these things, only "silence":

> When he opened the seventh seal, there was silence in heaven
> for about half an hour. (Revelation 8:1, WEB)

While silence seems odd to the ears of the modern reader, its meaning is anchored in the OT. The Minor Prophets associate silence with *divine judgment*. Beale writes:

> The OT associates silence with divine judgment. In Hab. 2:20–
> 3:15 and Zech. 2:13–3:2, God is pictured (as in Rev. 8:1) as
> being in His temple and about to bring judgment on the earth.
> That the temple is in heaven is to be assumed from texts such as
> Ezekiel 1. At the moment this judgment is to be delivered, God
> commands the earth to be silent. In Zeph. 1:7–18, silence is
> likewise commanded in connection with the "great day" of the
> Lord and of His judgment (Zeph. 1:14, 18 forming part of the
> OT background to the phrase "the great day of their wrath" in
> Rev. 6:17). These announcements of judgment from the Minor
> Prophets express cosmic end-time expectations (as implied by
> the pregnant word "all"), which is explicitly expressed in a uni-
> versal sense in Rev. 8:1. The thought is that this final judgment

of God is so awful that the whole world falls utterly silent in its presence. Thus the seventh seal is a continuation of the sixth.[317]

Reading "silence" as "punitive judgment" against God's adversaries illuminates John's intended meaning and dispels the mystery of the seventh seal. However, the language of the Minor Prophets is *secondary* in John's mind. The silence of eschatological judgment is retooled from two OT scenes: the Exodus and the Battle of Jericho, two key victories *God performed* for His people. First, note Exodus 14:12–14:

> Was this not the thing that we spoke to you in Egypt, saying, "Leave us alone so that we may serve the Egyptians. For it is better for us to be slaves to the Egyptians than to die in this wilderness." Now Moses said to the people, "Be courageous, stand firm! And observe the salvation that is from God, which he will perform for you today. For in the manner which you behold the Egyptians today, you will not continue any longer to see them forever. The Lord will do battle for you. *You keep silent!*" (LES)

Here, silence is associated with Egypt's defeat and Israel's redemption at the Red Sea.[318] So, silence in 8:1 is both a *precursor* to Christ's victory and a suitable *synonym* for the collapse of spiritual "Egypt" (Babylon) in Revelation.

As stated, John also borrows from Joshua 6, the account of the Battle of Jericho:

> But Joshua commanded the people, saying, "*You will not shout*, and you will *not let your voice be heard*; a word will *not go out from your mouth* until the day I say to you 'Shout!' Then you will shout." And at the seventh time the priests blew on the

trumpets, and Joshua said to the people, "Shout! For Yahweh has given you the city." (Joshua 6:10, 16, LEB; emphasis added)

Like the Exodus, the Battle of Jericho *typifies* the eschatological battle described in Revelation. Therefore, silence in Revelation 8:1 ensures the reader that *God is going to win the battle for His people*. However, there are more intertextual links between our passage and these OT accounts. Next, John writes:

I saw the seven angels who stand before God, and seven trumpets were given to them. Another angel came and stood over the altar, having a golden censer. Much incense was given to him, that he should add it to the prayers of all the saints on the golden altar which was before the throne. The smoke of the incense, with the prayers of the saints, went up before God out of the angel's hand. The angel took the censer, and he filled it with the fire of the altar, then threw it on the earth. Thunders, sounds, lightnings, and an earthquake followed. (Revelation 8:2–5, WEB)

The seven angels are undoubtedly the same group of seven angels in Revelation 1:20.[319] However, a *lone angel* is singled out as not being a part of the group of seven. This angelic figure has the golden censer so that he can offer the prayers of all the saints on the altar before the throne of God. The angel appears to be serving in the capacity of a high priest who hears the prayers of his people and answers them with a devastating judgment against the adversary.[320] Therefore, many scholars believe this angel represents Christ.[321]

Just before the commencement of the Battle of Jericho, Joshua is also confronted by a *lone angelic figure*, the commander of Yahweh's army. Scripture reveals this supernatural being to be God Himself (Joshua 5:13–15). In Revelation 8, John sees this same angel preparing his people for a spiritual battle at the eschatological Jericho. Interestingly, the *priestly activity* of John's angel also seems to mirror the language of Joshua 5, where it discusses ritual consecration, circumcision, and the Passover (Joshua 5:1–12) *prior* to the battle cry of the trumpets.[322] John embeds the motif of these markers into the activity of the priestly angel (Jesus), who prepares God's people for *spiritual* readiness in battle.

Next, John writes:

The seven angels who had the seven trumpets prepared themselves to sound. The first sounded, and there followed hail and fire, mixed with blood, and they were thrown to the earth. One third of the earth was burned up, and one third of the trees were burned up, and all green grass was burned up. The second angel sounded, and something like a great burning mountain was thrown into the sea. One third of the sea became blood, and one third of the living creatures which were in the sea died. One third of the ships were destroyed. The third angel sounded, and a great star fell from the sky, burning like a torch, and it fell on one third of the rivers, and on the springs of water. The name of the star is "Wormwood." One third of the waters became wormwood. Many people died from the waters, because they were made bitter. The fourth angel sounded, and one third of the sun was struck, and one third of the moon, and one third of the stars, so that one third of them would be darkened; and the day wouldn't shine for one third of it, and the night in the same way. (Revelation 8:6–12, WEB)

In *Decoding Revelation's Trumpets*, author Jon Paulien explains:

In a subtle manner the author of Revelation combines the plagues on Egypt with Joshua's attack on Jericho. As at Jericho, the trumpets precede the fall of a great city (cf. Rev 11 and 18) and the entrance of God's people into the promised land (cf.

Rev 21 and 22). As with the seven bowls, the trumpets are also part of what Strand calls the "Exodus from Egypt/Fall of Babylon" motif. While most of the plagues are based directly on the Exodus motif, we really have a blending of the Exodus with the Exile.[323]

Beale agrees, and fleshes out the typological layers the Apostle John sets forth:

Undoubtedly, the main OT passage in view here is the story of the fall of Jericho in Joshua 6, where trumpets announced the impending victory of a holy war. Seven trumpets were blown by seven priests, and here the trumpets are blown by seven angels who are priestly figures (see 15:6). The ark was present at Jericho (Josh. 6:11–13) and, in its heavenly form, is also present in the heavenly temple (Rev. 11:19). Interestingly, at the Jericho episode (Josh. 6:10–20), there was verbal silence directly linked to a climactic trumpet judgment, which is a pattern found in Revelation 8. The trumpets blown at Jericho by the priests, like the plagues on Egypt, are not warnings at all, but only indicate judgment. This shows further that the trumpets in Revelation primarily connote the idea of judgment rather than warnings designed to induce repentance.[324]

That John sees Jericho as a *prophetic type* of the fall of the "great city" of Babylon is further evidenced by the seventh trumpet.

At Jericho, likewise, the first six trumpets precede, but are a necessary preparation for the climactic judgment of the seventh. Likewise, the first six trumpets of Revelation are necessary primary woes leading up to the decisive judgment of the seventh trumpet at the end of history (see on 11:15–19), when the "great city" (11:8), of which Jericho is a prophetic type, will be decisively destroyed (see on 11:13).[325]

Reading Revelation 8 through the lens of the OT prophets also helps one identify that the first five trumpets are patterned after five plagues of the Exodus.

The first trumpet (hail, fire, and blood) corresponds to the plague of hail and fire (Exod. 9:22–25); the second and third (poisoning of the sea and waters) to the plague on the Nile (Exod. 7:20–25); the fourth (darkness) to the plague of darkness (Exod. 10:21–23); and the fifth (locusts) to the plague of locusts (Exod. 10:12–15). As with the Egyptian plagues, the plagues punish hardness of heart, idolatry (since each plague had a judgment suited to a particular Egyptian god), and persecution of God's people.[326]

Trailing back through these verses again allows several other things to jump off the page, the first of which is John's usage of the phrase "a third" to describe things that partially burn up or are affected by the trumpets. Again, John writes:

And the first blew the trumpet, and there was hail and fire mixed with blood, and it was thrown to the earth, and *a third of the earth* was burned up, and *a third of the trees* were burned up, and all the green grass was burned up. And the second angel blew the trumpet, and something like a great mountain burning with fire was thrown into the sea, and *a third of the sea* became blood, and *a third of the creatures* in the sea—the ones which had life—died, and *a third of the ships* were destroyed. And the third angel blew the trumpet, and a great star burning like a torch fell from heaven, and it fell on *a third of the rivers* and on the springs of water. And the name of the star was called Wormwood, and *a third of the waters* became wormwood, and many people died from the waters because they were made bitter. And the fourth angel blew the trumpet, and *a third of the sun* was struck, and a third of the moon, and *a third of the stars*, so that a third of them were darkened, and the day did not shine with respect to a third of it, and the night likewise. (Revelation 8:7–12, LEB; emphasis added)

These "thirds" are retooled from Ezekiel 5:

A third you must burn with fire in the midst of the city at the completion of the days of the siege, and *you must take a third*, and you must strike it with the sword around it, and *a third you must scatter to the wind*, and I will draw a sword behind them.… *A third of you will die* because of the plague, and because of the famine they will perish in the midst of you, and *a third will fall* through the sword around you, and *a third I will scatter* to every direction of the wind, and I will draw the sword behind them. (Ezekiel 5:2, 12, LEB; emphasis added)

Here, the Israelites are "weighed on scales" and divided up and punished in *thirds*. One-third is burned with fire, struck by the sword, and scattered into captivity.[327] In Revelation, the shoe is on the other foot; the wicked nations run by Babel's angels are divided into thirds and judged. This engine of chaos is the "great burning mountain" that sinks like an irretrievable rock in Revelation 8:8:

And the second angel blew the trumpet, and something like a great mountain burning with fire was thrown into the sea, and a third of the sea became blood. (Revelation 8:8, LEB)

Identifying Babylon as the "great burning mountain" becomes apparent when considering Revelation 18 and Jeremiah 51:

"Rejoice over her, heaven and the saints and the apostles and the prophets, because God has pronounced your judgment on her!" And one powerful angel picked up a stone like a great millstone and threw it into the sea, saying, "In this way Babylon the great city will be thrown down with violence, and will never be found again!" (Revelation 18:20–21, LEB)

"And I will repay Babylon, and all the inhabitants of Chaldea, all their wickedness that they have done in Zion before your eyes," declares Yahweh. "Look, I am against you, *O mountain of the destruction*," declares Yahweh, "the one that destroys the whole earth. And I will stretch out my hand against you, and I will roll you down from the cliffs, and *I will make you as a mountain burned away…. The sea has risen over Babylon*, she has been covered by the roar of its waves…. And then when you finish reading aloud this scroll, you must tie *a stone* on it, and you must *throw it into the middle of the Euphrates*. And you must say, '*Thus shall Babylon sink, and she will not rise*, because of the face of the disasters that I am bringing on her, and they will grow weary.'" Thus far the words of Jeremiah. (Jeremiah 51:24–25, 63–64, LEB; emphasis added)

Tossing "Babylon" as a rock into chaotic waters in Revelation 8 is a prophetic callback to Jeremiah's doomsday prophecy of the baleful nation in Jeremiah 51.[328]

In Revelation 7, John introduces his readers to the reality of the *Messianic army*. Transitioning now from the formation of an army to various targeted strikes in Revelation 8 is logical. Beale explains:

In light of the Jericho background, it is suitable that the trumpet judgments are placed immediately after ch. 7, where God's people have been portrayed as a fighting army (7:3–8), which conducts victorious holy war ironically by remaining faithful despite earthly suffering (e.g., 7:14). The trumpet inflictions coming on the heels of ch. 7 should be seen as another of the ways the saints carry on holy war: they pray that God's judicial decree will be carried out against their persecutors. The saints wage ironic warfare by means of sacrificial suffering, which makes their prayer of vindication acceptable to God.[329]

As the trumpets of war once sounded at the walls of Jericho, the seven trumpets of Revelation crumble Babylon's defensive walls. Without them, defeat is imminent.

Most interestingly, in *The Epic of Gilgamesh*, the southern Babylonian city of Uruk had *seven* walls. Uruk means "the walled or fortified city" and is considered by some as the capital of a kingdom contemporaneous with the earliest period of Babylonian history.[330] It's believed that its seven walls had a *cosmic* significance, imitating the seven concentric zones into which Babylonians perceived the world was divided.[331] Is it possible that John knew all of this and recycled the seven trumpets of Jericho to tear down the impenetrable, seven-walled city of Babylon? It's certainly feasible.

The Seven Angels of Balance

It is no secret the number seven is fundamental throughout Revelation. I argue that the seven angels who destroy Babylon with the seven trumpets are incredibly polemic to John's ancient audience. To understand why, we need to rabbit-trail through Second-Temple Judaism and ancient Mesopotamia.

Second Temple Judaism carved out seven angels who sinned *and* seven angels who didn't. The seven angels who sinned are from the days of Jared and are *primarily* responsible for the decay of morality *before* the Flood. They are named in 1 Enoch 8:1–4 and assigned a specific area of guilt. For example, Azael taught people to make weapons; Semiaza taught enchantments; Armaros taught spells of healing; Rhakiel taught astrology; Chochiel taught the science of symptoms; Sathiel advised man in the watching of the stars; and Seriel is specifically said to have taught the course of the moon.

It is believed the Jewish writer of 1 Enoch 6–11 was reorienting the Mesopotamian backdrop of the *apkallu* to fit a Genesis 6 world-view. As we discussed, *the Babylonian literature was well known among Jews and Christians, especially those in the Babylonian diaspora.*[332] Every aspect surrounding the Watchers of 1 Enoch is prefigured in the Meso-potamian context. The writer of Enoch sought to target the deeply held beliefs of Mesopotamia and reorient them as being harmful, not helpful, to humanity, as Genesis 6:1–4 depicts.[333] So, the seven Watchers of 1 Enoch are based on the seven *apkallu* gods who revealed divine wisdom and secrets to man. Their names are listed in Mesopotamian texts as follows:

- [In the tim]e of Ayalu the king, **U'an was apkallu.**
- [In the tim]e of Alalgar the king, **U'anduga was apkallu.**
- [In the time of] Ammelu'anna the king, **Enmeduga was apkallu.**
- [In the time of] Ammegalanna the king, **Enmegalamma was apkallu.**
- [In the time of] Enme' ušumgalanna the king, **Enmebulugga was apkallu.**
- [In the time of] Enmeduranki the king, **Utu'abzu was apkallu.**
- [After the flood(?)], in the reign of Enmerkar, **Nungalpiriggal was apkallu.**[334] (Emphasis added)

Interestingly enough, in all the ancient literature (Jewish, Christian, Grecian, Babylonian, etc.), these spirits were locked away in an underworld prison. The *apkallu* were locked in the *absu/abzu* in Sumerian texts, and the angels who sinned were locked under gloomy chains of darkness in Tartarus/the Abyss in the NT (2 Peter 2:4–5; Jude 1:6). The NT's confirmation of this event per 1 Enoch means the Mesopotamian stories aren't fictional; the seven *apkallu* really came to earth as ancient *alien* gods and were punished for their misdeeds.

But how does this relate to the seven priestly angels of Revelation?

In both Second Temple Judaism and the book of Revelation, the seven fallen angels/*apkallu* who left their dwelling are balanced by the seven angels who tend to God's Temple. This cosmic balance is present in 1 Enoch 20:1–8, where the seven archangels are listed. Uriel is said to be over the world and Tartarus. Raphael is said to be over the spirits of men. Raguel takes vengeance on the world of the luminaries. Michael is set over the best part of mankind and over chaos. Saraqâêl is set over the spirits who sin in the spirit. Gabriel is set over Paradise, the serpents, and the cherubim. Remiel is specifically said to set over those who rise.[335]

That seven *loyal* angels will destroy Babylon in the passage is fitting; it was the seven *rebellious* angels in 1 Enoch and the seven *apkallu* gods of Mesopotamia who spearheaded the transgression against Yahweh and accelerated wickedness on earth. John sees the cosmic damage of these seven spirits reversed by the seven angels who faithfully pour out God's wrath on Babylon the Great. This eschatological action will pave the way for the return of Eden, a cosmic place of purity filled with God's presence and His loyal agents.

LOOKING AHEAD

This chapter has explored Revelation's hidden images surrounding the eschatological fall of Babylon. Our final chapter will explore how the Messiah defeats Babylon's patron god Marduk and strips the Babylonian deity of his title as "king of the gods."

11

THE MESSIAH OVER MARDUK

I saw a new heaven and a new earth, for the first heaven and the first earth have passed away, and the sea is no more…. He who sits on the throne said, "Behold, I am making all things new." He said, "Write, for these words of God are faithful and true."

~REVELATION 21:1, 5, WEB

IN A NUTSHELL

This chapter covers Revelation 15:1–4, which depicts a *new exodus* for God's covenant people. After *conquering* the beast in "victory through sacrifice," the Lamb's followers cross over into eternity and sing a celebratory song akin to the songs of Moses (Exodus 15; Deuteronomy 32). This song is a clear callback to the Old Testament, which carries the notion of defeat for the nations and their gods. We will also discuss how the promise of *re-creation* after Babylon falls (Revelation 21:1–5) is the final blow for Marduk, "king of the gods."

DIGGING DEEPER

The Song of Moses and Victory Over the Gods

In Revelation 15:1, John writes:

> I saw another great and marvelous sign in the sky: seven angels
> having the seven last plagues, for in them God's wrath is fin-
> ished. (WEB)

These "last plagues" signal that John's vision is drawing closer to an end. You may recall the former judgments in the book: the seven seals and the seven trumpets. The plagues poured out from the seven bowls in Revelation 15–16 are the final round of shots fired at those aligned with the beast. This, of course, sets up John's readers for the conclusion and outcome of such judgments against evil—*victory* for God's elect. John then writes:

> I saw something like a sea of glass mixed with fire, and those
> who overcame the beast, his image, and the number of his
> name, standing on the sea of glass, having harps of God. They
> sang the song of Moses, the servant of God, and the song of the
> Lamb, saying, "Great and marvelous are your works, Lord God,
> the Almighty! Righteous and true are your ways, you King of the
> nations. Who wouldn't fear you, Lord, and glorify your name?
> For you only are holy. For all the nations will come and worship
> before you. For your righteous acts have been revealed." (Revela-
> tion 15:2–4, WEB)

The song of Moses and the Lamb here is *thematically* based upon the two songs of Moses in the OT (Exodus 15:1–21 and Deuteronomy 32).[336] *Structurally*, it also includes a conglomerate of multiple OT passages that link to and elaborate upon the two lyrical poems of Moses (see Psalms 86:9–10; 105; Isaiah 12; Jeremiah 10:7).

Let's discuss the songs of Moses.

The "Song of the Sea," as it's often called, was Moses' first song. Israel sang this after passing safely through the Red Sea (Exodus 15). The song emphasizes Yahweh's *superiority* and *salvation*. For example, it begins by stating that Egypt's chariots of war are no match for Yah, the man of war (Exodus 15:1–10). Next, Moses sings of God's power over the sea, a theological notion of "order out of chaos" in the ancient world (Exodus 15:8–10). Furthermore, Moses asks, "Who is like Yahweh among the gods?" (Exodus 15:11). This question is answered in Exodus 15:11–18, where Moses cites Yahweh's incomparable holiness, actions, love, and kingship. The song ends by elucidating the two outcomes of Israel and Egypt: Israel was saved and Egypt was slain.

The intended point for John's readers is that *Yahweh is superior to the gods of the nations and the system of chaos.* Thus, His people will be eternally saved from sin and the powers of darkness.

That John sees Israel's victory in Exodus 15 as *analogous* to Christ's end-times followers is a beautiful picture of hope for these martyrs. As they pass through the valley of the shadow of death (their Red Sea), they will not fear evil. Their passage from martyrdom to Heaven means their eternal peace is certain; they now stand in the presence of God by the calm, crystal sea, over which God and the Lamb are enthroned.[337] For these martyrs, the new exodus, or the *final* exodus, is now complete.

At the end of Moses' life, he sang another song commonly referred to as the "Song of Moses" (Deuteronomy 31:19–32:44). It, too, emphasizes Yahweh's *superiority* over the nation's gods and the *salvation* enjoyed by His people. At Babel, God gave the people what they wanted—other gods to follow (Deuteronomy 32:8). Israel tended to whore after these deities with sacrifices and drink offerings (Deuteronomy 32:17, 38). Moses sings of *God's judgment* that falls on all who follow other gods, including wayward Israel, whom He made His portion (Deuteronomy

32:9), the apple of His eye (Deuteronomy 32:10), and a nation where *no* foreign god was to be found (Deuteronomy 32:12).

The song of Deuteronomy 32 ends with Yahweh "sharpening His sword" and "taking hold of it in judgment," "for the blood of His servant He will avenge" (Deuteronomy 32:41–43). This narrative is precisely the surrounding context of Revelation 15:1–4. Sandwiched between the swinging sickles (Revelation 14) and the bowls of judgment (Revelation 15–16) is our passage that describes eternal victory.

So, the lyrics in Exodus 15 and Deuteronomy 32 speak to God's *superiority* over the gods and the *salvation* from evil entities He offers. The meaning behind John's citation of the Song of Moses in Revelation 15:1–4 is quite apparent.

Who among the gods is like Yahweh?

As the Egyptians drowned in the torrential waters, the nations in bed with the Beast won't escape. The wrath of God is coming for them (and their gods), like the punishing walls of the Red Sea.

Re-creation and the Impeachment of Marduk

The early chapters of Genesis reveal that God's original plan was to live in Eden with man. This much is clear. However, God's ideal home was destroyed by sin. Therefore, "Project Eden" was *seemingly* dismantled through the Serpent's dark deception. The Genesis 3 disaster spurs some rather important questions:

- Was the Garden of Eden God's ideal home?
- If sin never entered the world, how long would God have lived with man in Eden?
- Does God's original project still matter to Him?
- If God went to the creative "trouble" to launch physical Eden, why would He abandon it for something totally different?

- If God was forced to simply "move on" to a plan "B," does this mean God was unable to remedy His ideal home?

These questions are powerful.

John's readers are reintroduced to God's ideal home in the book of Revelation. In Revelation 2:7, conquerors in Christ are promised access to Eden's tree of life.

> He who has an ear, let him hear what the Spirit says to the assemblies. To him who overcomes I will give to eat from the tree of life, which is in the Paradise of my God. (WEB)

The word "paradise" (Greek: παράδεισος, *paradeisos*) is used in the Septuagint for "garden" as in "the Garden of Eden" (Genesis 2:8, 15, etc.). The Fall of man resulted in his being kicked out of the Garden, away from God's holy presence. The promise is that those who are faithful unto death (Revelation 2:10) will *once again* be in the Garden of Eden (Paradise) with their loving Creator, and they will eat of the tree of life.

According to Revelation 21:1–8, the Edenic utopia God originally envisioned returns on a global scale in the *new creation*.

> I saw a new heaven and a new earth, for the first heaven and the first earth have passed away, and the sea is no more. I saw the holy city, New Jerusalem, coming down out of heaven from God, prepared like a bride adorned for her husband. I heard a loud voice out of heaven saying, "Behold, God's dwelling is with people; and he will dwell with them, and they will be his people, and God himself will be with them as their God. He will wipe away every tear from their eyes. Death will be no more; neither will there be mourning, nor crying, nor pain any more. The

first things have passed away." He who sits on the throne said, "Behold, I am making all things new." He said, "Write, for these words of God are faithful and true." He said to me, "I am the Alpha and the Omega, the Beginning and the End. I will give freely to him who is thirsty from the spring of the water of life. He who overcomes, I will give him these things. I will be his God, and he will be my son. But for the cowardly, unbelieving, sinners, abominable, murderers, sexually immoral, sorcerers, idolaters, and all liars, their part is in the lake that burns with fire and sulfur, which is the second death." (WEB)

While our aim is not to referee the *literal vs. figurative* matchup or be exhaustive on the subject, we must recognize that an eschatological *re-creation* is in fact a major part of how the Bible ends. Not only does Revelation 21:1–8 conjure up images of Adam and Eve in the Garden of Eden, the language John employs is recycled material from the book of Isaiah 65–66.

Revelation 21:1–5, LEB	Isaiah 65:16–18, LEB	Isaiah 66:22, LES
And I saw a new heaven and a new earth, for the first heaven and the first earth had passed away, and the sea did not exist any longer. And I saw the holy city, new Jerusalem, coming down out of heaven from God, prepared like a bride adorned for her husband. And I heard a loud voice from	Whoever blesses himself in the land shall bless himself by the God of trustworthiness, and the one who swears an oath in the land shall swear by the God of trustworthi-ness, because *the former troubles are forgotten, and they are hidden from my eyes. For look! I am about to create new heav-*	

Revelation 21:1–5, LEB	Isaiah 65:16–18, LEB	Isaiah 66:22, LES
the throne saying, "Behold, the dwelling of God is with humanity, and he will take up residence with them, and they will be his people and God himself will be with them. And he will wipe away every tear from their eyes, and death will not exist any longer, and mourning or wailing or pain will not exist any longer. The former things have passed away." And the one seated on the throne said, "Behold, I am making all things new!" And he said, "Write, because these words are faithful and true."	*ens and a new earth, and the former things shall not be remembered, and they shall not come to mind. But rejoice and shout in exultation forever and ever over what I am about to create! For look! I am about to create Jerusalem as a source of rejoicing, and her people as a source of joy."*	"For just as the *new heaven and the new earth, which I am making*, remain before me," said the Lord, "so your seed and your name will be established."

Isaiah's prophecy caused many Jews in the Second Temple period to write about a future *remaking* of the cosmos. Jubilees 1:29:

And the angel of the presence, who went before the camp of Israel, took the tablets of the division of years from the time of the creation of the law and testimony according to their weeks (of years), according to the jubilees, year by year throughout the full number of jubilees, from [the day of Creation until] the day of the new creation when the heaven and earth and all of their creatures shall be renewed according to the powers of heaven and according to the whole nature of earth, until the sanctuary of the Lord is created in Jerusalem upon Mount Zion. And all of the lights will be renewed for healing and peace and blessing for all of the elect of Israel and in order that it might be thus from that day and unto all the days of the earth.[338]

Jubilees 4:26:

For the Lord has four (sacred) places upon the earth: the garden of Eden and the mountain of the East and this mountain which you are upon today, Mount Sinai, and Mount Zion, which will be sanctified in the new creation for the sanctification of the earth. On account of this the earth will be sanctified from all sin and from pollution throughout eternal generations.[339]

This Jewish expectation naturally makes its way into NT thought. Paul discusses it in Romans 8:18–23, where he corresponds the eschatological remaking of our dying bodies to the renovation of a groaning creation. While NT writers clearly leaned heavily on the OT when discussing the New Heavens, New Earth, and New Creation motif, Revelation 21:1–8 also takes a shot at Babylon and the supreme god Marduk. This has been overlooked.

Throughout our study of Revelation, we've continually discussed Marduk, the chief god in the Babylonian pantheon. As we learned, the city over which he presided was Babylon, that great cosmic enemy of God in Revelation. That Marduk lies in the background during John's vision should then be unsurprising. In chapter 6, we discovered Marduk is the demonic rider on the white horse in Revelation 6:1–2. In chapter 7 of our study, we discussed the Babylonian exorcistic incantation *Marduk-Ea* and how it influenced the content and literary flow of 1 Enoch. As we said, this matters because John alludes to 1 Enoch throughout the book as he takes aim at Babylon. In chapter 8, we discussed the Babylonian creation epic *Enuma Elish,* which framed Marduk as the liberator of the gods and the slayer of the cosmic sea serpent *Tiamat.* As the oldest *Chaoskampf* literature, the beasts of Revelation *ultimately* derive from Babylonian mythology. Through a biblical worldview, the gods of Babylon function as *Tiamat;* they're all chaotic beasts.

Now, as John concludes the book of Revelation in Revelation 21:1–8, he frames the Messiah as a "better Marduk." According to Babylonian mythology, Marduk's kingship was cemented by defeating the sea and *re-creating* the stars and cosmos. This is precisely how John frames Jesus in Revelation. Like Marduk, the Messiah will destroy the sea, displace the stars, and dismantle the cosmos. Like Marduk, the Messiah's *re-creation* will underscore His eternal kingship and bring Him glory.

But don't miss this point: The New Heavens and New Earth ultimately delegitimize Marduk's ancient claims and dismantle the foundation of Babylonian ideologies.

When Christ literally changes the cosmos on the Day of Yahweh, by the words of His power, the entire Babylonian pantheon will be forced to impeach their dark king and bow before the real master, the Messiah of Heaven and earth. For the gods of Babel, those angelic sons of the Most High who rebelled long ago, loyalty will be too late; they will die like men (Psalm 82:6–7).

LOOKING AHEAD

Indeed, the story of good versus evil is enamoring. However, this *story* has no spectators. Everyone chooses a side. The book of Revelation was written to make believers' choice simple: stay loyal and stay faithful. While I pray that the content of this book has made Revelation plain and has illuminated how the supernatural war of the Bible ends, I leave you with this exhortation: Though Babylon grows stronger each passing day, with the ferocity of a Judaic lion, the Messiah is coming, and He is coming to claim His own. Look to Jesus. Stay ready. Be mindful of temptation.

You are at war!

Many people love to discuss eschatology, but most ignore their battle in the present. Think of every temptation you face as an act of war. Who exactly are we fighting? Our fight is against fallen angels, against cosmic entities and dark demons. As Paul put it in Ephesians 6:12, we're warring "against rulers [*archē*], against the authorities [*exousia*], against the world rulers [*kosmokratōr*] of this darkness, against the spiritual forces [*pneumatikos*] of wickedness in the heavenly places." The powers of darkness to which Paul referred are the real enemy. Understand, they are well-organized and highly-trained assassins in the discipline of spiritual warfare. They've had thousands of years to perfect their craft and have slain countless souls. In light of this, here's a question: How, then, do modern humans, particularly laymen, stand a chance against them?

Studying Jesus' forty-day temptation teaches us a lot about the satanic profile. We learn the pattern of temptation is brought to fulfillment by three stages: suggestion, delight, consent. And we, in facing temptation, generally fall through delight, and then through consent.

Satan had hoped he could lead Jesus through these stages to consent, but he left disappointed. Jesus' wilderness temptation shows us Satan can be defeated; we don't have to consent to our desires and Satan's allurements. This scene also exposes Satan's strategy to weaken our assurance in our identity as children of God. Some forty days after Jesus heard His Father say at His baptism, "This is my beloved Son, with whom I am well pleased" (Matthew 3:17), Satan tried to get Jesus to doubt His sonship. He tried to put a wedge between Christ and the Father with the snarky comment, "If you are the Son of God…" (Luke 4:3). The inclusion of this small detail is huge. Doubt is one of many wedges Satan tries to sandwich himself between us and our Heavenly Father. Hell's armory of weapons is most impressive. If we charge into battle defenseless, our carcasses will likely rot in the desert of temptation. We must suit up for battle!

Paul concludes his letter to the church at Ephesus by admonishing them to be strong in the Lord by putting on the armor of God (Ephesians 6:10–18). Paul's words demonstrate that every soldier, even inexperienced ones, can stand strong against temptation. But without the armor of God, we're toast. Our weak spots are exposed. Soldiers of the cross who fully dress in the armor of light are fortified, protecting their weaknesses. Each piece of armor plays an integral part in our success: the belt of truth (v. 14), the breastplate of righteousness (v. 14), shoes shod with the gospel of peace (v. 15), the shield of faith (v. 16), the helmet of salvation (v. 17), and the sword of the Spirit (v. 17).

The powers of darkness fire shots at us every day. Being fully dressed in the armor of God at all times not only prevents us from being fatally wounded; it also allows us to take the fight to Satan and his minions, to be on the offensive, to fire back, to gain ground. But we don't need to worry. Our lack of experience and training is to be expected. God anticipated that. That's why He's given us something strong to wear in battle. Our armor has been forged to withstand the boiling flares of Hell's fire. We must put on the whole armor of God so we can win our war.

The Word of God will prove to be an invaluable ally; it will never let us down.

After Jesus was baptized by John the Baptist (Matthew 3:13–17), the heavens ripped open and the Spirit of God descended and rested on the Lord. What followed was a voice from Heaven proclaiming that Jesus was the consecrated Son. This marked the commencement of His task to save the nations.

Matthew, Mark, and Luke then reveal that Jesus was led by the Spirit out of the Jordan River and into the Judean desert, a place haunted with wild beasts and evil spirits (Leviticus 16:10; Isaiah 13:21; 34:14). The sequence of events that follows is actual dialogue between the Savior and Satan. Luke writes:

Jesus, full of the Holy Spirit, returned from the Jordan and was led by the Spirit into the wilderness for forty days, being tempted by the devil. He ate nothing in those days. Afterward, when they were completed, he was hungry. The devil said to him, "If you are the Son of God, command this stone to become bread." Jesus answered him, saying, "It is written, 'Man shall not live by bread alone, but by every word of God.'" (Luke 4:1–4, WEB)

Satan's first temptation focused on Jesus' physical needs. He had been fasting for forty days and forty nights and was physically famished. However, His fasting strengthened His devotion and connection with His Father. This is evidenced by His constant use of the Word of God to respond to all three of Satan's alluring temptations. Satan was hoping he could appeal to Jesus' weakened humanity first. The temptation was for a starving Jesus to physically sustain Himself. To become self-sufficient. To act like a grown-up who's independent and not in need of Daddy to put food on the table. To rebel and become like Satan. Jesus rejected independence and denied His hunger by quoting Deuteronomy 8:3: Man lives by every word that comes from the mouth of God. It was precisely the Word of God that Jesus would continue to fire at Satan's temptations.

In my book *Gospel Over Gods,* I discuss at length the power the Word of God has over the enemy. This power is not some abstract force; it's literal power over literal evil beings. Jews considered Psalm 91 an exorcistic psalm—a psalm for exorcising demons and defeating the powers of darkness.[340] Commentators' suspicion that Psalm 91 possessed protection from demonic powers was confirmed in the Dead Sea Scrolls, where it was bundled with three other psalms of exorcism.[341]

Together, these psalms functioned much like when David expelled an evil spirit from Saul when playing his melodic lyre (1 Samuel 16:23). Skimming Psalm 91 leaves us wondering why it is a psalm for exorcising demons, seeing as no demons are mentioned in the chapter. Grammatically, they are listed, but they're masked by our English translations in an attempt to demythologize the Bible.

David actually lists specific demons or evil spirits from whom Yahweh will deliver His children.

Psalm 91:3–6 (ESV)	Psalm 90:3–6 (LES)
For he will deliver you from the snare of the fowler and from the deadly *pestilence* [*deber*]. He will cover you with his pinions, and under his wings you will find refuge; his faithfulness is a shield and buckler. You will not fear the *terror of the night* [*paḥad laylâ*], nor *the arrow that flies* [*ḥēṣ yā 'ûp*] by day, nor *the pestilence* [*deber*] that stalks in darkness, nor *the destruction* [*qeṭeb*] that wastes at noonday.	because he will rescue from the trap of hunters and from a terrifying word. With his shoulders he will overshadow you, and under his wings you will have hope; with a shield his truth will surround you. That one will not be afraid from fear by night, from the arrow flying by day, from the deed carried out in darkness, from mishap and *demon* [*daimonou*] at midday.

King David starts by addressing a demon called Deber, or "the pestilence," an evil nocturnal deity in Canaanite religions who was viewed as the master of epidemics. Deber is listed twice in Psalm 91 (vv. 3, 6). Secondly, David lists "the terror of the night," or *paḥad laylâ*, in Hebrew. He balances out the list of night demons with his mention of Qeteb, a daytime demon of destruction. In the Ugaritic text *KTU 1.5 ii:24*, Qeteb is listed as a kinsman, or accomplice, of Mot, the Canaanite deity of death. In Psalm 91:5, David is likely alluding to the feared demonic archer of antiquity—Resheph (the "arrow" that flies by day). The Bible mentions Resheph seven times in the Old Testament (Deuteronomy 32:24; 1 Chronicles 7:25; Job 5:7; Psalms 76:3; 78:48; Song of Solomon 8:6; Habakkuk 3:5). Like other demons and deities, Resheph is masked in English translations by words apropos to his nature, such as "arrows," "fiery," "flame," "fire-bolt," "pestilence," and "plague." Psalm 76:3 describes Yahweh as putting an end to war by the "arrows of Resheph." The language of the biblical writers is clear: While demons are rebellious and vile entities, Yahweh is still Lord over every single one of them. None of the powers of darkness can usurp or undercut the God of Heaven. They are wielded by the finger of God whenever He chooses.

The point is the Word of God can help us defeat evil in more ways than one.

MORE FROM THE AUTHOR

Familiar Bible stories have captivated countless generations. Stories of a talking serpent and ancient gardens. Whispers of a watery flood and tales of a tower built to the heavens. Rumors of giants in the Promised Land and Israelites in the Red Sea. You've wondered, and been in wonder, of angels from Heaven and demons from the deep. The Bible is fascinating…and it is in no way fiction. Although we didn't walk the holy mountains with Elijah or watch Jesus bleed, we believe (John 20:29). But let me ask you a question—have you ever felt like something in the Bible was missing? Primarily, a common thread that ties the entire narrative together from Genesis to Revelation? I certainly did.

That missing link was the war of the unseen realm. I write all about it in my best-selling book *Gospel Over Gods*.

The supernatural struggle between God and His fallen angels had always seemed obscure in the biblical narrative, if not completely absent altogether. Admittedly, reading the Bible felt a bit like watching a failed blockbuster movie where the hero and villain rarely cross paths, let alone interact or confront one another in battle. Instead, the entire "film" was seemingly nothing but random scenes of a supporting cast merely filling space and time. This often left me asking, "Wait, that's it? There has to be more to the story, right? Is the Bible really just a collection of unrelated accounts that seem to have little to no bearing on one another? Is there no metanarrative in the Bible, no detailed storyline that captures the big picture?" I'm embarrassed to say Bible study soon became a "required" burden instead of a real blessing. As a Christian minister, this was a "Houston, we have a problem" moment!

My theological world was rocked when a dear friend challenged my grasp of Jesus' good news and its supernatural implications by asking me several pointed questions. I began to dig deeper, much deeper than I ever had before, to find answers to those questions. In Jesus' Sermon on the Mount, He told His disciples, "You have heard that it was said, but I say unto you…" For many months, I felt like I lived on that mountain, listening to Jesus' words on repeat. Like the disciples, I too was in the classroom of the master Teacher, experiencing the hardest part of learning: unlearning. What I discovered on my journey truly changed me. The Bible wasn't missing anything—*I* was. I was missing the "eyes to see" (Matthew 13:16). I was missing my first-century glasses.

The reality is "your gospel" (Galatians 1:8) is too modern; it's filtered through hundreds of years of opinions and traditions, just like mine was. Unknowingly and unintentionally, Jesus' sheep have been led to brown pastures by many well-intentioned preachers and teachers. The epidemic of the modern gospel has invaded all of Christendom, including your church. I wrote *Gospel Over Gods* to lead a new generation back to the beginning, back to the green pastures, and back to the original good news.

Gospel Over Gods will lead you to the ancient world, a world very different than the one you call home. Like Abraham, you will be faced with the decision to raise your knife and sacrifice something you hold dearest at the turn of every page—your beliefs, your convictions, and your context. I assure you, studying *Gospel Over Gods* will make your faith soar to the heavens, and so will your love for reading the Bible.

In my book, I retrace the biblical narrative and point out important (and often overlooked) markers along the way—clues the inspired biblical writers, ancient Israelites, first-century Christians, the church fathers, and even historians left for seeking souls to find (Matthew 7:7). As I reveal, the connectivity of all Scripture is shocking, and so is the forgotten story of the ancient gospel.

But what is the ancient gospel? Well, I'm so glad you asked. It's breathtaking and life-giving. It's supernatural and saving. It's gospel over gods.

NOTES

1. Rick Brannan et al., eds., *The Lexham English Septuagint* (Bellingham, WA: Lexham Press, 2012).

2. *The Holy Bible with Deuterocanon/Apocrypha* (M. P. Johnson, 2020), ii.

3. Eugene H. Peterson, *The Message: The Bible in Contemporary Language* (Colorado Springs, CO: NavPress, 2005).

4. G. K. Beale and Sean M. McDonough, "Revelation," in *Commentary on the New Testament Use of the Old Testament* (Grand Rapids, MI; Nottingham, UK: Baker Academic; Apollos, 2007), 1132.

5. Michael J. Vlach, *The Old in the New: Understanding How the New Testament Authors Quoted the Old Testament* (Woodlands, TX; Sun Valley, CA: Kress Biblical Resources; Master's Seminary Press, 2021), viii.

6. Steve Moyise, "The Old Testament in the Book of Revelation," ed. Stanley E. Porter, vol. 115 of *Journal for the Study of the New Testament Supplement Series* (Sheffield: Sheffield Academic, 1995), 14.

7. Richard Bauckham, *The Climax of Prophecy: Studies on the Book of Revelation* (London; New York: T&T Clark: A Continuum Imprint, 1993), x–xi.

8. Moyise, *Old Testament in the Book of Revelation*, 13–14.

9. Brian J. Tabb, "All Things New: Revelation as Canonical Capstone," ed. D. A. Carson, vol. 48 of *New Studies in Biblical Theology* (London; Downers Grove, IL: IVP Academic: An Imprint of InterVarsity Press; Apollos, 2019), 16–17.

10. David E. Aune, Revelation 1–5, vol. 52A, *Word Biblical Commentary* (Dallas: Word, Incorporated, 1997), 75.

11. Tabb, *All Things New*, 16–17.

12. Vlach, *The Old in the New*, 218.

13. Aune, Revelation 1–5, vol. 52A of *Word Biblical Commentary*, 108–109.

14. Michael Heiser, *John's Use of the Old Testament in the Book of Revelation: Notes from the Naked Bible Podcast* (p. 243). Naked Bible Press. Kindle Edition.

15. Steven Grabiner, "Revelation's Hymns: Commentary on the Cosmic Conflict," ed. Chris Keith, vol. 511 of *Library of New Testament Studies* (London; New Delhi; New York; Sydney: Bloomsbury, 2015), 176–177.

16. Beale and McDonough, "Revelation," in *Commentary on the New Testament Use of the Old Testament*, 1134.

17. Ibid.

18. G. K. Beale and David H. Campbell, *Revelation: A Shorter Commentary* (Grand Rapids, MI; Cambridge, U.K.: William B. Eerdmans, 2015), 172–173.

19. R. H. Charles, ed., *The Book of Enoch or 1 Enoch: Translation*, trans. R. H. Charles (Oxford: Clarendon Press, 1912), 43–45.

20. Beale and Campbell, *Revelation: A Shorter Commentary*, 41–42.

21. Grant R. Osborne, "Revelation," *Baker Exegetical Commentary on the New Testament* (Grand Rapids, MI: Baker Academic, 2002), 65.

22. Craig S. Keener, "Revelation," *NIV Application Commentary* (Grand Rapids, MI: Zondervan, 1999), 71.

23. Joel R. Beeke, "Revelation," eds. Joel R. Beeke and Jon D. Payne,

Lectio Continua Expository Commentary on the New Testament (Grand Rapids, MI: Reformation Heritage Books, 2016), 33.

24. Michael B. Hundley, "Divine Presence in Ancient Near Eastern Temples," *Religion Compass* 9.7 (2015): 205–207, doi: 10.1111/rec3.12154.

25. Beale and McDonough, "Revelation," in *Commentary on the New Testament Use of the Old Testament*, 1158.

26. Sigve K. Tonstad, "Revelation," ed. Mikeal C. Parsons, Charles H. Talbert, and Bruce W. Longenecker, *Paideia Commentaries on the New Testament* (Grand Rapids, MI: Baker Academic: A Division of Baker Publishing, 2019), 76.

27. Buist M. Fanning, "Revelation," ed. Clinton E. Arnold, *Zondervan Exegetical Commentary on the New Testament* (Grand Rapids, MI: Zondervan Academic, 2020), 136.

28. Aune, Revelation 1–5, vol. 52A of *Word Biblical Commentary*, 182–183.

29. G. K. Beale, *The Book of Revelation: A Commentary on the Greek Text, New International Greek Testament Commentary* (Grand Rapids, MI; Carlisle, Cumbria: Eerdmans; Paternoster Press, 1999), 249.

30. Beale and Campbell, *Revelation: A Shorter Commentary*, 66.

31. Beale and McDonough, "Revelation," in *Commentary on the New Testament Use of the Old Testament*, 1094.

32. Tonstad, "Revelation," *Paideia Commentaries on the New Testament*, 79.

33. Stephen S. Smalley, *The Revelation to John: A Commentary on the Greek Text of the Apocalypse* (London: SPCK, 2005), 70.

34. Beale, *The Book of Revelation: A Commentary on the Greek Text*, 260.

35. Aune, Revelation 1–5, vol. 52A of *Word Biblical Commentary*, 203.

36. Robert H. Mounce, *The Book of Revelation, The New International*

Commentary on the New Testament (Grand Rapids, MI: Eerdmans, 1997), 87.

37. Beale and McDonough, "Revelation," in *Commentary on the New Testament Use of the Old Testament*, 1095.

38. Michael S. Heiser, *The Unseen Realm: Recovering the Supernatural Worldview of the Bible*, First Edition. (Bellingham, WA: Lexham Press, 2015), 158–159.

39. Fanning, "Revelation," *Zondervan Exegetical Commentary on the New Testament*, 156.

40. Heiser, *The Unseen Realm*, 312–313.

41. Roger Ellsworth, *Opening Up Revelation, Opening Up Commentary* (Leominster: Day One, 2013), 39.

42. Tonstad, "Revelation," *Paideia Commentaries on the New Testament*, 89.

43. Mounce, *The Book of Revelation*.

44. Beale and Campbell, *Revelation: A Shorter Commentary*, 80.

45. Beale, *The Book of Revelation: A Commentary on the Greek Text*, 276.

46. Keener, "Revelation," *NIV Application Commentary*, 144–145.

47. b. Yoma 19A and m. Middoth 5:4.

48. Jacob Neusner, *The Babylonian Talmud: A Translation and Commentary* (Peabody, MA: Hendrickson, 2011), 58.

49. Beale and McDonough, "Revelation," in *Commentary on the New Testament Use of the Old Testament*, 1096.

50. Beale, *The Book of Revelation: A Commentary on the Greek Text*, 277.

51. Mounce, *The Book of Revelation*, 96.

52. Beale, *The Book of Revelation: A Commentary on the Greek Text*, 281.

53. Mounce, *The Book of Revelation*, 108.

54. George Eldon Ladd, *A Commentary on the Revelation of John* (Grand Rapids, MI: Eerdmans, 1972), 64–65.

55. Joel R. Beeke, "Revelation," 159.

56. Beale and Campbell, *Revelation: A Shorter Commentary*, 90.

57. Beale, *The Book of Revelation: A Commentary on the Greek Text*, 303.

58. Aune, Revelation 1–5, vol. 52A of *Word Biblical Commentary*, 258.

59. Beale, *The Book of Revelation: A Commentary on the Greek Text*, 302.

60. William Hendriksen, *More Than Conquerors: An Interpretation of the Book of Revelation* (Grand Rapids, MI: Baker Books, 1967), 76.

61. Tonstad, "Revelation," *Paideia Commentaries on the New Testament*, 98.

62. Beale and Campbell, *Revelation: A Shorter Commentary*, 92.

63. Beale, *The Book of Revelation: A Commentary on the Greek Text*, 306.

64. Aune, Revelation 1–5, vol. 52A of *Word Biblical Commentary*, 260.

65. Mounce, *The Book of Revelation*, 113.

66. Aune, Revelation 1–5, vol. 52A of *Word Biblical Commentary*, 262.

67. Osborne, "Revelation," *Baker Exegetical Commentary on the New Testament*, 215.

68. Beale and Campbell, *Revelation: A Shorter Commentary*, 55–56.

69. Tabb, *All Things New*, 102.

70. Beale, *The Book of Revelation: A Commentary on the Greek Text*, 237–238.

71. Mounce, *The Book of Revelation*, 73.

72. Aune, Revelation 1–5, vol. 52A of *Word Biblical Commentary*, 175.

73. Beeke, "Revelation," 76.

74. Keener, "Revelation," *NIV Application Commentary*, 115.

75. 1QHa Col. x:22; Michael O. Wise, Martin G. Abegg Jr., and Edward M. Cook, *The Dead Sea Scrolls: A New Translation* (New York: HarperOne, 2005), 180.

76. Grabiner, "Revelation's Hymns," 64.

77. Beale and Campbell, *Revelation: A Shorter Commentary*, 62–63.

78. Hendriksen, *More Than Conquerors*, 64.

79. Vern S. Poythress, *The Returning King: A Guide to the Book of Revelation* (Phillipsburg, NJ: P&R Publishing, 2000), 87.

80. Beale, *The Book of Revelation: A Commentary on the Greek Text*, 284.

81. Mounce, *The Book of Revelation*, 102.

82. Osborne, "Revelation," *Baker Exegetical Commentary on the New Testament*, 197.

83. Ibid., 196.

84. Tonstad, "Revelation," *Paideia Commentaries on the New Testament*, 95.

85. Aune, Revelation 1–5, vol. 52A of *Word Biblical Commentary*, 242.

86. Ladd, *A Commentary on the Revelation of John*, 63.

87. Grabiner, "Revelation's Hymns," 196.

88. Charles Gieschen, *Angelomorphic Christology: Antecedents and Early Evidence* (*Arbeiten zur Geschichte des antiken Judentums und des Urchristentums* 28; Leiden: Brill, 1998).

89. Heiser, *John's Use of the Old Testament in the Book of Revelation*, 185–186.

90. Gieschen, *Angelomorphic Christology*.

91. Douglas Mangum, *Lexham Glossary of Theology* (Bellingham, WA: Lexham Press, 2014).

92. Walter A. Elwell and Barry J. Beitzel, "Angel of the Lord," *Baker Encyclopedia of the Bible* (Grand Rapids, MI: Baker Book House, 1988) 90.

93. Alan Segal, *Two Powers in Heaven: Early Rabbinic Reports about Christianity and Gnosticism* (SSEJC, 25; Leiden: E.J. Brill, 1977).

94. Exodus 3:1–4, The Aramaic Bible, Volume 2: *Targum Neofiti* 1: Exodus and Targum Pseudo-Jonathan: Exodus; italics in original.

95. Heiser, *The Unseen Realm*, 148.

96. James M. Hamilton Jr., *With the Clouds of Heaven: The Book of Daniel in Biblical Theology*, ed. D. A. Carson, vol. 32 of *New Studies in*

Biblical Theology (Downers Grove, IL; England: Apollos; InterVarsity Press, 2015), 203–204.

97. Beale, *The Book of Revelation: A Commentary on the Greek Text*, 213.

98. Justin Bass, *The Battle for the Keys: Revelation 1:18 and Christ's Descent into the Underworld* (Paternoster Biblical Monographs) (p. 49). Paternoster. Kindle Edition.

99. J. N. Bremmer, "Hades," *Dictionary of Deities and Demons in the Bible* (Leiden; Boston; Köln; Grand Rapids, MI; Cambridge: Brill; Eerdmans, 1999), 382–383.

100. KTU 1.4:8:15–20; N. Wyatt, "Religious Texts from Ugarit," 2nd ed., *Biblical Seminar*, 53 (London; New York: Sheffield Academic, 2002), 113.

101. Aune, Revelation 1–5, vol. 52A of *Word Biblical Commentary*, 104–105.

102. Bass, *The Battle for the Keys*, p. 69.

103. Osborne, "Revelation," *Baker Exegetical Commentary on the New Testament*, 248.

104. Fanning, "Revelation," *Zondervan Exegetical Commentary on the New Testament*, 212.

105. Beeke, "Revelation," 194.

106. Tonstad, "Revelation," *Paideia Commentaries on the New Testament*, 114.

107. Aune, Revelation 1–5, vol. 52A of *Word Biblical Commentary*, 374.

108. Beeke, "Revelation," 194.

109. Tonstad, "Revelation," *Paideia Commentaries on the New Testament*, 113.

110. Beale and McDonough, "Revelation," in *Commentary on the New Testament Use of the Old Testament* 1101.

111. Craig R. Koester, *Revelation and the End of All Things* (Grand Rapids, MI; Cambridge, U.K.: Eerdmans, 2001), 76–77.

112. Keener, "Revelation," *NIV Application Commentary*, 184–185.

113. Tonstad, "Revelation," *Paideia Commentaries on the New Testament*, 111.

114. Osborne, "Revelation," *Baker Exegetical Commentary on the New Testament*, 251–252.

115. Hendriksen, *More Than Conquerors*, 89.

116. Fanning, "Revelation," *Zondervan Exegetical Commentary on the New Testament*, 216.

117. Beeke, "Revelation," 196–197.

118. Dana M. Harris, "4 Ezra and Revelation 5:1–14: Creaturely Images of the Messiah," in *Reading Revelation in Context: John's Apocalypse and Second Temple Judaism* (Grand Rapids, MI: Zondervan Academic, 2019), 59–60.

119. Fanning, "Revelation," *Zondervan Exegetical Commentary on the New Testament*, 217–218.

120. Mounce, *The Book of Revelation*, 132.

121. Fanning, "Revelation," *Zondervan Exegetical Commentary on the New Testament*, 99.

122. Mounce, *The Book of Revelation*, 58.

123. Fanning, "Revelation," *Zondervan Exegetical Commentary on the New Testament*, 101.

124. Beale, *The Book of Revelation: A Commentary on the Greek Text*, 283.

125. Osborne, "Revelation," *Baker Exegetical Commentary on the New Testament*, 187.

126. G. K. Beale, *John's Use of the Old Testament in Revelation*, ed. Stanley E. Porter, vol. 166 of *Journal for the Study of the New Testament Supplement Series* (Sheffield: Sheffield Academic, 1998), 121–122.

127. Tabb, *All Things New*, 220–221.

128. Isaiah 22:22, The Aramaic Bible, Volume 11: The Isaiah Targum.

129. John D. W. Watts, "Isaiah 1–33," Revised Edition., vol. 24 of *Word Biblical Commentary* (Nashville: Thomas Nelson 2005), 347.

130. Beeke, "Revelation," 144–145.

131. Keener, "Revelation," *NIV Application Commentary*, 149–150.

132. Beale and Campbell, *Revelation: A Shorter Commentary*, 83–84.

133. Beale, *The Book of Revelation: A Commentary on the Greek Text*, 284.

134. Fanning, "Revelation," *Zondervan Exegetical Commentary on the New Testament*, 84.

135. Smalley, *The Revelation to John*, 39–40.

136. Mounce, *The Book of Revelation*, 51.

137. Koowon Kim, "Rider on the Clouds," ed. John D. Barry et al., *Lexham Bible Dictionary* (Bellingham, WA: Lexham Press, 2016).

138. Wyatt, *Religious Texts from Ugarit*, 65.

139. Moyise, *The Old Testament in the Book of Revelation*, 59.

140. WiseAbegg, and Cook, *The Dead Sea Scrolls,*, 148.

141. Ibid., 146–147.

142. J. Lust, "Gog," *Dictionary of Deities and Demons in the Bible* (Leiden; Boston; Köln; Grand Rapids, MI; Cambridge: Brill; Eerdmans, 1999), 375.

143. Ibid., 374.

144. Aune, Revelation 6–16, vol. 52B of *Word Biblical Commentary*, 460.

145. Beale and McDonough, "Revelation," in *Commentary on the New Testament Use of the Old Testament*, 1108.

146. Tabb, *All Things New*, 104–105.

147. Jon Paulien, *Decoding Revelation's Trumpets: Literary Allusions and the Interpretation of Revelation 8:7–12*, vol. XI of *Andrews University Seminary Doctoral Dissertation Series* (Berrien Springs, MI: Andrews University Press, 1988), 348–349.

148. Tabb, *All Things New*, 104–105.

149. Ibid., 102–103.

150. John J. Davis, *Biblical Numerology: A Basic Study of the Use of Numbers in the Bible* (Baker Book House, 1968), 76.

151. Bauckham, *Climax of Prophecy*, 217.

152. Ibid.

153. Ibid., 218–219.

154. 1QM; Ibid., 217.

155. Beale and McDonough, "Revelation," in *Commentary on the New Testament Use of the Old Testament*, 1107.

156. R. H. Charles, ed., *The Book of Enoch or 1 Enoch: Translation*, 28–29.

157. Terel Manikam and Jan A. Du Rand. "The 144,000 Undefiled Levites of Revelation 14:1–5 and the Link to the Defiled Watchers of 1 Enoch 1–36," *Ekklesiastikos Pharos* 94.1 (2012): 123–136 (esp. 125). Citing D. C. Olson, "Those Who Have Not Defiled Themselves with Women": Revelation 14:4 and the Book of Enoch, *The Catholic Biblical Quarterly*. Vol. 59:3 (1997), 492–510.

158. Michael S. Heiser, *Reversing Hermon: Enoch, the Watchers and the Forgotten Mission of Jesus Christ* (Bellingham, WA: Lexham Press, 2017), 167–168.

159. Tammi J. Schneider, *An Introduction to Ancient Mesopotamian Religion* (Grand Rapids, MI; Cambridge, U.K.: Eerdmans, 2011), 26.

160. Ibid.

161. Morris Jastrow Jr., *The Religion of Babylonia and Assyria* (Boston, MA: Ginn & Co., 1898), 26.

162. Schneider, *Introduction to Ancient Mesopotamian Religion*, 141–143.

163. Alan Bandy, "The Prophetic Lawsuit in the Book of Revelation," (PhD Dissertation, Southeastern Baptist Theological Seminary, 2007), 228–229.

164. Michael S. Heiser, "Divine Council," *Lexham Bible Dictionary* (Bellingham, WA: Lexham Press, 2016).

165. Grabiner, "Revelation's Hymns," 49–50.

166. Ibid., 51–52.

167. Bandy, "Prophetic Lawsuit," 229–230.

168. Heiser, *John's Use of the Old Testament in the Book of Revelation*, 81.

169. Ibid.

170. Andrew E. Hill, "Malachi: A New Translation with Introduction and Commentary," vol. 25D of *Anchor Yale Bible* (New Haven; London: Yale University Press, 2008), 31–32.

171. Meira Z. Kensky, *Trying Man, Trying God: The Divine Courtroom in Early Jewish and Christian Literature* (WUNT 289 Reihe 2; Tübingen: Mohr Siebeck, 2010), 37.

172. Bandy, "Prophetic Lawsuit," 226–227.

173. Ibid., 230–231

174. Beale and McDonough, "Revelation," in Commentary on the *New Testament Use of the Old Testament, 1139*.

175. Ibid., 1137.

176. Ibid.

177. Ibid., 1140.

178. Ibid., 1140.

179. Ibid., 1141.

180. Ibid.

181. Ibid.

182. Ibid., 1142.

183. Ibid.

184. Heiser, *John's Use of the Old Testament in the Book of Revelation*, 259.

185. Tonstad, "Revelation," *Paideia Commentaries on the New Testament*, 123–124.

186. Heiser, *John's Use of the Old Testament in the Book of Revelation*, 119.

187. Michael Snearly, "Astrology," *Lexham Bible Dictionary* (Bellingham, WA: Lexham Press, 2016).

188. Amar Annus, "Divination and Interpretation of Signs in the Ancient World," Number 6 of The Oriental Institute of the University of Chicago Seminars (Chicago: University of Chicago, 2010), 87.

189. Wayne Horowitz, *Mesopotamian Cosmic Geography*, ed. Jerrold S. Cooper, vol. 8 of *Mesopotamian Civilizations* (Winona Lake, IN: Eisenbrauns, 2011), 166.

190. Ida Fröhlich, "Mesopotamian Elements and the Watchers Traditions," in *The Watchers in Jewish and Christian Traditions*, ed. Angela Kim Harkins, Kelley Coblentz Bautch, and John C. Endres (Minneapolis, MN: Fortress Press, 2014), 19.

191. Bruce J. Malina and John J. Pilch, *Social-Science Commentary on the Book of Revelation* (Minneapolis, MN: Fortress Press, 2000), 111.

192. Kihlman, *Star of Bethlehem*, 5.

193. Ibid., 5–6.

194. Ibid.

195. Morris Jastrow, Jr., *Aspects of Religious Belief and Practice in Babylonia and Assyria* (New York; London: Putnam's Sons, 1911), 217.

196. Schneider, *An Introduction to Ancient Mesopotamian Religion*, 57.

197. Jeffery M Leonard, *Creation Rediscovered: Finding New Meaning in an Ancient Story* (p. 212). Tyndale House. Kindle Edition.

198. Beale, *The Book of Revelation: A Commentary on the Greek Text*, 507.

199. Ibid.

200. Beale and McDonough, "Revelation," in *Commentary on the New Testament Use of the Old Testament*, 1115.

201. K. van der Toorn, "Euphrates," *Dictionary of Deities and Demons in the Bible* (Leiden; Boston; Köln; Grand Rapids, MI; Cambridge: Brill; Eerdmans, 1999), 315.

202. Ibid.

203. Ibid., 315–316.

204. Ibid., 314.

205. Kihlman, *Star of Bethlehem*, 5.

206. Amar Annus, "The God Ninurta in the Mythology and Royal Ideology of Ancient Mesopotamia," vol. 14 of State Archives of Assyria

Studies (Helsinki: The Neo-Assyrian Text Corpus Project, 2002), 201.

207. Heiser, *John's Use of the Old Testament in the Book of Revelation,* 209.

208. Ibid., 212–213.

209. Heiser, *Reversing Hermon,* 66.

210. "Yale University." CCP 3.8.2.A - *Iqqur īpuš, série mensuelle* (Tašrītu) A | Cuneiform Commentaries Project. Accessed October 1, 2022. https://ccp.yale.edu/P461210.

211. https://www.livius.org/articles/concept/calendar-babylonian/.

212. Schneider, *An Introduction to Ancient Mesopotamian Religion,* 85.

213. Jastrow Jr., *The Religion of Babylonia and Assyria,* 462–463.

214. Ibid., 71–72.

215. K. van der Toorn, "The Babylonian New Year Festival New Insights from the Cuneiform Texts and Their Bearing on Old Testament Study," in Congress Volume. Leuven 1989, Brill, 1991, pp. 331–344

216. Kenton L. Sparks, *Ancient Texts for the Study of the Hebrew Bible: A Guide to the Background Literature* (Peabody, MA: Hendrickson, 2005), 166.

217. K. van der Toorn, "The Babylonian New Year Festival," 331–344.

218. Sparks, *Ancient Texts for the Study of the Hebrew Bible,* 166.

219. Wesley Crouser, "Bel," *Lexham Bible Dictionary* (Bellingham, WA: Lexham Press, 2016).

220. Sparks, *Ancient Texts for the Study of the Hebrew Bible,* 167.

221. "Yale University." CCP 3.8.2.A - *Iqqur īpuš, série mensuelle* (Tašrītu) A | Cuneiform Commentaries Project. Accessed October 1, 2022. https://ccp.yale.edu/P461210.

222. Jastrow, Jr., *The Religion of Babylonia and Assyria,* 84.

223. Ibid., 186.

224. Ibid.

225. Heiser, *Reversing Hermon,* 41.

226. J. C. Greenfield, "Apkallu," *Dictionary of Deities and Demons in the Bible* (Leiden; Boston; Köln; Grand Rapids, MI; Cambridge: Brill; Eerdmans, 1999), 72–73.

227. Michael S. Heiser, *Demons: What the Bible Really Says about the Powers of Darkness* (Bellingham, WA: Lexham Press, 2020), 135–136.

228. Heiser, *Reversing Hermon*, 41.

229. Matthew Neujahr, *Babylonian Scribalism and the Production of Apocalypses and Related Early Jewish Texts* (Hebrew Bible and Ancient Israel 5.3, 2016), 221.

230. Annus, Amar. "On the Origin of the Watchers: A Comparative Study of the Antediluvian Wisdom in Mesopotamian and Jewish Traditions." *Journal for the Study of the Pseudepigrapha* 19.4 (2010): 289–291.

231. Neujahr, *Babylonian Scribalism*, 222.

232. Heiser, *Demons: What the Bible Really Says*, 121.

233. Aramaic term yryn, "the wakeful ones," for both good angels and the Watchers....

234. Fröhlich, "Mesopotamian Elements and the Watchers Traditions," 17.

235. Heiser, *Demons: What the Bible Really Says*, 118.

236. Henryk Drawnel, "Enoch 6–11 Interpreted in the Light of Mesopotamian Incantation Literature." *Early Judaism and Its Literature* no. 44: pg. 282–284.

237. Heiser, *Reversing Hermon*, 38.

238. Ibid., 45.

239. Heiser, *John's Use of the Old Testament in the Book of Revelation*, 176.

240. Bass, *The Battle for the Keys*, 122–123.

241. Genesis 6:4 The Aramaic Bible, Volume 1B: Targum Pseudo-Jonathan: Genesis.

242. Beale, *The Book of Revelation: A Commentary on the Greek Text*, 494–495.

243. Ibid., 496.

244. Beale and McDonough, "Revelation," in *Commentary on the New Testament Use of the Old Testament*, 1114.

245. Beale, *The Book of Revelation: A Commentary on the Greek Text*, 498.

246. Beale and McDonough, "Revelation," in *Commentary on the New Testament Use of the Old Testament*, 1114.

247. Beale, *The Book of Revelation: A Commentary on the Greek Text*, 500–501.

248. Louis Ginzberg, Henrietta Szold, and Paul Radin, *Legends of the Jews*, 2nd ed. (Philadelphia: Jewish Publication Society, 2003), 524.

249. Beale and McDonough, "Revelation," in *Commentary on the New Testament Use of the Old Testament*, 1114.

250. Heiser, *Reversing Hermon*, 164–165.

251. Beale, *The Book of Revelation: A Commentary on the Greek Text*, 494.

252. Heiser, *John's Use of the Old Testament in the Book of Revelation*, 178.

253. 1QHa Col. Xi of the DSS; Geza Vermes, *The Dead Sea Scrolls in English*, Revised and extended 4th ed. (Sheffield: Sheffield Academic, 1995), 197.

254. 4Q504 Frags. 1–2 viiv.

255. Ibid., 252.

256. 1Q33 Col. xv:12 of.

257. Wise, Abegg, and Cook, *The Dead Sea Scrolls*, 162.

258. Beale, *The Book of Revelation: A Commentary on the Greek Text*, 502–503.

259. 4Q286 Frag. 7 ii:10 in DSS.

260. Wise, Abegg, and Cook, *The Dead Sea Scrolls*, 374.

261. R. H. Charles, ed., *The Book of Jubilees or The Little Genesis: Translation*, trans. R. H. Charles (London: Adam and Charles Black, 1902), 78–81.

262. Beale and Campbell, *Revelation: A Shorter Commentary*, 267.

263. Beale and Campbell, *Revelation: A Shorter Commentary*, 218.

264. John D. Currid, *Against the Gods: The Polemical Theology of the Old Testament* (Wheaton, IL: Crossway, 2013), 25–26.

265. Eric Ortlund, *Piercing Leviathan: God's Defeat of Evil in the Book of Job*, ed. D. A. Carson, vol. 56 of *New Studies in Biblical Theology* (London; Downers Grove, IL: Apollos; IVP Academic: An Imprint of InterVarsity Press, 2021), 138.

266. Elaine A. Phillips, "Serpent," *Lexham Bible Dictionary* (Bellingham, WA: Lexham Press, 2016).

267. C. Uehlinger, "Leviathan," *Dictionary of Deities and Demons in the Bible* (Leiden; Boston; Köln; Grand Rapids, MI; Cambridge: Brill; Eerdmans, 1999), 511.

268. Sidney Greidanus, *From Chaos to Cosmos: Creation to New Creation*, ed. Dane C. Ortlund and Miles V. Van Pelt, *Short Studies in Biblical Theology* (Wheaton, IL: Crossway, 2018), 30.

269. Walter A. Elwell and Barry J. Beitzel, "Enuma Elish," *Baker Encyclopedia of the Bible* (Grand Rapids, MI: Baker Book House, 1988) 702.

270. B. Alster, "Tiamat," *Dictionary of Deities and Demons in the Bible* (Leiden; Boston; Köln; Grand Rapids, MI; Cambridge: Brill; Eerdmans, 1999), 867.

271. Ibid.

272. Hermann Gunkel and Heinrich Zimmern, *Creation and Chaos in the Primeval Era and the Eschaton: A Religio-Historical Study of Genesis 1 and Revelation 12*, trans. K. William Whitney Jr. (Grand Rapids, MI; Cambridge, UK: Eerdmans, 2006), 75–76.

273. William Arndt, et al., *A Greek-English Lexicon of the New Testament and Other Early Christian Literature* (Chicago: University of Chicago Press, 2000), 386.

274. Currid, *Against the Gods*, 35.

275. John Anthony Dunne, "Enuma Elish," *Lexham Bible Dictionary* (Bellingham, WA: Lexham Press, 2016).

276. N. Wyatt, *Space and Time in the Religious Life of the Near East*, vol. 85 of *The Biblical Seminar* (Sheffield, England: Sheffield Academic Press, 2001), 64–65.

277. Greidanus, *From Chaos to Cosmos*, 30.

278. Currid, *Against the Gods*, 34.

279. Irenaeus of Lyons, *The Writings of Irenæus*, ed. Alexander Roberts and James Donaldson, trans. Alexander Roberts and W. H. Rambaut, vol. 2 of Ante-Nicene Christian Library (Edinburgh; London; Dublin: T. & T. Clark; Hamilton & Co.; John Robertson & Co., 1868–1869), 137–138.

280. Heiser, *Reversing Hermon*, 162.

281. Ortlund, *Piercing Leviathan*, 71.

282. Phil Logan, "Molten Sea," *Holman Illustrated Bible Dictionary* (Nashville, TN: Holman, 2003), 1148.

283. Carol Meyers, "Sea, Molten," *Anchor Yale Bible Dictionary* (New York: Doubleday, 1992) 1061.

284. David Shapira, "The Molten Sea Revisited," *Vetus Testamentum* (2020): 1,9.

285. Gunkel and Zimmern, *Creation and Chaos*, 108.

286. Shapira, "Molten Sea Revisited," 1, 9.

287. Meyers, "Sea, Molten," 1062.

288. Shapira, "Molten Sea Revisited," 8.

289. N. T. Parker, "Marduk," *The Lexham Bible Dictionary* (Bellingham, WA: Lexham Press, 2016).

290. Gunkel and Zimmern, *Creation and Chaos*, 108.

291. Meyers, "Sea, Molten," 1061.

292. Matthew A. Thomas, "Bull," *Eerdmans Dictionary of the Bible* (Grand Rapids, MI: Eerdmans, 2000), 202.

293. Ibid., 202–203.

294. For more details, see Tyler Gilreath, *Gospel Over Gods: Jesus Christ, the Fallen Angels, and the Supernatural War of the Bible* (Gilreath Publishing, 2021), 435–438.

295. Shapira, "Molten Sea Revisited," 7.

296. Ibid., 6.

297. Joe E. Lunceford, "Lotus," *Eerdmans Dictionary of the Bible* (Grand Rapids, MI: Eerdmans, 2000), 825.

298. Michael Kuykendall, "Sea of Glass," *Lexham Bible Dictionary* (Bellingham, WA: Lexham Press, 2016).

299. Schneider, *An Introduction to Ancient Mesopotamian Religion*, 68.

300. Horowitz, *Mesopotamian Cosmic Geography*, 132–133.

301. Heiser, *John's Use of the Old Testament in the Book of Revelation*, 225.

302. James H. Charlesworth, *The Old Testament Pseudepigrapha* (New York; London: Yale University Press, 1983), 40–42.

303. Brant Pitre, *Jesus and the Last Supper* (Grand Rapids, MI; Cambridge, U.K.: Eerdmans, 2015), 456–458.

304. Leonard, *Creation Rediscovered,* 113–114).

305. Beale and McDonough, "Revelation," in *Commentary on the New Testament Use of the Old Testament*, 1118.

306. Beale and Campbell, *Revelation: A Shorter Commentary*, 218.

307. Ibid.

308. Bryan E. Beyer, "Zerubbabel (Person)," *Anchor Yale Bible Dictionary* (New York: Doubleday, 1992), 1084–1085.

309. Victor Harold Matthews, Mark W. Chavalas, and John H. Walton, *The IVP Bible Background Commentary: Old Testament*, electronic ed. (Downers Grove, IL: InterVarsity Press, 2000), Zechariah 4:14.

310. E. Ray Clendenen, "The Minor Prophets," in *Holman Concise Bible Commentary*, ed. David S. Dockery (Nashville, TN: Broadman & Holman, 1998), 385.

311. Beale and Campbell, *Revelation: A Shorter Commentary*, 221.

312. Sara Ferry, "Tyre," *Lexham Bible Dictionary* (Bellingham, WA: Lexham Press, 2016).

313. Ibid.

314. Beale and McDonough, "Revelation," in *Commentary on the New Testament Use of the Old Testament*, 1141.

315. Stanley N. Helton, "Jehoshaphat, Valley of," *Lexham Bible Dictionary* (Bellingham, WA: Lexham Press, 2016).

316. W. Harold Mare, "Decision, Valley of (Place)," *Anchor Yale Bible Dictionary* (New York: Doubleday, 1992) 121.

317. Beale and Campbell, *Revelation: A Shorter Commentary*, 164.

318. Beale and McDonough, "Revelation," in *Commentary on the New Testament Use of the Old Testament*, 1110.

319. Paulien, *Decoding Revelation's Trumpets*, 310.

320. Ibid., 312–313.

321. Beale and McDonough, "Revelation," in *Commentary on the New Testament Use of the Old Testament*, 1111.

322. E. Tod Twist, "Holy Ground," in *Study Like a Pro: Explore Difficult Passages from Every Book of the Bible*, ed. John D. Barry and Rebecca Van Noord (Bellingham, WA: Lexham Press, 2014).

323. Paulien, *Decoding Revelation's Trumpets*, 345–346.

324. Beale and Campbell, *Revelation: A Shorter Commentary*, 172–173.

325. Ibid.

326. Ibid., 171.

327. Beale and McDonough, "Revelation," in *Commentary on the New Testament Use of the Old Testament*, 1112–1113.

328. Beale, *The Book of Revelation: A Commentary on the Greek Text*, 475–476.

329. Beale and Campbell, *Revelation: A Shorter Commentary*, 172–173.

330. Jastrow Jr., *The Religion of Babylonia and Assyria*, 472.

331. Ibid.

332. Fröhlich, "Mesopotamian Elements and the Watchers Traditions," 21.

333. Heiser, *Reversing Hermon*, 49.

334. Richard J. Clifford, *Proverbs: A Commentary*, First edition., *The Old Testament Library* (Louisville, KY; London; Leiden: Westminster John Knox Press, 1999), 26.

335. R. H. Charles, ed., *The Book of Enoch or 1 Enoch: Translation*, 43–45.

336. Sigve K. Tonstad, *Saving God's Reputation: The Theological Function of Pistis Iesou in the Cosmic Narratives of Revelation*, ed. Mark Goodacre, vol. 337 of *Library of New Testament Studies* (London; New Delhi; New York; Sydney: Bloomsbury, 2012), 152–154.

337. Bauckham, *Climax of Prophecy*, 296–297.

338. James H. Charlesworth, *The Old Testament Pseudepigrapha and the New Testament: Expansions of the "Old Testament" and Legends, Wisdom, and Philosophical Literature, Prayers, Psalms and Odes, Fragments of Lost Judeo-Hellenistic Works* (New Haven; London: Yale University Press, 1985), 54–55.

339. Ibid., 63.

340. M. Abegg, Jr., P. Flint, and E. Ulrich, trans. *The Dead Sea Scrolls Bible: The Oldest Known Bible Translated for the First Time into English* (New York: HarperOne, 1999), 539.

341. *Celebrating the Dead Sea Scrolls: A Canadian Contribution*, eds. Peter W. Flint, Jean Duhaime, and Kyung S. Baek, vol. 30 of *Early Judaism and Its Literature*. (Atlanta: Society of Biblical Literature, 2011).

USE THE QR-CODE BELOW TO ACCESS MANY SPECIAL
DEALS AND PROMOTIONS ON BOOKS
AND FILMS FEATURING DISCOVERY,
PROPHECY, AND THE SUPERNATURAL!